THE

AMERICAN GOLFER

Novels by Anthony Robinson

A DEPARTURE FROM THE RULES
THE EASY WAY
HOME AGAIN, HOME AGAIN
THE MEMBER-GUEST
THE WHOLE TRUTH

ISBN: 143926970X
ISBN-13: 9781439269701

"Sooner or later one has to take sides."

The Quiet American

Graham Greene

For my wife, Tania,
who has made my life complete.

THE

AMERICAN GOLFER

A NOVEL

Anthony Robinson

A BLUESTONE BOOK

CHAPTER 1

On his first evening in Ireland, shortly after seven o'clock, Charlie walked into a pub in the West Cork village of Castlebantry. Couples were seated at upholstered banquettes having dinner and four or five men were standing at the bracket-shaped bar. The woman behind the bar, seeing the new arrival, came over.

"May I help you?"

"Murphy's please."

The settling, topping off and re-settling of the stout were distinct steps, and she gave each its due. When she delivered the pint, Charlie asked her if she was Fiona Dennehy.

"I am."

"Frank Bailey, the real-estate agent, said you served great food."

"That was kind of Frank."

"My name is Charlie."

"Pleased to meet you, Charlie."

He asked her if she had a menu. She didn't but she could give him his choices for the evening. "Roast loin of pork, beef stew, or mackerel fresh from the sea. Each with stewed tomatoes, broccoli, and potatoes."

"Thank you."

"Just let me know."

To Charlie, she looked forty or thereabouts. Brown eyes, light-brown hair piled atop her head. Preoccupied, maybe just overworked. Fiona went away to serve a customer and Charlie picked up his pint, glad his day of travel was over. It had begun with a two-hour delay leaving Atlanta, then a sleepless trans-Atlantic flight to Shannon, a hop to Dublin and a ninety-minute wait to catch a smaller jet to Cork, and finally a forty-mile taxi ride to the cottage he had rented, sight unseen, in this small Irish town. Dead tired, Charlie had taken off his shoes and stretched out on the odd-sized bed in the small, boxy bedroom...and next thing he knew a buzzing sound was dragging him out of a deep sleep. Where in hell was he? He reached out, fumbling with the receiver. Agent Bailey wanted to welcome him to Castlebantry. How was he finding the house? Half-asleep, Charlie said it seemed OK. A bit rustic. He'd have a better feel for the place in the morning. Was there a pub or restaurant close by?

Now here he was in McCurtain's having his first beer. A young man pushed open an interior door and came out with a tray of steaming dishes and bowls. He went through an opening in the bar proper and delivered the order to a man and woman at one of the banquettes. Just then a man in blue wearing a checkered cap walked in, taking a place near Charlie. Fiona chatted with him while the stout swirled, then put the pint—a rich black topped with a crisp white halo—before him on the bar.

Across the room Charlie noticed an alcove with several chairs in it and a variety of musical instruments high on a shelf. All in all, McCurtain's seemed like a great place for food and drink and he was glad having it a quarter-mile from his house. Even if he moved and he was considering it—the water pressure in his cottage was weak, the refrigerator was on its last legs, and, most disconcerting of all, he seemed to feel a presence in the house as if someone was watching him, judging him—he'd likely come back.

"Excuse me, sir."

Charlie turned. The man wearing the checkered cap was looking at him. In a rich brogue, "Not to be overly personal, might ye be Charlie Kingston?"

"That's my name."

"The American golfer?"

"I play."

The man's rough, sun-brown face broke into a grin. "The Open at St. Andrews! Everyone in the pub is rootin' for ye to beat the bloody Englishman, Nick Faldo. Ye went shot for shot with him in the final round, and when ye teed off on the seventeenth, the infamous Road Hole, ye were tied for the lead."

Charlie was astounded and charmed as well. "That's true. I was."

"Then the bad kick on your approach and ye end up in the Road Hole bunker," the Irishman went on. "The infamous 'Sands of Nakajima,' your ball snug against the wall so ye can't take your stance. A lie from hell! But ye play it lefty, flip the face of your sand wedge, and take a mighty swing, and God Almighty ye end up on the green. Ye have a twenty-foot putt and your ball keeps the line and dies an inch from the hole. It was a groan heard round the world. Faldo moved ahead by one stroke and beat ye by one stroke."

"I seem to recall," Charlie said.

The man came closer and they shook hands. "I'm Dennis O'Hea. Are ye here for a tournament?"

"No, just visiting. My great-grandmother lived in Castlebantry."

"I wouldn't say ye were visiting, I'd say ye were coming home!"

Charlie laughed. Then, seriously, "I'd like to find her grave."

"Now that shouldn't be too difficult," O'Hea said. "Stop by the mayor's office on Doolin Square and ask for Ellen Burke. She's kept the public records nigh on fifty years." He had a swallow of stout, wiped a speck of foam from his lip with a rough knuckle. "Also, each church has its own burial ground. Then ye have family plots scattered about—mostly in the Castlebantry Hills."

"Where are the Castlebantry Hills?" Charlie inquired.

"At the crossroads, right here at McCurtain's, take the road to Croghanvale," Dennis O'Hea went on. "You'll see narrow byways leading into the hills. Follow one, follow another, graveyards will surely spring up. And if one day ye work up a thirst, there's a fine old pub in Croghanvale. Pharr's. Emily Pharr is a woman ye won't soon forget."

"I'll be sure to stop in."

O'Hea lowered his voice. "Ye should understand there's no love lost between Pharr's and McCurtain's. Both pubs go back many years, each claiming Michael Collins had his last pint under their roof."

"Forgive me, Dennis. I'm not familiar with the name."

"Michael Collins—the man who made Ireland," O'Hea said with pride. "Beat the English in our War of Independence in 1920. After seven centuries under British rule, we became a Free State."

Fiona stopped by and Charlie ordered a new round. When she delivered it, Dennis said, "Fiona, I am sitting here with the great American golfer, Charlie Kingston. Came within a whisker of beating Nick Faldo in the Open."

"Did he now?" She gave Charlie a quiet look. "Have you decided on what you'd like for dinner?"

"I think the beef stew."

"And a wise choice it is," Dennis O'Hea put in. "I'll say without fear of contradiction that Fiona's beef stew is the finest in all of West Cork."

"Thank you, Dennis," she said. "But if you think the next Guinness is on the house, think again."

She took the order to the kitchen, and Dennis said, "It pains me poor heart how much I love that woman. Aye, she's married, but her husband's a mean-spirited, no-good individual. I keep telling myself one day she'll come to her senses, but how long can a man wait?"

Charlie smiled, amused; he liked Dennis O'Hea. He asked him what he did for a living.

"I'm a golf course superintendent, thirty-five years now," O'Hea said, "at Bandon, Kinsale, Old Head, and now at Whitridge Manor here in Castlebantry."

"My taxi driver told me there was only one course in Castlebantry, O'Brien's," Charlie said.

"O'Brien's is not a golf course, it's a battlefield. Playing it ye take your life in your hands," O'Hea came back. "Balls go whistling by your head like cannon fire. The Whitridge is private, a Sean Harrigan design."

"He did The Bobcat in South Carolina," Charlie said, "just outside of Charleston."

"I'm sure it's a great layout, but none of Harrigan's courses touch The Whitridge for sheer beauty," O'Hea said. "That doesn't make it his top-ranked course, ye understand; it's only nine holes. Mr. Brotherton wanted a 'family gem,' as he instructed Harrigan—and he has one. Harrigan gave each hole two distinct tees, so in a way there's a front and a back nine."

Charlie was becoming genuinely interested. "Who's Mr. Brotherton?"

"The owner of Whitridge Manor, a Scot, one of the wealthiest men in the U.K. Hard to work for but he pays well. We do have a problem, however. In Mr. Brotherton's opinion, his 'family gem' has a flaw. He and Harrigan had a falling out over it, he fired the man, and the Brothertons' first guests are coming in two weeks for The Whitridge grand opening."

"What's the flaw?"

"Maybe nothing," Dennis said. "But if Mr. Brotherton says something's wrong, there's something wrong. There's one hole he doesn't like and he wants *me* to fix it. I'm a greenskeeper, Charlie, not a golf-course architect!"

"Then why doesn't he bring one in?"

"By the time an architect got around to coming out, we'd be well into the fall." O'Hea adjusted his cap, pushed it back a little. "Charlie, I hardly know ye, but I've known of ye for years. Would ye be willing to take a look? I'd prize your opinion."

"Sure—just don't tell me which hole it is," Charlie said. "I'll play the nine. If something jumps up at me I don't like, I'll tell you about it and we can take it from there."

"My gratitude is too great for words," O'Hea said. "When might ye be coming by?"

"Give me a day or two to settle in."

At the waiter's request, Charlie moved to a banquette, and in a few minutes the young man —on closer look, a boy in his teens—came up with a tray and set the beef stew and a number of side dishes on the table. He had a great shock of reddish-brown hair and a lingering bruise on his cheek. He turned to go away—

"What's your name?" Charlie asked.

"Kevin."

"Thanks, Kevin. Food looks great. I'm Charlie."

The lad gave a perfunctory nod and Charlie started his dinner, eating slowly, remembering his indecision as he was leaving his condo in Atlanta. Should he bring his clubs? Golf wasn't why he was going to Ireland; if anything, it was to get away from golf. But as he was walking out the door—all of one day ago now—he had a change of heart. How could a golfer go to Ireland and *not* bring his clubs? And so he had, with one proviso—a pledge to himself and to the memory of his young daughter that any golf he played in Ireland would be for the fun of it only. No competition, no stress.

At the bar O'Hea was settling up with Fiona—in Charlie's opinion, trying to make a little time while at it. On his way out the superintendent stopped by Charlie's banquette. "I'll leave your name with Pat Joe at the Whitridge Manor gate."

"OK."

"Now then, Charlie, how many wins have ye on the PGA Tour? Mr. Brotherton will surely ask. He's very big on credentials."

"Six."

"Plus your second at St. Andrews—and let's not forget your win at Mount Juliet in the Irish Open. A splendid record indeed."

"Thank you, Dennis."

O'Hea left McCurtain's and soon, in the alcove across the room, musicians were getting ready to play. They were talking among themselves, laughing quietly. A young woman with dark hair, a fiddle in her lap; a man with a graying beard holding an instrument that resembled a guitar; a stout woman with a button accordion; a man about 20 with a pennywhistle; an old-timer in black, drum on his knees, a single double-headed stick in his hand.

Then, without sign or signal, they started. The fiddle beginning, the other instruments entering in—and the beat took hold. The man with the graying beard sang in a clear tenor voice, and the lyrics and melodies, in one ballad after another, swept Charlie along, touching him deeply.

He finished his meal, slid away from the banquette. Fiona came over and met him at the bar. "The stew was delicious," Charlie said.

"I'm glad you liked it."

He gave her a couple of Irish notes and she came back with change, telling him that service was included. "How long will you be with us?" she asked.

"All of May."

"Then we'll be seeing you again," she said.

"I'm sure you will. Good night, Fiona."

"Good night, Charlie."

For the first time that evening she smiled; it wasn't a big smile but it brought a lovely change to her face, warming it. He left something extra for the youth, then continued to the door. Passing through the hall, he spied a bronze plaque beneath the large, grainy photograph of the military officer he'd noticed earlier. He went over and read the inscription:

> **Michael Collins**
> **General of the Army, Irish Free State**
> **Born in Sam's Cross, 16 October 1890**
> **Killed in an Ambush at Beal na mBlath,**
> **22 August 1922**

He stood for a long moment looking at the man striding down a city street. Charlie had the feeling that Collins was trying to catch his eye. *"You, to arms!"*

Sorry, it's not why I'm here, General, Charlie thought. Outside, he stood on the crossroads, viewing a sign that pointed in four direction: *Croghanvale—5 km; Castle-bantry—2 km; Ballincarrig—7 km; Sam's Cross—1 km.* He gazed down one road, then another, each blending into a murky dusk, and started in the direction of Castlebantry, passing two other buildings in the immediate area, both smaller than McCurtain's and both dark. One, Monahan's, had the look of a general store. The second had a sign outside, "Surgery." Charlie rounded the bend in Pearse Road and after two hundred yards stood across from his cottage. Stone sides cobbled loosely together, slate roof, a small door and a pair of little windows, empty window boxes. He crossed Pearse Road and walked down the weeded path, hesitating at the door; then he tripped the latch....

CHAPTER 2

Shortly after ten in the morning on his third day in Castlebantry, Charlie stepped out of his cottage and walked to the taxi idling on Pearse Road. When he reached the car he pushed in his golf bag, then got in and closed the door. "Whitridge Manor," he said to the driver.

"You'll forgive me, sir, but I believe the course at Whitridge Manor is closed to the public," the driver said, turning around in his seat. He had a thick, straw-like mustache.

"I know the course superintendent," Charlie said.

"Now that's different," the driver said, letting out his clutch. "Not that I'm familiar with Whitridge Manor, but I do a bit of golfing myself and it's well known it's private. I was afraid ye might be disappointed."

"I appreciate that. Where do you play?"

"O'Brien's. It has a fine view of Castlebantry Bay but a God-awful design. Each bunker doubles as a foxhole."

Charlie laughed. "I've heard."

"Actually my game is hurling," the driver went on, "or was. Three times West Cork champions we were—"

"Hurling?"

"It's an old Irish sport, very fast—mix Gaelic football and lacrosse, you might have it. Fifteen players on a team. You have a stick, there's a ball—goal posts. But it's for younger men, so I took up golf. When did you start?"

"The summer I was twelve."

"Maybe ye can tell me something."

"Go ahead."

"I'm still using my hurling grip, left hand low on the handle, and my golfing mates laugh at me. But I can hit that little white ball a mile."

"Some golfers use a cross-handed grip in putting," Charlie said, "but if it works for you—"

"Do you think I should change?"

"Try it. See what happens."

Looking out his window, Charlie saw grazing cows and sheep in great rolling fields, endless shades of green. The Emerald Isle. As they drew near the village, houses began appearing, and in a few minutes they were in downtown Castlebantry. On one corner rose a huge cathedral and on the opposite corner a large, brick structure: the Bank of Ireland. Sturdy two- and three-story buildings, many painted bright colors—reds, greens, yellow—lined the main street, with shops and stores and pubs at sidewalk level. Pearse Road was now Wolfe Tone Way. Crowds going in and out of doorways, window shopping, walking quickly along. Traffic started, stopped; started, stopped. Finally the taxi reached the lower end of Wolfe Tone Way where Charlie noticed the Castlebantry Hotel and the early stages of a shopping plaza. Just ahead, a traffic circle. The driver bore left and headed west on a highway in the direction of Cork.

Almost immediately he said, "On the other side of the road, the wall that follows it along? That's Whitridge Manor."

The wall, ten feet high, was constructed of solidly stacked stone, much of it covered with a thick network of vines and plant life. "Runs for almost a mile, then circles around, takes in the whole estate," the driver said. "Here we are now." He slowed, gave a careful look, then cut across the Cork road and came to a stop at an ornately forged black iron gate, as tall as the great wall on both sides of it. Charlie thought he might have to cross a moat to get to the course. He paid the driver, who introduced himself as Jimmy O'Sullivan, then handed Charlie his card.

"I've a pub in Ballincarrig. Come by and see us, there'll be a good pint waiting for ye."

"Thank you, Jimmy. I'm Charlie Kingston."

He slipped the card into his wallet, then stepped out with his clubs. The gate swung open—gratefully, no creaking of hinges—and a man in blue trousers and shirt, with sunglasses, came forward.

"You must be the American golfer. Welcome to Whitridge Manor."

They shook hands, introduced themselves. "Dennis said you'd be coming by once you got settled in," Pat Joe said. "Let me give you directions to the course. Stay on the main driveway here. It runs past the garage and then the Manor House. At that point you'll see a path of white stones. Follow it to the first tee."

"Thanks."

"Have a good game."

Charlie hoisted his golf bag to his shoulder and began walking. The cobblestone drive curved downward beneath dark boughs and soon went by a large, six-bay garage. A man in the identical blue of the gate keeper was polishing a Rolls Royce out front. Inside the open garage doors, like thoroughbreds waiting their turn for grooming, were a BMW, a yellow Saab convertible, a Land Rover and a Jaguar coupe. The man gave a friendly wave. Charlie raised his hand and continued on the same steady downslope, passing in a few minutes a two-story mansion of dark stone that stood at the end of a deep, magnificent lawn. A U-shaped driveway, trimmed with shrubbery and flowering plants, passed in front of the Manor House. Parked there and adding a spark of color to the somber building was a red Mustang convertible.

Charlie saw the path of white stone and followed it to the course. On his right, a wide but shallow river burbled over rocks, and a hundred yards from the far bank the great Whitridge Manor wall he'd seen from the taxi rose up. A practice green was close to the first tee. Tempting as it was to test the nature and speed of the greens, Charlie decided it wasn't necessary, wasn't why he was playing The Whitridge.

Twenty-five yards behind the first tee, to the left and considerably higher, was a second teebox. Blue markers. The "tenth hole." Here, on the first hole, the markers were white. On the far side of the tee was a topographical depiction of the hole carved in fine wood, maybe teak. Two fairway bunkers, two greenside bunkers, fairway bending left, elevated green. Beneath the carving in bold print: "**The Whitridge. Hole 1—par 4—355 yards**."

Charlie looked down the first fairway. What struck him was the natural roll and flow of the land, nothing artificial to jar the eye. It was as if Harrigan had employed no bulldozers, no dump trucks, no backhoes; hadn't disturbed so much as a mole hill. But of course he'd moved tons of earth. He was a superb "editor" of the land, fellow architects said.

The dogleg, Charlie saw, started at about 250 yards. Keeping his driver in the bag, he pulled out his 3-wood, teed a ball, did a couple of stretches, then made a smooth, easy swing. The ball flew straight and deep, bore left at the dogleg and bounced toward the green. Bag on his shoulder, Charlie started walking, the fairway crisply mowed, springy to the step. Sixty yards along he noticed a third teebox, markers in red. Evidently women didn't get to play from alternate tees the second time around.

When he reached his ball, he had either a 9-iron or a pitching wedge to the pin. He chose the wedge. The hole itself wasn't visible, just the flagstick, and when he reached the putting surface he didn't see his ball. He poked around in the rough on the far side of the green. Nothing. After three or four minutes he dropped a ball in the long grass, hit a delicate pitch to seven feet and, before putting, pulled the flag. A golf ball lay in the hole. Charlie reached in, pulled it out. His. No ball mark in the immediate vicinity. He had to laugh. It wasn't every day you flew an approach dead into the cup.

Charlie followed another white-pebbled path to the second tee. On each hole, as he played along, he looked for a problem, or for what Wesley Brotherton might consider a problem. But he saw nothing awkward or unattractive. Just magnificent golf holes. The lake on the par-3 third had swans swimming on it. One thing he particularly liked was the isolation of each hole. You weren't likely to knock a ball onto another fairway; you couldn't see another fairway. Two different streams feeding into the river wound their way through the land. Compared to courses on the PGA Tour,

The Whitridge was short; short, however, didn't mean easy. Harrigan always had something up his sleeve; you had to think on a Harrigan course. The greens were difficult to read, with any number of conflicting rolls, and the bunkers, each in a modernistic design, were superbly placed—to snag an errant shot.

After sinking a 20-footer on the fourth green, Charlie followed a directional arrow and found himself walking through a grove of trees and flowering plants. On most courses, connecting paths functioned solely to get you from the last green to the next teebox. Not at The Whitridge. The path he was on now was a wondrous, magical stroll, clubs weightless on his shoulder. He might have forgotten he was playing golf.

Charlie, the mission. You're here on a mission.

The fifth was a long par 4, uphill all the way. He hit a good drive but his 6-iron approach veered left from the start. His ball lay in a bunker, a very deep bunker. A sand wedge put him twelve feet from the hole but he missed the side-hill putt. Bogey.

He had reached the highest point on the course, and the sight of Castlebantry Bay and the ocean was spectacular. Charlie reinserted the flagstick, moved toward the sixth tee, having to remind himself, still again, that he was here to help Dennis, not to lose himself in the pleasure of playing a superb course. Back to the job at hand. Suddenly Charlie stopped short. Just ahead, sitting on a park bench taking in the view, was a woman.

"Excuse me," he said, drawing a little closer.

She looked at him. "Charlie Kingston, I presume."

"Yes."

"I'm Lora Brotherton."

He took a few steps, drawing closer. She had an accent—if more English or more Irish, he didn't know. Rich, dark-red hair, ocean-green eyes. "It's a pleasure meeting you, Mrs. Brotherton."

"Are you liking the course?" A silver-gray golf bag with eight or nine clubs in it was leaning against the bench.

"Very much," Charlie said. "It wants a golfer to play well."

"What a nice way to say it." She had full lips, no lipstick, no makeup at all. On her cheeks a mild smattering of freckles. "I know you're 'on assignment' for Dennis," she went on, "but sit for a moment."

"Thank you." He lowered his bag to the ground. "The question is, are you liking the course?"

"So far, very much; it's actually my first time playing it," Mrs. Brotherton said. "Yesterday my husband and I were going to christen The Whitridge but the weather turned dismal, and today he got called back to London."

"So you're christening it on your own," Charlie said.

"I got to this point and stopped." She had on tan shorts and a white, short-sleeved shirt with a curved collar. An exquisite gold pendant hung from her neck on a gold chain.

"I can see why." To Charlie the ocean, several miles away, had the appearance of a wall, a sparkling bluish-green wall, rather than a flat expanse. "I take it that's the Atlantic."

"Actually it's the Celtic Sea," she said. "If you continued straight, you'd hit Spain." She pointed to her right. "America is that way."

"America, that way. Thanks."

She smiled. "Are you on holiday?"

"Not really a holiday. Just getting away for a month, a change of pace. My great-grandmother was born in Castlebantry."

"That makes you part Irish, at least."

"Half. How about you?"

"All." Strands of her hair, touching her shoulders, responded to a breeze. "But for the past ten years I've lived in London. I'm something of a hybrid, I'm afraid."

"You must still have family here."

"I do, in County Mayo, Kilcarney. I'll probably drive over tomorrow and spend the day."

"In your Mustang?"

She laughed. "Pretty, isn't it?"

"Very. Out of curiosity—when you go with your husband, do you take the Rolls, Jag, Saab, or Land Rover?"

"He never comes with me."

"That's too bad, nice ride through the country to visit your folks. What's the problem?"

"Wesley and my parents don't get along, and he's not particularly fond of Ireland."

"That's interesting, he bought a beautiful place here."

"I asked him to."

"You have a very generous husband, Mrs. Brotherton. What kind of town is Kilcarney?"

"Scenic, historic. Home of Ireland's Pirate Queen, Grace O'Malley."

"Ireland's *Pirate Queen*?"

"Granuaile Uí Máille, in Irish," Lora said. "She lived about 400 years ago. As a girl, I fashioned myself the 'new Granuaile,' sailing on Clew Bay looking for hapless victims to plunder. Of course, I didn't fool anyone. I was Tom Fitzgerald's daughter, play-acting as usual."

"Are you an actress?"

"I love the stage but by profession—I do have a profession—I'm a graphic designer. What about you?" Adding quickly, "I mean, besides golf."

"My high school adviser said I should go into accounting," Charlie said. "I'm good with numbers, supposedly. But to sit behind a desk all day? In college I shifted majors a couple of times—civil engineering, geology. By then, everything was secondary to golf anyway."

"So golf's your life."

"I have a love for golf-course architecture," Charlie said. "When I finally put away the sticks, it's something I'd like to do. But it's still golf. So, yes, it's my life."

"Shall we play in?"

"I'd love to, Mrs. Brotherton."

"Please, call me Lora."

They followed the path to the next tee. Hole six, virtually all of it downhill, offered a great view of the village and surrounding countryside: the innermost cove of Castlebantry Bay (swans on it looking like snowflakes), St. Matthew's Cathedral, Pearse Road leading out of town, rolling fields framed by hedgerows—

"I'll play from the men's tee," Lora said.

She pulled a driver from her bag, teed a ball, took the club back smoothly, made an excellent shoulder turn, and transferred her weight on the downswing—but not completely. In advance, Charlie knew what the ball would do, how it would respond. It sailed away smartly but began tailing off, fading, and settled into the first cut of rough. OK distance and only minor trouble.

"Good shot," Charlie said.

"I'm in play. That's about it."

He teed a ball and hit it deep and straight: with the help of the downslope, 300+ yards.

"I'm impressed," Lora said, "but not intimidated."

As they walked along, he asked her where she'd learned to play. When she wasn't sailing on Clew Bay as a kid, she said, her father would drag her to the course, rain or shine. She'd never had a lesson, just coaching from dad.

"He coached you well. What does he do?"

"He's a doctor in Kilcarney."

"Now you golf with your husband," Charlie said.

"Occasionally. I don't give him enough challenge, he says. Wesley played on the Walker Cup team—one of the few Englishmen, that year, to win his matches."

****

On the ninth green Lora sank a breaking 12-foot putt to give her a bogey five, a good score considering she'd had a wayward drive. She was delighted with herself, raised her hand and Charlie gave it a congratulatory slap. They left the green and walked on an unpaved access road away from the course. Lora pointed out the practice range on the right; it was also the site of the helipad, she said. Soon they came to a clearing surrounded by heavy trees. Hulking in the middle of it was a large, barnlike building, with two tractors and a greens-cutter parked at one end. With a younger man, near the machinery, stood Dennis O'Hea.

Charlie stopped. "This is as far as I go."

"Will you give me a rematch?"

"Definitely, I'll practice up."

She laughed and continued on. Charlie veered toward the barn. As he drew near, the superintendent came over. "I see ye made the most of your round, Charlie. And how might ye be describing Mrs. Brotherton's swing?"

"Words fail me, Dennis."

"Sure it's a thing of beauty. I weep just thinking about it."

Charlie laughed and O'Hea pulled open a door. It was a large room, the part of the barn, O'Hea said, where grooms had kept tack. The barn had once had upwards of twelve horses. When the barometer was just so, you could still detect a faint aroma.

"Tea, Charlie?"

"Sure."

The superintendent made up two mugs—the water was already hot—and delivered them to the low table; he and his guest sat down. Charlie said, "It's a gem, Dennis, every detail. The Whitridge is a great small course."

"Was there anything ye *didn't* like?"

Charlie kept to himself that he'd forgotten his mission; after meeting Lora, it had vanished from his mind. "Not really, but I think I know what Mr. Brotherton is referring to. We were on the eighth hole, the par 5, a big sweeping left-to-right off the tee. A natural for Mrs. Brotherton, who hits a fade, and she hit her best drive of the day. My tee-ball hugged the curve. I figured I had a 4-iron to get home. Only when we got out there, neither ball was in sight."

"Because they'd hit the slope of the fairway and bounded and rolled and hopped incessantly!" Dennis said.

"Her ball was in the deep rough, mine was in the woods."

"It's a hole that unfairly penalizes a player, to quote Mr. Brotherton."

"In my opinion it's the best hole on the course," Charlie said, noting the look of surprise on Dennis's face. "Let me explain. On the teebox on eight you say to yourself, OK, a big power fade. A Lee Trevino special. But the drive to hit on eight isn't a fade, because with fade spin it won't hold.

That's Harrigan for you, the old double-cross. The shot to hit is a draw or a straight ball *into* the slope. Hit like that, a ball won't hop or bound. Mrs. Brotherton and I both went back and hit second drives."

"But Charlie, you're a pro!" O'Hea said. "Who among the Brothertons' guests can hit the draw? With exceptions, we're looking at weekend golfers. Basically they slice—their tee shots on eight will end up in the trees."

"True, so here's my idea, in deference to Mr. Brotherton," Charlie said. "About 150 yards from the teebox and ten steps into the rough, construct a berm with three to five degrees reverse slant, enough to stop a rolling ball." Charlie moved his hand like a bird swooping in, then gently rising. "Run the berm along for a hundred yards or so. How many truck-loads of fill will you need? Eight? Grade, cover with sod. You're in business."

O'Hea was delighted. "Excellent. In case I want to talk, where are ye staying, Charlie?"

"On Pearse Road, a small stone house just shy of McCurtain's."

"Now that's the McGarrity house," Dennis said. "Empty these twenty years. Empty and forlorn. Mairead and Kieran. Ah, she loved her flowers. Irish Ale—the name of a lily—grew by her door. I used to tease her about it. 'How's your Irish Ale today, Mairead? Invite me in for a pint!'"

Charlie grinned. "Where are they now?"

"It's a long a story, and right now I have a berm to build." Dennis got to his feet. "Come back and play the alternate tees, whenever the fancy strikes."

They shook hands and Charlie went out. There was something about the McGarritys that people didn't want to talk about. As he neared the end of the access road, he noticed a stone house, nearly twice the size of his and in much better condition; maybe, at one time, home to the stable master. A mere thirty steps farther along, Charlie found himself back on the cobblestone driveway. First tee to the left, Manor House straight ahead—still parked at the door, the red Mustang convertible. Main gate to the right.

Charlie shifted his golf bag from one shoulder to the other and started the uphill trek.

CHAPTER 3

Walking on the side of Pearse Road, toting his clubs, Charlie was visualizing Lora Brotherton's swing; really, Lora Brotherton. Emulating her idol, Granuaile, she had pirated his heart, but not, he would readily admit, against his will. She could plunder as she chose, when she chose, as often as she liked—

A car was slowing, then came to a stop next to Charlie. A man was speaking to him through an open window. "Where might ye be going, lad?"

Probably to hell, Charlie thought, seeing the clerical collar of a priest. "To the crossroads."

"Well, hop in."

Charlie put his golf bag in back and opened the passenger door. "Thank you, Father."

"I'm Preston Byrne, pastor at St. Matthew's."

"Charlie Kingston."

In his fifties, the priest had closely cut brownish-gray hair and a ruddy complexion. Charlie got a whiff of after-shave, perhaps Old Spice. Preston Byrne put his Toyota through the gears. "Where was it ye were playing golf?"

"At Whitridge Manor."

"Don't get me going on Whitridge Manor."

But Father Byrne got going on it anyway. "The arch-diocese wanted to make it into a retreat for priests," he said, "but Wesley Brotherton outmaneuvered the bishops—that is, outbid them—at every turn. The man was unrelenting in his goal to buy the property. He's no friend of the com-munity, I might add. Helicopters flying in and out, wreaking havoc on the peace and quiet of Castlebantry. Ah, it was a sad day when Brotherton acquired Whitridge Manor. An Orangeman in our midst. But forgive me, Charlie. Clearly you and Wesley Brotherton are friends, and it's not becom-ing of a Christian to cast aspersions on someone's friend."

"I've never met the man," Charlie said.

"Then how it is ye got to play?"

"I know the greenskeeper."

"Ah, Dennis O'Hea," spoken with enthusiasm, perhaps love. "That puts a different light on it. He's a very fine man, a fine but lonely man, lost his wife of many years. I told him, 'I'd like to see ye at Holy Communion on a more regular basis.'" They were passing Charlie's house. "'Let the Sacrament help ye through these difficult times.' He tried, I won't say he didn't try; but Dennis's devotion to the holy virtues is sporadic, at best."

Soon the priest was braking directly across from McCurtain's. "Well, here we are, Charlie. I'm going out on a limb, I'm taking ye as a Catholic."

"I was raised one."

"I have the eight and ten every Sunday at St. Matt's. Come celebrate the Mass with us."

"I appreciate that, Father. Thanks for the lift."

Charlie grabbed his bag from the back and Father Byrne drove off. He carried his clubs across the road, wanting to see if McCurtain's was open; he'd have a good lunch here instead of a PB&J at his house. But the pub was dark and he started walking. He hadn't taken five steps when a woman came out of Monahan's carrying a string sack weighted with groceries. He thought it was Fiona, but with her hair let down, falling to her shoulders, he wasn't sure.

"Charlie," she said, "you've played golf and are looking for a little sustenance. Am I right?"

It was Fiona, just with a different look. "Unfortunately your place is closed."

"My house isn't." The building had two doors—the more elaborate pub entrance and the family door, separated one from the other by thirty steps. "I'll make you a bite."

"Fiona, that's kind of you, but—"

"It will be my pleasure, Charlie."

He followed her into a large sitting room—a couple of upholstered easy chairs, a sofa with a dark-green slipcover, coffee table, a small bookshelf and a television. "If you'd like to freshen up a bit, it's down the hall," Fiona said.

Charlie propped his golf bag next to an umbrella stand, found the bathroom. When he returned, Fiona wasn't around, and he sat on the sofa thinking it curious, if not unsettling, that a priest had pulled over and spoken to him exactly as he was having delicious thoughts of Lora Brotherton. Now here he was in another married woman's house, wondering what he'd say if her husband happened to walk in. How about: "Hi, Mr. Dennehy. Your wife's rustling me up a little lunch. Won't you join us?"

Soon Fiona came in with a lacquered tray and set it on the low table. On his plate were three cuts of ham, lettuce, slices of cheese and tomato. Dark bread lay on a smaller plate. A dish of potato salad and a jar of mustard were on the side. As was a glorious pint of stout.

"Fiona, this is far more than a bite!"

"I know a hungry man when I see one. Were you playing O'Brien's?"

"No. At Whitridge Manor. Dennis extended the invitation."

"Did he now?" Fiona sat in an armchair near the sofa. "I hear it's a beautiful course, not that I know anything about golf. Unlike my son, Kevin."

Charlie smiled. "You can imagine my surprise when I went to Monahan's yesterday morning for a few groceries and there's my waiter from McCurtain's holding down a job."

"He said he carried a sack of peat to your house for you."

"He did," Charlie said. "We had a good talk."

"You're in the McGarrity house."

"So I'm learning."

"Mairead and I were very close," Fiona said. "We grew up together here in Castlebantry. My brother wanted to marry her but she tied the knot with Kieran McGarrity. Eddie was more dashing, she said, but Kieran won out. A beautiful tenor voice he had, melted many a heart."

"Including yours?" Charlie asked.

"No one could compete with Mairead. Wisely, I stayed out of it."

"Is your brother still in town?"

"Oh, yes," Fiona said. "He joined the Castlebantry Garda at twenty-five, now he's the chief. Eddie Dunn. Highly respected, loves his job. Secretly, he fashions himself a writer. From his youngest days he was always coming up with great ideas for a screenplay or novel. As for my son—" Fiona paused, her expression and tone suddenly somber, "—he's giving us problems. About a month ago he went to school with bloodshot eyes, none too steady on his feet, and they sent him home. He'd been golfing with men on holiday at O'Brien's, drinking with them at the hotel pub. And it wasn't the first time either. He'll be sixteen next month, young barmaid never questioned him. Smoking, cutting classes. His grades took a dive. When his father got home he picked up one of Kevin's clubs and chased him out the door, swinging it wildly. Kevin ducked just in time and Donal wrapped the club around a tree. It was just a terrible, awful scene. He could've killed his own son then and there! Now Donal has Kevin working three jobs—he does yard work for Dr. Mulrooney—thinking what he needs is discipline."

"Where's his father now?" Charlie asked.

"In Germany," Fiona said. "He owns and operates Irish pubs. He has one in Hildesheim, one in Hanover, and he's opening a third *Dennehy's* in Wolfsburg. He's motivated but at what expense? Brigid, our daughter, is starting to think of him as a stranger. And Donal and Kevin are at war; there's no other way to say it."

As Fiona went on, Charlie thought he could now start his lunch.

"When we first bought McCurtain's, about ten years ago, we were a family," she said. "Donal put up the photograph of Michael Collins, and we became known as the pub where Collins had his last pint. I knew it wasn't true but my husband's not one to argue with. Our business picked up—Collins was born just a mile away in Sam's Cross; but Donal wanted more. Then he had an idea about pubs in Germany and now everything's changed. Deteriorated, really. Brigid isn't sleeping well. She has a *feis* coming up and needs her rest."

"What's a *feis*?"

"An Irish dance competition. She's very good, very talented. Kevin's a different story," Fiona said "He's threatening to run away—with his girlfriend. Donal says golf ruined his judgment, corrupted his morals, made him think it was OK to cut classes and start drinking and have sex out of wedlock." Fiona stopped momentarily, then, with painful earnestness, "Can golf do that to someone, Charlie?"

He had a swallow of Murphy's, washing down a delicious bite of his sandwich. "Here's what I think, Fiona," he said. "If you're the swearing type, golf will give you plenty to swear about. If you're somebody who gets down on himself, you'll have ample opportunities to get depressed. If you like to smell the flowers, here's your chance. Golf never judges; it just brings out who you are. Your husband is wrong. It's not golf that's hurting Kevin."

"I know that to be true," Fiona said, "but Donal won't admit to any faults in himself." She was quiet for a moment, then, her eyes warming, she asked Charlie to tell her something about himself.

"I wouldn't know where to begin," he said.

"Begin with golf."

He was starting to feel relaxed, especially knowing that Donal Dennehy was taking care of business in Germany. "This may seem like a roundabout answer," Charlie said. "My father was an assembly-line worker for Ford Motor Company, a union man—the UAW. Endless meetings in smoke-filled rooms. I remember his awful hack when he'd get up in the morning. The thing was, he was a good athlete in his day—had a tryout with the Tigers, a baseball team in Detroit. He knew golf. He helped me with my tempo when I was a kid. Tempo means a graceful, even stroke.

I had a tendency to jump at the ball. Not good. My dad had me say 'Old Tom Morris...*Bobby Jones*.' Old Tom Morris on the backswing, nice and easy; then *Bobby Jones* on the downswing, with emphasis, power. It worked for me; it made my game. My father would shag balls for me in a big field next to our house when I was kid. I loved my dad but I was angry at him. I didn't respect what he was doing—killing himself so *others* could have a better life? What about you, Dad? How about a better life for you and mom? Like maybe a nicer house, a new car. Eugene Debs, the Socialist labor organizer in the twenties—he was my father's hero. I didn't get it, didn't understand it. Still don't, really. I got into Wake Forest University on a golf scholarship. In one of my courses we read Ralph Waldo Emerson, a couple of his essays, and something he wrote has always stayed with me: 'Trust yourself, every heart vibrates to that iron string.' That was it, that was golf—trusting yourself. To others maybe the line means something else. I don't know, Fiona. I just know my dad's lifestyle and views weren't for me; or his politics. I argued with him, we fought, he wouldn't change. I wanted to show him what a successful life was—you did it by taking care of Number One. He became seriously ill at fifty, doctors told me he wasn't going to make it. I wanted to win my first tournament before he died, but that didn't happen."

"How very sad," Fiona said.

"I miss him. I still fight with him," Charlie said.

They sat quietly. He did a little work on his lunch. Finally Fiona said, "Are you married?"

"I was. I'm divorced."

"Do you have any children?"

Charlie didn't answer right away; then he gathered himself and said, "Debby, my wife, couldn't stay pregnant.

A couple of miscarriages, then she had an ectopic pregnancy, almost died. That was it for trying. We adopted a little girl, four months old. April. God blessed us, it's the only way we could explain it. I was playing good golf, picking up a few wins, a number of top tens, a second at St. Andrews. Then, for whatever reason, my game started falling off. Not for lack of effort. I worked out, practiced long hours, linked up with an instructor, one of the best in the business. It was all an ordeal for Debby and she got tired of hoping, worrying, no money coming in. I was giving too much time to golf with too few results. The only joy I had was with April, then six. I'd come home on a Friday—if you come home on a Friday you've missed the cut, no check—and April and I would talk. She knew all the golfing terms. She gave me reason to keep my dream alive—of sinking the winning putt and having her run across the eighteenth green and jump into my arms."

Charlie was quiet for while, wondering if he could go on; wondering if he should. Then he said, "It was in the spring, just two years ago now. Buddy Hewitt, my instructor, called me one evening. Instead of eleven tomorrow morning could I get to the club at eight? He had to leave for the Coast. No problem. We were getting somewhere and I didn't want to miss the session. I ran out of the house at 7:45 and while Buddy and I were working, my cell phone buzzes. It's Debby. April took a nasty spill on her bicycle, her training wheels collapsed—her helmet wasn't on snug and she'd hit her head on the curb. I raced to the hospital, praying—fearful that she was seriously injured; but it was the guilt, the waves of it that kept pounding me. The evening before, April had told me her training wheels were wobbly. I said I'd tighten them in the morning. But in the morning I was in a hurry to meet Hewitt, and I just plain forgot to do it. Debby meets me in the lobby and we go into a little private room. April is in a coma with bleeding of the brain, undergoing an operation as we talk. I'd die for her, Fiona. God, take me, just save April. Debby keeps saying to me, Charlie, how could it have happened? She's beside herself with pain, the agony of it is tearing at her, tearing at both of us. *How could it have happened, Charlie?*"

He made a fist, clasped it with his other hand. "I almost told her but held off. Why throw my guilt, my horrendous lapse, into the mix? It may have pushed Debby over the edge. I called it a terrible accident. We prayed, we held each other. The doctors came out, said our daughter had suffered a huge trauma; she had a fifty-fifty chance of surviving. She never regained consciousness and died six weeks later. Our marriage wasn't that strong, it couldn't sustain the tragedy, I went into counseling with a priest and he said I had to tell her the truth, and I did. Debby flew at me violently. Charlie Kingston and his career. Well you and golf can rot in hell! she screamed at me, and after that she never spoke to me again. She was crazy with vindictiveness, threatened to bring reckless endangerment charges against me. The charges didn't hold up but she got a big settlement, and I was in a bad way. I fell off the money list, lost my card. Phil Reardon, the priest I told you about, said I should go somewhere for a rest, a change. Hadn't my great-grandmother lived in Ireland? I should go to her village, look for her grave, and invite my soul."

"Atonement," Fiona said.

"If one can ever atone."

"You will. I know you will, Charlie."

"It's nice of you to say so," he said. "But to answer your question, Fiona. I wish I *could* blame golf. I can't. It's never golf."

CHAPTER 4

O n his first two forays into the Castlebantry Hills to find his great-grandmother's grave, Charlie came across several rural cemeteries, but no stone of the many he examined bore her name. Now, once again, he followed the sign at the crossroads for Croghanvale, walked along the narrow two-lane road, ignoring the first byway branching off as already traveled, then the second. Ten minutes farther along he spotted a narrow dirt lane leading upward through a meadow.

He followed it, going deeper and higher into the hills, the land becoming little more than a grassy trail. Up ahead, a farmer was driving ten or twelve head of cattle. Charlie stood to the side as they passed. The Irishman, smoking an old pipe, gave his cap a tip, and Charlie, pretending to have one on, touched his.

Well past the meadow, now in higher country, he came to a scattering of old stone buildings, a barn, a couple of sheds, and in the background a stucco house, long ago white; adjacent to the barn were several pens, connected one to the other by chutes. In one pen twelve or more cattle, not fully grown, milled about. Singly, they were shunted to another pen, where a young man with massive forearms grabbed each animal by the head while a second farmhand applied a long-handled cutter to the steer's stubby horns, lopping off one, then the other, as if trimming the limbs of a sapling. It was a battle each time, fierce bellowing of beast and swearing of man. Then the freshly shorn creature, blood oozing from the severed horns, was sent to a larger, fenced-in area, and a new steer was prodded in.

Charlie walked away, moving higher into the hills, beginning to think that finding Margaret Russell's grave, by random ventures, was unlikely. Nothing rode on the success or failure of the search; no one at home was waiting for a report. If Phil Reardon hadn't suggested it, Charlie couldn't say he'd even be looking. But he couldn't deny it was a nice way to spend an afternoon, walking in the countryside, looking at old gravestones; he would probably continue doing it.

The trail was becoming steeper, and finally Charlie spotted a path leading away from it. Following the path, he came to an ill-maintained patch of land dotted with gravestones. He stopped at the closest stone, rough and gritty, spotted with lichen; had to lean down to read the name: Barbara Clancy, 1842-1915. Next to her lay Neil Clancy, 1837-1902. Charlie wandered about. One marker, a stone cross, belonged to Martin Kilcannon, 1811-1879. A similar cross close to it: Lucille Kilcannon, 1815-1882. The graveyard seemed to have no discernible beginning or end, no front or back; it had simply spread out like ivy. Here lay James P. Delaney, 1807-1879. Here, Joseph O'Toole, 1899-1920.

He kept looking, moving about, respectful of the ground. At a small stone almost completely overgrown, he stopped; he wasn't sure why. All he could make out was the given name: Tamara. He pushed aside the grass and soil, bringing the full name to view.

Tamara Joyce, 1921-1927.

Charlie dropped to his knees and brushed away every last remnant of sod and weed from the unknown child's stone. So brief a life. Looking up, he saw field after field, always the grazing cows, endless hedgerows, a couple of farmhouses and barns, cumulus clouds in the sky. Farther away, a stretch of grain was bending in the wind, as if a great hand were sweeping through, flattening it; and then it sat up again, smiling at the sun. Off to his right a village, really a hamlet—probably Croghanvale; and farthest away of all, to the south, Charlie caught a bluish-green glimmer of the Celtic Sea.

****

In time he was on the main road again, but instead of heading back to Castlebantry, Charlie decided to continue on. The road began sloping downward, curving and winding. A few houses, small, very modest, popped up, then a number of houses in quick succession. One of them was a B&B called Rod & Creel. Dark-green door, sparkling windows softly curtained, window boxes flowing over. Not far ahead a steel bridge with a plank roadbed crossed a river, and on the other side the road resumed and rose into the country. Charlie didn't see anything that resembled a pub, unless it was the old, rambling, dull-white building with an odd variety of rooflines that sat on the river's bank.

Before finding out, he decided to walk to the bridge; halfway across he stopped and looked down at the water. It had a familiar character, as if he'd seen it before–not this exact spot but water similar to it, not very wide, not very deep, crisply moving around boulders. Two men in boots were casting flies upstream. Hands on the bridge railing, Charlie watched them for several minutes. The taller and younger had a strike and, after playing the fish for a couple of minutes, brought in a trout maybe twelve inches long. Charlie remembered his boyhood days fishing the ponds and creeks near his home in Willow Falls, until the summer he turned twelve and picked up his first golf club. Basically, that ended fishing.

He retraced his steps. Above the door that seemed an entrance to the meandering structure, a faded sign read: Pharr's. Charlie went in. Several men stood at the long bar, three of them at one end huddled together in earnest talk. The banquettes, in black vinyl, had splits here and there with white stuffing showing through. Behind the bar hung a large pegboard with a hundred items on it, many of them related to fishing. Compared to McCurtain's, Pharr's seemed like a poor cousin. In McCurtain's you were a guest in someone's living room; in Pharr's you weren't so much a guest, Charlie got the impression, as a family member home from the hills or the sea, rough clothes and all.

A young woman, the barmaid, came over, and he asked for a Murphy's. She drew the stout, perhaps rushing the process; it wasn't fully settled when she placed the pint before Charlie. Maybe Fiona's perfect presentations had set too high a standard, but he wasn't going to give it a second thought. Nicer to contemplate was the barmaid.

Dreamy brown eyes, curly auburn hair, in rose-colored cords and a peasant blouse with a low scoop neckline. Twenty. "Here for the fishing?" she asked.

"No. But it's a nice river. What is it?"

"The Argideen."

"Right, of course," Charlie said.   "It runs through Whitridge Manor."

"It might. I know it goes into Castlebantry."

Charlie was about to continue on the theme of the river. Ask her if she liked fishing. But before he could say another word, the men at the end of the bar suddenly raised their voices—no mere difference of opinion—and stayed at it a good while.

The barmaid gave them a glance, and Charlie asked her what was going on.

"Good Friday," she said.

"Good Friday? In May?"

She seemed amused. "The Peace Agreement with Ireland, Northern Ireland and England, so called because that was when it was signed, last month."

Charlie had never heard of it. "Why the argument?"

"For some it leaves a lot to be desired. It's in our Constitution that Ireland has inalienable rights to the six, and in the agreement that clause is deleted."

"The *six*?"

"The counties that make up Northern Ireland."

"Oh. Well, it doesn't seem right. I wouldn't like it either."

"That puts you in the minority."

"So most people think it's OK?"

"Ninety-five percent of Irish today say let England stay."

"I always thought the Irish were fighters," Charlie said.

"We were fighters," she said. "But now that everyone is making money—Ireland has become a prosperous na-tion—no one cares."

A new lifting of voices. "Someone seems to care," Charlie said.

"This is Pharr's, don't forget."

He couldn't forget what he didn't know.

In a hushed voice she said, "Two of those men are with the Southern Command."

"Are they now?"

"The Provos are hanging in but it's a dead issue. No one cares."

"Right." Charlie didn't have a clue as to what she was talking about.

She glanced at her watch. "God, I'm late. Have to run. Nice talking with you."

"Nice talking with you," he said. "What's your name?"

"Mary McAleer."

"I'm Charlie Kingston."

"Come back again."

He said he would. She started to leave and he asked her if she knew Emily.

"I think so, she's my grandmother."

"I'm supposed to look her up."

"I'll tell her you're here."

She left the public room, pushing through an inner door. The men at the far end of the bar seemed to have reached a certain truce, talking quietly among themselves. Charlie studied the items for sale on the peg board. He could use a combination bottle opener and cork screw. How about a flashlight? A selection of dry flies? A pearl-handled pen-knife? Sunglasses? Bug repellent? Playing cards?

The inner door swung open and a woman came out, spotted Charlie and walked over. She had a good many years on her but clearly didn't consider herself old. "Mary said an American was asking for me," she said in a strong voice. "That has to be you."

"It is. I'm Charlie Kingston."

"Emily Pharr. Mary's my granddaughter."

"She told me," Charlie said. "She just educated me on Good Friday."

"Oh, she's a smart one, studying political science at university in Cork," Emily Pharr said, "but like so many today, especially the young, full of misconceptions . The whole country is riding the back of the Celtic Tiger. Now who said you should look me up?"

"Dennis O'Hea."

"Ah, Dennis." Her eyes brightened in a smile. "I won't say how many years he and I go back, you wouldn't believe me. How is it you know each other?"

"We met in McCurtain's."

Emily gave her head a disapproving shake. "Pharr's is his local, always was," she said. "His wife died and he took a shine to Fiona. A splendid woman, loyal as the day is long. Her husband's an opportunist, an out-and-out charlatan, mounting a photograph of Michael Collins in the foyer of McCurtain's and claiming it's where he had his last pint!"

Charlie's elbows were on the bar but the force of Emily's words caused him to stand somewhat straighter. Just then a middle-aged man and woman, both ruddy-faced, walked in. Emily greeted them warmly. By their accents Charlie took them as Scandinavian. They mentioned how much they were enjoying the Rod & Creel and they'd both had a good day on the Argideen. Emily served them a couple of Jamesons and came back to Charlie.

"It was right here at this bar," she said, picking up where she'd left off. "Castlebantry Wrastler it was—of course I didn't know it at the time, I was a child. Michael Collins standing right where you're standing now, my mother at his side. Ah, the look of joy on her face. And his. Later on he took me on his knee and sang me a song about my father, who was killed in the war with England. 'A Brave Soldier,' that was the name of it. Then after a while he was kissing my mum goodbye, and he picked me up in his arms. The future of our young nation lay on his shoulders as he and his entourage headed back to Dublin. We all prayed for him and for Ireland, and next morning the news came in. I cried and cried, my mother cried and cried. Endless tears. Michael Collins shot dead at Beal na mBlath."

"Who did it, why?"

Just then one of the men spoke up. "Emily, me love, be a good woman now and take care of us. We're dying of thirst here."

She filled new pints, took away the empties, returned to Charlie. "The war with England was over but there were those against the treaty Collins signed," Emily went on. "It wasn't a clean break with Britain, certain allegiances held. Counties in the north stayed under English rule, a bone of contention to this day. As if Good Friday, eighty years later, will put that issue to rest! There were those, back then, namely Éamon de Valera, who thought the treaty was wrong and were against Collins. Civil war broke out. In the ambush that night, only Collins was killed. Many saw it as a conspiracy, still do. But this much I know, Charlie. It was Michael Collins who delivered Ireland to the Irish after centuries of suppression." She smiled in recognition of a great moment in the history of her country. "But let me get you another. Guinness, Murphy's?"

"Murphy's."

Emily worked the tap and placed a fresh pint before him. "Are you staying here in Croghanvale?"

"In Castlebantry. I'm renting a house on Pearse Road."

"Sure, it's a fine road to live on," Emily said. "Are you familiar with Pádraig Pearse?"

"I can't say I am."

"When I was a child we learned the Irish Proclamation, read by Pearse at the Easter Rising. Tell me if you don't think these are beautiful words: 'Irishmen and Irishwomen in the name of God and of the dead generations from which she receives her old tradition of nationhood, Ireland, through us, summons her children to her flag and strikes for her freedom.'"

"They are, they're very beautiful words," Charlie said.

"Easter Monday, 1916," she said, adding with quiet pride, "the year I was born. A rebellion against British rule, bound to fail; but it was a start, the first step on our road to independence."

"What happened to Pearse?"

"He faced an English firing squad with fourteen others, all brave Irishmen," Emily Pharr said. "There's a line from an Irish poet describing it. 'A terrible beauty is born.' You can't say it better than that."

CHAPTER 5

Occasionally a chill gust of wind would sneak though the cobbled siding of Charlie's house. Rain was falling hard and a corner of the ceiling was becoming stained; so far no leaks. His living room, thanks to a fire in the hearth, was staying warm; not exactly cozy but, everything considered, comfortable. Odd, to Charlie, was the color of the tiny flames licking the edges of the peat. Most everything in Ireland was green, but *fire*?

He was trying to catch up on Irish history and to understand current issues; at the moment was reading an article in the *Cork Examiner* on the Celtic Tiger, the pros and cons of the economic change sweeping the nation. For many, according to the article, the times were excellent; but for all the benefits of a booming economy, of the increase in per capita wealth, taxes were higher, the number of homeless was growing, housing costs were shooting upward. That stated, Ireland was no longer a poor, scrape-along farming country but a nation soon to be admitted to the European Union, more economically sound than many of the nations already a part of it.

Charlie leafed through the paper, stopping when he came to an article on Northern Ireland. Probably on the Good Friday Peace Agreement. It was on everyone's lips, in the papers on almost a daily basis. Most politicians and writers were calling it a "turning point in Irish history." Charlie began reading, only to realize that the article wasn't about Good Friday at all. It was about the upcoming "marching season" in Northern Ireland and the likelihood of renewed hostilities between supporters of the Orange Order parade, Protestants celebrating King William's victory over Catholic King James II at the Battle of the Boyne in 1690, and Catholic families who lived on Garvaghy Road, the parade's route. A year ago (the article went on) violence broke out. Three policemen were shot, 30 civilians injured, 900 baton rounds fired; and it was feared that violence this year would even be greater—

Someone was knocking and Charlie set the paper down. He went to the door; pulling it open he saw a woman in a yellow slicker looking at him and smiling. For a second he didn't recognize her, or couldn't believe what he saw, didn't trust his eyes—

"Hello, Charlie."

"Lora. How nice."

"Am I intruding?"

"Not at all. The rain doesn't want to stop. How did you know where I lived?"

"Dennis told me."

She slipped out of her slicker; taking it, he hung it on a hook on the door. Lora looked about. "What a snug, wonderful place!"

"Any minute now I expect the roof to start leaking."

They sat in the chairs before the fire. In her hand was a small package wrapped in silver paper, which she handed him. "This is for you, Charlie."

"Thank you." He removed the paper, revealing a slender book of William Butler Yeats's poems. He wasn't much into poetry but was touched by the thought, the gesture.

"I thought you might appreciate a glimpse into the Irish soul," she said.

"This is very kind of you, Lora." He laid the book on the low table. "Would you like a cup of tea?"

"I'd love one."

He went to the range, and Lora said that she and her husband were having a grand opening at The Whitridge a week from Saturday. "Wesley wants to know if you'd be willing to play an exhibition round for our guests," she said. "He'd play along with you to give it the 'appearance of a match,' his expression. Nine holes. For a professional fee, of course."

Charlie was caught off guard. Brotherton might *say* he'd play along to give it the appearance of a match but, as a former Walker Cup player, he would dearly love to beat the visiting American pro. It was precisely the kind of golf Charlie didn't want to play while here. But how could he refuse? "Tell your husband I'm looking forward to it."

"He'll be pleased. So will our guests."

He brought over two cups on different saucers. Lora, glancing about, asked him if he knew the history of his house. "Only that a young Irish couple lived here twenty years ago," he said, "the McGarritys. "I don't think they like me."

"Why do you say that?"

"I'm stomping on their turf. It's like—this is their place, what's an American golfer doing here?"

"The Irish love golf."

"It's a feeling I have, I really can't explain it," Charlie said. A drop of rain fell through the ceiling near the front window, hitting the floor. "How are you, Lora?"

"I just got back from Kilcarney," she said. "My father and I had our traditional nine-hole match. I'm getting tired of losing to him."

"I'm surprised your husband and dad don't get together occasionally to tee it up," Charlie said. "They might decide they like each other."

"In all these years they've met twice, and that's counting the wedding. I don't believe they'll ever meet again."

"Why not?"

"Politics. Wesley's an Orangeman," Lora explained. "His mother's a Blackhall from Glasgow. You can't get more conservative than that. She's often called the U.K.'s Barbara Bush."

Another drop fell and Charlie got a saucepan and set it on the floor. Before returning to his chair, he put a new chunk of peat on the fire.

"My father is anything but a Sinn Féin republican but he loves his country," Lora went on. "Wesley's loyalty is to the crown, specifically Northern Ireland. Deep down he'd like to see the old days come back when England ruled *all* of Ireland."

"So your husband's not too fond of Michael Collins."

"One mentions the name around Wesley at great risk."

"I'll take that under advisement," Charlie said with a laugh. "Where do you stand in this political mix, Lora?"

"Remember the day we met, I told you I was some-thing of a hybrid? That was the short answer," she began. "When I was a sixteen I was one with the great women in Ireland's war with England, Maud Gonne and Countess

Markievicz, among others. I kneeled in the waters of Clew Bay with my boyfriend and we wept for the lads on hunger strike in Northern Ireland's prisons. My father blamed Desmond—my boyfriend, Desmond McClure—for turning my head. Des had a job lined up in Killybegs, County Donegal, and we'd go there, get married, and have a life together. We ran away, got ourselves a flat, were happy— they were the happiest, the freest days of my life. But things took a bad turn. Des lost his job, I had a terrible miscarriage, got very sick and almost died. I didn't know it until later but he'd called my father, who came for me with another doctor and took me out of bed. I was too weak to fight and wondered why Des wasn't saying anything—he just stood there, looking at me. I had great care at home and pulled through, but for weeks and weeks I'd wake up crying."

"But you saw him again." Charlie said.

"I never did. He went to Australia."

"You were married," Charlie pointed out.

"We didn't get married." Raindrops kept hitting the pan. "For years I was upset that my father had come for me."

"You may have died, Lora."

"Something in me did die," she said. "On my twentieth birthday I made plans to study art in London, as a way of moving on."

"And met your future husband."

"In a pub near the National Gallery."

"From Desmond McClure to Wesley Brotherton," Charlie said.

"I know."

Lora was quiet for a while, fingers on her gold pendant.

"That's a beautiful piece," Charlie said.

"It was uncovered in Carraigahowley, Granuaile's castle," Lora said. "Likely belonged to her, experts say." She pulled the pendant away from her chest. "Here, feel it."

He hesitated a second, then leaned across the arm of his chair, their faces almost touching—her eyelash brushed the bristle on his chin—and felt the pendant's contours.

"Is anything happening?" Lora asked.

"Not yet."

"Give it time."

He would give it forever, breathing her in, his wrist gentle on her breast. Then he said, "I'm beginning to feel—warm."

"She's coming through. She likes you, Charlie."

"I like her." He held the pendant for another few seconds, then let it slip from his fingers. "The Pirate Queen," he said, sitting back in his chair.

Faint images of peat flames flickered on Lora's eyelids. "There's more to Grace O'Malley than that," she said.

"Tell me."

Rain and wind smashed into the side of his house. "Granuaile was the chieftan of a powerful clan in County Mayo in the late part of the Sixteenth Century," Lora went on. "Of course, all of Ireland was under the rule of England at that time. The English governor of the western region of Ireland, a Sir Richard Bingham, pursued Granuaile relentlessly with his men to arrest her; she had too much sway. He didn't catch up with her but he arrested her two grown sons. In one of her galleys with twenty oarsmen pulling, Granuaile went to London to petition Queen Elizabeth for their release. She was finally presented to Elizabeth and didn't bow when they met. She was after all a queen herself and definitely didn't consider Elizabeth the queen of Ireland. They met as equals and she won Elizabeth's respect."

Lora's eyes met Charlie's. "The petition was granted," she said. "Her sons were released and Sir Bingham was removed from his post."

"That's quite a story," Charlie said.

Lora glanced at her watch. "I should be going. That was a very fine cup of tea."

"Thank you, and thank you for the book."

At the door he helped her on with her slicker. "Remember, a week from Saturday," Lora said. "Oh, there's a party that evening, starting at seven."

She ran out to her car. Charlie watched through the window. When she pulled away, he sat down in his chair watching tiny emerald flames in the hearth, then reached for the book of poems.

CHAPTER 6

There wasn't much to see in Sam's Cross—a small stone building, a bronze bust of Michael Collins, a handsome plaque with highlights of his life and career; but Charlie was deeply moved as he walked about the Irishman's birthplace. Why he felt a connection with Collins, he wasn't sure. Pro golfers kneeled at the altar of flag, values, and the status quo. As one of them his entire adult life, Charlie couldn't imagine too many Tour players taking to the man who put a gun to England's head demanding independence.

A few tourists came in, looked quickly around, left. Charlie lingered a good while trying to make sense of his feelings. The place was getting to him; puzzled, but not unhappy about it, he headed back to the crossroads.

As he passed in front of McCurtain's the family door opened and two girls, maybe eight years old, came out in school uniforms—green-plaid skirts with dark-green knee socks and white blouses. One of the girls was tall and thin with light-brown hair; the other, smaller, had dark hair and reminded Charlie—he was stunned by the similarity—of April: what his daughter might look like today. The girls began practicing a dance step on the paved area before the door, arms at their sides, feet striking the hard surface rapidly and in unison. Their shoes had taps, and the routine caused a good bit of clatter.

When it ended, Charlie clapped; both girls smiled, the smaller of the two more openly. He continued by, stopping in Monahan's to pick up his laundry and a few items from her shelves. Mrs. Monahan was cordial, she liked his business, but he was beginning to sense that her opinion of him was souring. He remembered his first morning in Castlebantry, coming in for groceries and a bag of peat— she'd spoken of herself freely. Her husband, a great fisherman, lost his life three years ago when a sudden squall capsized his boat in the Celtic Sea. She'd been the first to mention the couple who had lived in his house, Mairead and Kieran McGarrity. Like Dennis, she had clammed up when Charlie had pressed her to go on. Now, as he paid for his laundry and selected items, Mrs. Monahan, a stolid woman of fifty, gave him a thank you and a tight little smile.

At his house he laid the paper-wrapped clothes on his bed, put away a couple of jars and cans, then opened the back door and sat down on one of the metal chairs. A breeze was blowing in from the rising field. The entire herd of cattle grazed near the crest, and Charlie was starting to relax— somewhat relax—here in his stone cottage. But he hardly felt at ease and had begun facing the bedroom door while at his table as the only way he could relax while eating; in his mind the McGarritys were always there, looking out at him. He'd spoken to Mr. Bailey on one occasion after his original call and had mentioned the outmoded plumbing and appliances—aspects of the rental the agent would understand—and Bailey said he would start looking around for another place, if Mr. Kingston wanted him to. Charlie had responded with a single word: Please.

A knocking on the front door broke Charlie's train of thought. He went through the house. Standing on the front path was Kevin Dennehy.

"Do you have a minute, Mr. Kingston?"

"Sure. Come in," Charlie said.

He led the way through the living room. "Sit down, Kevin," Charlie said, indicating one of the metal chairs. "What's up?"

"I thought maybe we could have a talk."

"Of course we can."

The boy had big hands, one holding the other between his knees. "Dr. Mulrooney only took me on for two weeks," he said. "My time with him is up and I was wandering around, thinking how much I wanted to play golf but Dick O'Brien would ring up the house, sure as hell, following my father's orders. My mum said she wouldn't cover for me again. My da almost killed me with a golf club once, and next time he'd likely succeed. Mr. Kingston, I don't mean to lay my troubles on you—"

"You're not, Kevin. Go ahead, keep on. Call me Charlie."

"I was walking by your house just now, hoping you were in. Next month I'll be sixteen—my whole life ahead of me, right? I feel like I'm in a sand trap with a buried lie."

"A buried lie is playable," Charlie said.

"Not this one. It's hell in the house, my da coming home, putting me down at every turn. If he ever hits me again, I'll lay into him, and I don't want that to happen. I could avoid the whole thing by leaving, by going away—"

"For how long?"

"A year, five years. Who knows?"

"What would you do?"

"I'd get a job at a golf course—cutting the rough, mowing fairways," Kevin said. "I'm strong, they'd take me on, and I could play and practice in my off hours. Here, golf is out. My da says it's ruining my life. How he makes it sound you'd think I was hooked on drugs! I don't want to give the game up, Charlie, not for him, not for anyone. It's something I love."

"Your father's absolutely wrong about golf," Charlie said. "But is he wrong about your failing grades, hanging out at O'Brien's, drinking with older men? How do you answer that, Kevin?"

"I was doing it to spite him—for leaving my mum alone to run the pub, working herself sick while he's in Germany, then coming home and—"

"It's a hell of a way to get back at him, isn't it?" Charlie said.

"Maybe it is, I don't care."

"You don't care about yourself?"

"I used to but he beat it out of me."

"So you're giving up."

"Giving up is staying home."

"To me, giving up is running away," Charlie said.

"Right now you sound just like my da! What did I come here for anyway?"

"To talk. We're talking, right?"

"I was hoping you'd understand."

"I do understand. The question is, do you?"

Just then the phone rang and Charlie stood up. "Excuse me, Kevin." He went into the bedroom and picked up the receiver. "Hello."

"Mr. Kingston, Frank Bailey speaking."

"Yes, Mr. Bailey." From where Charlie sat on his bed, he could see the terrace but only one chair—his, not Kevin's.

"As I said, rentals have been very tight," Bailey said. "But ten minutes ago something fell in my lap and I'm calling you at once."

Charlie pressed lightly on his forehead. "Yes, go ahead."

"A couple from Norway just canceled their reservation for a lovely apartment in Holiday Homes, a new development here in Castlebantry," Bailey said. "Nothing rustic about it, and I think more to your liking. All modern conveniences: washing machine and dryer, microwave oven, electric heat, color TV. Facing Castlebantry Bay. You can see the swans and fishing boats from your living room window. As for the rent, it's more than you're paying now but well worth it, and to show good faith I'll give you partial credit for the time already spent on Pearse Road. I could swing by in ten minutes and show you the unit."

Suddenly Charlie had different feelings. "Mr. Bailey, I've decided to stay where I am."

"A week ago you were saying—"

"I know. I want to thank you for your extra time and effort."

"Well, I'm glad you're happy, Mr. Kingston. I always thought the cottage on Pearse Road was everything you'd asked for: quiet, peaceful, away from the bustle of town."

"Thanks again, Mr. Bailey."

Charlie set the receiver down and went quickly out, his eyes going to Kevin's chair: empty. He liked the kid and wanted to help him, one golfer to another, and was disappointed he hadn't stayed. But the next moment Charlie spotted the boy at the stone wall and walked over.

Kevin turned, facing him. "You're not like my da, I didn't mean that," he said.

"It's OK. In certain ways all fathers are alike."

Several of the cattle had stopped grazing and were looking at the two figures at the wall.

"Here's what I want to say, Kevin," Charlie said. "Sixteen is young. I want you to be realistic about your age. I think you should continue living at home. I'm offering you a job."

Charlie turned from the boy and faced the back of the cottage. "I'd like the weeds in the front walk pulled, window boxes planted, weeds on the back terrace pulled." Charlie made a sweeping motion with his arm. "This whole area behind the house cut short, fairway length. So we'll have a really good place to practice pitching and chipping. I'm offering you lessons."

"Mr. Kingston, I can't afford lessons."

"They won't cost you anything."

"That's isn't right."

"Hear me out," Charlie said. Almost all the cattle were now watching and beginning to come closer. "For every hour you work, you'll earn a half hour of instruction," Charlie said. "If lessons weren't on the table, I'd pay you four pounds an hour. With lessons, I'll give you three. But you have to promise me something."

"What is it?"

"First, go to your principal and tell him, or her, that you're turning a new leaf and want a second chance."

"OK."

"And second, that you'll stick with it, no back-sliding, no lapses."

"I promise, you have my word on it, Charlie."

"Great."

The herd of cattle was plodding ever closer toward the wall. Charlie said tools were inside the shed, old but they looked serviceable. "If you feel like working and I'm not here," he said, "just go in and take what you need. Keep a work sheet. Hours worked, dates—"

"When can I start?"

"When do you want to?"

"How about now?"

Charlie was delighted. "Fine, but we have to shake hands on this, Kevin, to make it official. All we need is a witness."

"I can run home and get Brigid."

The cattle were plodding closer. "Not necessary. In another minute or two we're going to have upwards of fifty," Charlie said.

CHAPTER 7

Ten or so people were in McCurtain's when Charlie walked in early one evening toward the end of the week. Dennis O'Hea, standing at the bar, put out his hand. "I was hoping you'd come in, Charlie. We're making great progress on the berm. Eight truckloads of dirt, leveled and shaped—four to five degrees reverse pitch. Tomorrow we're laying down sod. Mr. Brotherton popped over from London and liked what he saw."

"Good. It never hurts to please the boss."

Fiona came by and set a Murphy's in front of Charlie. She greeted him but didn't stay to talk. Dennis said, "Donal is home. Poor woman, she's miserable."

"I'm sorry about that. Maybe she'll smarten up and leave him."

"Now wouldn't that be grand?"

"I met Emily Pharr," Charlie said.

"That's a brighter note."

"I mentioned the controversy over Michael Collins's 'last pint.'"

"Sure she set you straight."

"It was a 'Castlebantry Wrastler.'"

"A fine lager in its day. The brewer, Gus O'Toole? His grandson owns a pub in the village."

"The place itself—I mean Pharr's—it's not your everyday local," Charlie said. "Mary threw out a lot of names, phrases, like Southern Command and Provos. Right over my head."

"Sweet lass that she is," Dennis said with a smile. Then, "Southern Command means the southern branch of the I.R.A. Provos goes back a bit. At the start of the Troubles in Northern Ireland, start1ng in 1970—which really echoes your civil rights movement in the States—the original I.R.A. had good intentions but had no teeth to it. Its members were socialists, by and large. So a splinter group was formed that took up arms, believed in force, as in Michael Collins's day, and they called themselves the *Provisional* I.R.A. Provos. Today the Provos *are* the Irish Republican Army."

"Mary said only a small percentage of Irish put any stock in the I.R.A."

"Times are different," Dennis said, "and Mary's a young person, she looks to the future. But if the republican spirit is dead, why do the Castlebantry garda keep an eye on Pharr's?" O'Hea continued in a quieter voice. "Fiona's brother, Eddie Dunn—he's the chief, you know—has wanted to raid the place for the past ten years."

"What keeps him from doing it?"

"Emily, by being Emily."

Charlie ordered the corned beef and cabbage and another round of stout. His talk with Dennis turned to topics more immediately at hand—the completion of the berm and the golf weekend fast approaching.

Later that evening, after dinner and a little music, Charlie settled up with Fiona at the bar. As he was about to leave, she asked him if he could stop by tomorrow afternoon for tea; something had come up and she wanted his opinion.

"Isn't Donal here?"

"He's leaving in the morning. I'll call you if he stays on."

"I'd appreciate that, Fiona."

"Good night, Charlie."

****

Mrs. Monahan was in front of her shop arranging a display of hand-held tools and potted plants when Charlie walked by the following afternoon. She greeted him with a certain formality—any cheerfulness was gone—and he could feel her eyes on his back all the way to McCurtain's. At the Dennehy family door, he didn't look over his shoulder—wouldn't give her the satisfaction. Charlie lifted the brass knocker, let it fall. The door opened and Fiona was standing there.

"It's nice of you to come by, Charlie," she said.

"Having tea with you is a treat."

"Sit down. I'll bring it right in."

And she did, coming in with a flowered teapot, two cups and a dish of assorted treats: tiny cakes, scones, jams. She set the tray down; beside him on the sofa, she filled their cups. After a while she told him that Donal wanted them to come to Germany.

"To visit?"

"To live."

"Permanently?"

Fiona was biting her upper lip. "Yes."

"How do you feel about it?"

"Does that matter?"

"Fiona, of course it matters."

"Father Byrne says my responsibility is to my marriage."

"That's what he says. Are you happy with Donal?"

"When he comes home and we're in bed, I grit my teeth."

He was stunned by the directness of her reply. "Then that answers the question."

"Does it?"

"Of course it does."

"Father Byrne—"

"Father Byrne speaks from set and fast rules, Fiona. What else would he say?"

A truck pulled into McCurtain's parking lot. Fiona used a napkin on her eyes, stood, and looked out the window. "Excuse me, Charlie. It's a delivery I've been waiting for. I won't be long."

She walked out and he finished a scone and drank his tea, imagining a real-time scenario: Donal Dennehy hadn't returned to Germany at all. He'd spent the day in Cork and even now, as the American golfer sat in his house, he was heading back to Castlebantry and any minute would come bursting in—

Charlie's fantasy was interrupted by the sound of giggling. Looking over he saw two young girls coming into the living room from a different part of the house. Holding hands, they went to the family door, talking brightly. He recognized them as the girls he'd seen on an earlier occasion. In his mind, they were probably headed outside to practice a step, but then he realized they were simply saying goodbye. The girl with auburn hair, whom he had taken as Fiona's daughter, went out. The smaller, dark-haired girl, turning, looked startled at the sight of a man on the sofa.

"I'm waiting for your mum," Charlie said.

Her face softened. "We saw you before. You were walking by."

"And you were dancing. I'm Charlie."

"My name is Brigid."

"Your mum made a very nice tea, Brigid. Please, join me."

She smiled, sat on the sofa and reached for a sweet. Charlie said, "Your mother told me you're entering a dance competition." Then, remembering the term, "A *feis*."

"Yes, I am."

"Is it your first one?"

"Oh, no. It's my third. Two years ago I was a beginner, then an advanced beginner, now I'm a novice."

"That's very impressive," Charlie said. "You're moving up fast."

"The first levels are easier," she explained. "A first, second or third place moves you up. But when you're a novice you have to win or you stay a novice."

"Then what do you become, if you win?"

"A prizewinner."

"A prizewinner," Charlie repeated, liking the sound of the word. "I'm sure you'll do great."

They both reached for the same cookie, Charlie a split-second earlier. He put it in her hand. She smiled again, popped it into her mouth. "My mum says you live in the little house on Pearce Road."

"I do."

"Whenever I see that house it reminds me of a bunch of crooked teeth."

"Maybe I should call the dentist."

Brigid's laugh had a jingle to it, like far away sleigh bells.

"It's a house with many problems," Charlie said. "The roof leaks. The other day I had to put down a kitchen pot on the floor. Each time a drip hit, it went 'plink.'"

"Plink?"

Charlie nodded. "Plink."

"What else is wrong with it?" Brigid asked.

"It has a squeaky bed that doesn't know if it's a twin or a full."

"Well, send it to school then."

"Now that's an excellent suggestion."

"What else?"

"It has a rusty old shower. The water trickles out like a sprinkling can. It takes forever to rinse away the soap."

"That's dreadful. What else?"

"A big herd of cows comes up to a wall and looks at you when you're having tea," Charlie said. "Do you know why?"

"No."

"Because cows love tea parties. Especially the cookies!"

She was laughing gaily. "What else?"

"There's a spooky shed. Inside are lots of old tools, and the floorboards are broken, and no matter how bright it is outside, it's always dark and gloomy inside."

He thought she might ask "what else?" still again, and he was working to come up with another silliness. What she asked filled Charlie with joy. Would he come to her feis?

"I'd love to," he said.

"That's wonderful. Well, I have to go," she said. "I have schoolwork."

"See you again, Brigid."

She went away and Fiona came in, apologizing for her own absence.

"I met your daughter. She invited me to her feis. I accepted, but I may have spoken too soon," Charlie said

"Why do you say that?"

"I'm here for the month. When is it?"

"The second week in June."

Charlie raised his hands. "I'll be gone."

"That's too bad." She wasn't speaking just for her daughter. Then, returning to their earlier talk: "What am I going to do, Charlie?"

"You're asking me a huge question."

"Your views are important to me. I think you see things clearly."

He laughed to himself. "Fiona, I wish I did."

"Tell me how you see it."

Charlie had a last sip of tea. "Fiona, my father had the United Auto Workers, you have the Church. All I can do is tell you what I told him—don't get so buried in union affairs that you forget yourself. Personally, I can't see you going to Germany with Donal."

They talked for a while longer. At the family door, as he was leaving, Fiona thanked him for coming over. "I think it's wonderful that you've given Kevin work," she said.

"He's doing a great job. Did he mention the lessons?"

"He did."

"Are you all right with that?"

"He's a different boy, Charlie. I think it's wonderful."

****

At his house of crooked teeth, minutes later, Charlie went through to the back door. The whole backyard was cut, if not to fairway length, close to it. To the left of the shed stood a seven-foot bamboo stick. Kevin was attaching a bright yellow flag to the top of it. Nearby, a green, gas-driven mower squatted like a huge frog.

Charlie walked over. "Kevin, I'm beyond impressed."

"I asked my mum for a square of cloth. When I told her why, she hemmed the edges and sewed in grommets."

As if she has time to kill, Charlie thought. "Whose mower is it?"

Kevin finished securing the flag. "A friend of mine brought it over. His older brother has a truck. We threw the weeds and long grass over the wall."

"Good. Get your clubs."

Kevin went into the shed and came out with his golf bag.

"Now we have something to aim for," Charlie said, looking at the flagstick.

****

They worked for almost an hour on pitches to the green—the knock down, the lob, the bump and run. The boy had a natural rhythm, a good attitude, and Charlie had the feeling that he'd become a fine player. His clubs weren't much. Evidently someone had forgotten them at O'Brien's, had never claimed them, and Kevin had bought the whole set for £15. It was about all they were worth.

When the lesson ended they sat on the terrace, each with a glass of Orangina. "Pay day," Charlie said. "What do I owe you?"

"I have five hours on the books."

He drew a ten- and a five-pound note from his wallet. "Here you go. Terrific work, Kevin. Listen, will you be free to caddie for me tomorrow? I'm playing at Whitridge Manor."

"I'd like to, Charlie, but I don't know much about it."

"Don't worry. You'll do fine."

"Is it a tournament?"

"No, nothing like that," Charlie said. "Casual, a stroll in the park."

CHAPTER 8

On the great lawn before the Manor House a luncheon party was in progress—six tables draped in white with an elegant centerpiece on each, four people to a table, wine glasses sparkling, a string quartet playing on the terrace. Charlie gave a glance at the festivities, spied Lora—her red hair made it easy—then, with Kevin, who was carrying his golf bag, veered left onto the access road. In the vicinity of the stone cottage ten golf carts were parked, in no particular order, abandoned after the morning golf.

Shortly, they came to the practice range. Divots in the turf, hundreds of golf balls dotting the ground (near and far), dark-blue cloth bags, many still containing balls, scattered about. Kevin stood Charlie's clubs in a chrome rack and Charlie spilled a nearby bag and began hitting lofted shots, if he could call them shots. He didn't like one of them. The sound of club face striking ball was off key: more clunk than click. He went to an 8-iron, then a 5. He might have been splitting logs, for all the feel he had. He hit six balls off the turf with his 3-wood and two balls, sitting on tees, with his driver.

"That's it, Kevin."

They sat on one of the benches. Past the 300-yard marker, high on a distant hill on Whitridge Manor property, Charlie saw a red flag fluttering in the breeze. Probably the pin on the fifth hole. It looked more like a danger signal. Travel here at your own risk.

"I'm nervous about caddying," Kevin said.

"You put the bag on your shoulder, you watch where the ball goes—"

"There's more than that to it."

"True. Don't talk, whistle or jingle loose change when a player is addressing his ball."

"What about the flagstick?"

"Kevin, Mr. Brotherton will have his caddie. You're my caddie. If I want the flagstick out, I'll say pull the flagstick. If you're in doubt about something, ask."

"OK."

Charlie gave Kevin a slap on his arm. "Come on, it's tee time."

They started back. The lawn before the Manor House was deserted, except for staff members clearing the grounds. Charlie and Kevin bore left on the pebbled path sloping downward to the first tee. Waiting there, half of them in golf carts, were the Brothertons' guests. Lora emerged from the group and greeted Charlie, offering her hand, smiling. "Hello, Charlie," she said. "I'd like you to meet my husband, Wesley." Then to the man at her side, "Wesley, this is Charlie Kingston."

"Well, I've heard a lot about you," Brotherton said as he extended his hand. Bald, he had muscular arms and a full, round chest, tufts of gray-black hair showing at the neck of his brown and orange shirt. "Welcome to The Whitridge."

Charlie sensed power in the man's grip, not that Brotherton applied pressure; but the power was there. He also knew that Brotherton wouldn't be the one to break eye contact, and rather than force the issue, he didn't make it one. "It's my pleasure, Wesley," Charlie said. "This is my caddie, Kevin Dennehy."

"I have a caddie somewhere here myself," Brotherton said. "Oh, here he is now."

A tall, sinewy man with a thick, well-trimmed mustache and high cheekbones, sporting wraparound shades, came up toting a shiny black golf bag. He was Reggie MacNair, Brotherton said, from Buckhaven, Scotland. He was carrying the bag backwards, clubs pointing over his shoulder, as if the bag were a quiver and each club an arrow. Which made Charlie think MacNair wasn't a caddie at all, except as Brotherton called him one. MacNair didn't say a word. Perfunctory handshakes all around.

"Well, let's get started," Brotherton said. He spoke to his gathered guests. "Friends, I'd like to introduce American golfer Charlie Kingston, here in Castlebantry on holiday. A six-time winner on the PGA Tour, he won the Irish Open at Mount Juliet and came within a stroke of beating Nick Faldo at St. Andrews. I'll be keeping him company on our round." People laughed, applauded.

He turned to Charlie. "For the record—match play, stroke play? What's your pleasure?"

"Hole by hole."

"Then match play it is. The honor is fittingly yours." Brotherton again put out his hand.

Charlie and Kevin walked onto the teeing ground, where Kevin slid the bag from his shoulder and held it while Charlie selected his 3-wood. Club in hand, he teed a ball, stood behind it to determine his line, then, taking into account the dogleg, set up for a right-to-left shot: his patented draw. The ball started out OK but too soon began curving left, sharply left. It took four or five nasty bounces shy of the dogleg and settled into deep grass behind a grove of trees.

From the gallery, mostly silence; a few murmurings of disappointment. Charlie picked up his tee and moved to the side of the teebox with Kevin.

Wesley Brotherton's turn. He didn't fool with a 3-wood; from his bag he pulled his 45-inch Big Bertha with a black and gold graphite shaft. His stance was something of a crouch. No waggle, no fiddling with his grip, no forward press to initiate his swing. He snapped the club back as if yanking his hands out of a fire. When his arms were belt high, he cocked his wrists, then shifted his weight to the left: hips thrusting, hands lashing downward, wrist staying hinged almost until contact. The ball rocketed away, going deep and straight, curved at the dogleg and bounced (out of sight) toward the green.

He stood, shaft wrapped around his back, looking after the ball, which he hadn't so much hit as murdered. He acknowledged the applause, then made a gesture to Charlie to join him in walking.

They moved off the tee, MacNair at Brotherton's side, Kevin at Charlie's. Those of the gallery in carts started engines and followed along, as did those on foot. All proceeded down the first fairway. Brotherton said to Charlie, "I was struggling all morning. Finally got it going on the seventh hole, finished birdie, par, birdie—for a two-over thirty-eight."

"Very nice," Charlie said.

"Your berm on the eighth hole works like a charm," Brotherton said. "I played for a draw but my swing double-crossed me—I hit a push-fade. Bloody ball hit the slope and bounded like a bat out of hell for the trees. Charlie Kingston's berm to the rescue! I hit 5-iron to escape, then a neat 7 to twelve feet and drained the putt. Instead of a double bogey, I made par."

"Excellent playing," Charlie said.

"Did you ever design a course?"

"Not on my own. A couple of years ago I sprained my wrist hitting from a tangle of roots, and a well-known Chicago architect, Lew Warnecke, took me on—"

"I hired Sean Harrigan to do The Whitridge," Brotherton said, "but I got tired of fighting the pig-headed Irishman and let him go. Right now I have 300-plus acres in County Clare. It's going to be a great course, hard on the Atlantic—huge dunes, crashing surf. The routing is giving us a headache."

"Who's the architect?"

"Nick Jarvis, the American."

"Sure. The Mink Hollow course in Rye, New York—"

"Myself, I'm disappointed in him," Brotherton said. "He lacks imagination." They kept walking, their caddies keeping pace. "What do you think of Clinton?"

"Clinton?"

"Your president, Bill Clinton?"

"Oh. I didn't vote for him."

"Good. I can't stand the man."

"I'm not really that political," Charlie said, "but I vote Republican."

"In Ireland," Brotherton said, "if you're a republican—small 'r'—it links you with Sinn Féin and the I.R.A. Fucking terrorists, I'd send every bloody member to the gallows and be done with it. So a word to the wise. While you're here, don't say you're a republican. It sends the wrong message."

Someone from the gallery was calling Wesley's name. "Excuse me, Charlie," he said, going over to walk with an elderly couple. The man's pale green trousers complemented the woman's yellow, broad-brimmed hat.

"How're you doing?" Charlie said to Kevin.

"If I ever played here I'd be afraid of taking a divot."

Brotherton remained with his guests and Kevin and Charlie approached the area where his ball had finally stopped. After a short search Kevin found it nestled in thick grass. Rough. With a perfectly hit, tree-clearing, left-bending 8-iron, Charlie could reach the green. The gallery was gathered about, wanting the golfer who'd almost beaten Nick Faldo to go for it. Only problem was—Charlie didn't have it in him to execute the shot. He selected a 7-iron and punched safely to the fairway.

Still away, he took aim at the flagstick with a pitching wedge. He couldn't see the hole, just the top half of the pin. He wanted to get within ten feet, but the hit was off line from the start and stayed off line, falling short as well. Silence among the gallery, not even a groan.

For his second shot Brotherton selected a 60-degree wedge, chopped down on the ball as if beheading a snake. The ball rose at a steep angle, landing on the green to cheers and clapping.

MacNair retrieved the divot and tamped it down with his shoe, and both players started up the incline. Charlie's ball was 25 feet from the pin, Brotherton's twelve. Farther away, Charlie putted first, his ball stopping seven feet from the hole. Brotherton gave his putt a perfunctory read, then promptly holed out—birdie. He gave his gold-plated putter a kiss to laughter and applause and walked off the green.

Wesley Brotherton, 1-up.

He had taken the honor and, as if saying he had no intention of relinquishing it, the Whitridge Manor host rocketed his drive on the second hole, easily clearing the stream. Excellent position. Charlie cleared the stream also but his ball again veered left, ending up in a fairway bunker. As on the first hole, the two men walked together with their respective caddies. The former Walker Cup player had a quick, energetic step, and Charlie's clubs were rattling on Kevin's shoulder as the lad hustled to keep up.

"I've wanted my own course for years," Brotherton said. He had a large mouth but line-thin lips and a forehead that almost seemed a weapon, to be used for bumping one's way through a crowd or butting aside executives in a boardroom. "I have five-star resorts around the world, four all told, each with championship layouts built mostly around castles," he said. "When Lora and I show up we're given the 10:20 slot in the morning, say. We own the fucking place and we have tee times. I hate tee times. Even if a man owns Big Ben, he wants his own watch."

"I can see that," Charlie said.

"A few years ago I played Augusta National," Brotherton said. "A good friend I have on Wall Street is a member. I finished Amen Corner and said 'Amen'— three times. Came in with a 77, quite pleased with it actually. You've played in the Masters."

"I have," Charlie said.

"How'd you do?"

"One top five, three top tens, missed the cut four times."

"Lora says you're part Irish."

"I am."

"She likes telling people she's related to Grace O'Malley. As if that's a recommendation," Brotherton said. "The woman was a bloody pirate, robbing and killing her own people. The Celts were arrogant dreamers. Didn't have the brains to join hands and create a united front against the English. By birth I'm a Scot—loyal to the crown, always have been, always will be. When we put our mind to it, back then, we knocked the Celts off like tins on a fence, clan by fucking clan. Here's your ball."

Charlie walked into the bunker with a 5-iron, trying to clear his brain; he worked his feet into the sand. With a clean hit, he could reach the green. But he didn't have a clean hit. He caught the ball heavy, taking too much sand, and it fell short of the green. Brotherton's approach was low, a partial top, but it bounced and skipped onto the putting surface, well past the flag. Charlie's pitch was long; it needed backspin but the spin didn't materialize. Brotherton lagged to 14 inches and Charlie conceded the putt. His own right-to-left 15-footer skidded by the hole. Another bogey.

Brotherton, 2-up.

On the path to the next teebox, the host walked with his guests; he was in an expansive mood, chatting it up. Taking two holes from the American pro was an accomplishment—he was doing all right, more than holding his own. When they reached the teeing ground of the 3-par, Brotherton asked MacNair for a hat; his head had taken quite enough sun. From the side pocket on Brotherton's bag, the Scotsman pulled a bright orange cap and Brotherton put it on. Someone said, "Wesley, this is Ireland. Wrong color," to laughter. Brotherton tugged at the cap's visor and tomahawked a 4-iron over the shimmering pond and the swans swimming benignly on it. The ball, terrified, did as goddamn well told, landing pin high. Charlie couldn't shake his malaise. He sent his ball upward in a big lazy arc; it landed on the bank near the green, stayed for a couple of seconds, then trickled into the water.

Brotherton, 3-up.

Guests were starting to talk among themselves, shaking their heads. This was the golfer who almost beat Nick Faldo? On the fourth hole, a par five reachable in two, both golfers cleared the ravine, but Charlie's second shot, a 3-wood, died, his ball burrowing into a clover-leaf greenside trap. Brotherton's third shot, a chip, took him to ten feet of the hole. Charlie, blasting to get out, didn't put sufficient charge in the shot, and his ball barely made the green. Away, he putted to two feet. Brotherton's putt hit the hole, and fell.

Brotherton, 4-up.

Kevin wasn't saying anything but he was glum as he walked with Charlie on the magical path through the forest that led to the fifth tee. Not far ahead, guests were talking. A gentleman was telling Brotherton if he wasn't careful he'd close the American pro out on the next hole; another man said he should give Kingston a break, let him win a hole for Anglo-American relations. Wesley was walking with Lora, his arm casually on her shoulder. Perhaps he had instructed MacNair to reverse his bag because he was now carrying it correctly while trudging along four or five steps behind the Brothertons, or more exactly behind Mrs. Brotherton, a forward tilt to his head. On every third breath his nostrils seemed to contract, like someone sniffing the air.

Why are you lollygagging along? Charlie asked himself, suddenly conscious. Losing to Brotherton is losing to the creep dogging Lora's tracks! So you made a pledge to your daughter. Forget the pledge, she'll understand. Win this one, for April....

On the teeing ground, he waited for Brotherton to hit. The fifth hole was a steady rise to the green, 448 yards away, the highest spot on the course; and a tough par 4. Brotherton powered his ball straight up the middle. Pleased with the shot, with himself, he stepped back. All yours, Charlie.

Kevin put the driver in his hand and Charlie perched a ball on a tee, made an easy practice stroke—then took his stance and swung. The ball exploded off the club face, going high and deep, landed thirty yards past Brotherton's, took two big hops, and stopped.

Silence: Where did *that* come from?

"Good hit," Brotherton said, and began walking with MacNair.

Brotherton hit his second shot a touch heavy and the ball fell short of the green. He mumbled under his breath. Charlie nailed a 5-iron to seven feet, and Brotherton made a great up-and-down for par. Charlie gave his putt a good read, inside left edge, and the ball dropped for a birdie.

Brotherton, 3-up.

Charlie won the next hole with a birdie.

Brotherton, 2-up.

And the next with a birdie.

Brotherton, 1-up.

They went to the eighth tee, the second par 5 on the course. Charlie knew how to play the hole—a solid draw into the slope. He executed it perfectly. Brotherton, knowing how to play the hole, executed the shot poorly. His drive didn't bend to the left; it veered right, hit the sloping fairway, and bounced for the trees. Thanks to a certain berm, his ball stayed in play, but he was still upset and cursed the bloody Irishman who designed the hole to start with. No one was talking now. As Brotherton and MacNair headed for the berm, Charlie, observing his host, saw a will to prevail etched more sharply on his face than he could ever recall seeing on the face of a Tour competitor. Brotherton would not allow his four-hole lead over the American golfer to vanish.

He recovered well from the berm, sent his next shot to the putting surface. Charlie had only thirty yards for his third shot; a little bump and run got him to six feet. Brotherton's putt went wide (par) and Charlie sank his (birdie).

Match, all square. One hole to play.

A guest commented, as the party made its way to the ninth tee, that this was getting good.

Nine was an exceptionally beautiful hole at The Whitridge, and the most challenging in Charlie's opinion: a par 4 measuring 435 yards that fell into a valley, then curved to the right and simultaneously rose to a small green surrounded by traps, trees in the background and on the right. The stream that meandered through the course cut this fairway as well, some 230 yards from the tee.

"What do you think, Kevin?" Charlie said. "Three-iron or driver?"

"Do you want to tie or do you want to win?"

Charlie put out his hand. "Driver."

He set up, made a good swing, he thought; but the ball started right and kept right. Straight, just off line. It flew the stream, plenty of distance, ending up in the extreme right rough. Not good. Not good at all. In fact, terrible.

Brotherton promptly exchanged his driver for a 5-wood: less chance for error. Nicely struck, the ball landed thirty yards short of the stream and stopped ten feet shy of it, leaving him a clear approach. He was smiling as he walked off the tee. Charlie knew what Wesley was thinking: even *halving* the match with Kingston, a touring pro, would be a victory of sorts; but Brotherton would much rather prevail. He was the first to hit, and it was easily his best shot of the day, a scorched 3-iron dead to the green.

Charlie and Kevin trudged on, crossed the stone bridge, and cut to the right into the rough. Where the hell was it? At last Kevin spotted the ball and Charlie, peering down, saw it hiding in deep grass. From where he stood, the green wasn't visible; all he saw was a grove of trees.

Kevin was standing next to him, holding the golf bag. "I could pitch out," Charlie said, "or I could try and bend one."

"Brotherton's looking at a par, isn't he?" Kevin said.

"He's lying two, I don't think he has twenty feet to the cup."

"Go for it, Charlie."

"Six-iron."

Kevin handed him the club.

Charlie set up for a left-to-right shot, a big fade. He put all he had into the swing. The ball soared upward, began curving, and almost at once Charlie saw he'd over-cooked it. Too much fade. Ball was headed into the woods. Win a few, lose a few. But at the last instant it nicked a branch and caromed left, toward the green.

Brotherton, standing in the middle of the fairway, glanced at Charlie. The Whitridge host said nothing but it was easy to read his thoughts, and they weren't pretty.

The players and gallery moved up the fairway. When they arrived at the green, Charlie saw that both balls were on the putting surface, on diametrically opposite sides; it wasn't easily discernible which was closer. MacNair said he'd pace it off. Brotherton's ball was seven steps to the hole, Charlie's just over six. Golfer farther away putted first.

Brotherton stroked a beauty, his ball sliding by the cup and stopping. Eighteen inches.

"That's good," Charlie said, conceding the putt. Brotherton picked up.

His own putt was a treacherous one, mostly downhill—get it going too fast and he could find himself with ten or fifteen feet coming back...to halve. Plus, as Charlie crouched behind the ball, he saw, or thought he saw, three separate breaks. He sized up the putt from the opposite side—and saw the breaks differently. Knowing the dangers of an over-read—you began second-guessing yourself—he returned to his ball, determined to give the line one final look, regardless. On one knee, he studied the roll, the bend of the grass, still hesitant to commit. To clear his mind, he took his eyes entirely off the putting surface, looked up. Standing on the fringe of the green directly in his line of sight was Lora.

Her hand lay on her chest, her fingers moving; she appeared to be holding a small, gold object, rubbing its surface. For a second, as he watched, it glinted in the sun. Charlie addressed the ball. As if on its own, the putter blade opened ever so slightly, became still, and he made the stroke. The ball, rolling smoothly, followed one break, then another, began slowing, edged slightly to the left, and, on its final revolution, fell. From the fringes of the green came cheers and applauding. Charlie raised his putter in response; he walked to the cup and lifted his ball out, then approached Brotherton.

They shook hands, though with Brotherton it was more of a grab and release. "Good match," he said, saying what he had to say, and strode off the green. To a guest, with a laugh, "What was I supposed to do, *beat him?* He almost won the Open!"

Guests came up to congratulate Charlie. Slowly, then, they all began walking in, Lora among them. As she was leaving, she looked over, giving him a wave and a happy smile.

"Five birdies in a row!" Kevin said.

"We caught a couple of breaks." He gave Kevin the ball, who made to return it to the zippered pouch.

"No, keep it."

"Really?"

"And here." He pressed two twenty-pound notes and one ten into Kevin's hand.

"What's this?"

"It's called pay. Put it in your pocket," Charlie said.

CHAPTER 9

A florid-faced man in Whitridge Manor blue, who introduced himself as Eamon, welcomed him at the main gate at seven that evening, and Charlie, in ironed khakis and a blue dress shirt open at the neck, took the now familiar down-sloping entranceway past the garage to the great circular drive before the Manor House. He followed it in, soon picking up strains of lively music coming from behind and below the mansion. Rounding the building on a footpath, he came to a grand terrace overlooking the Argideen River, a broad stretch of lawn, and a huge white tent, beneath which a five-piece band was playing. The Brothertons' guests were dancing or walking about or sitting at saffron-topped tables, sampling hors d'oeuvres presented on silver trays and drinking from crystal glasses. Charlie took it all in and started down the stone stairway.

Near the base of it a bar was set up. Charlie walked over and asked for a vodka and tonic. He looked around and spied Brotherton at one of the tables talking with an elderly man in a pink blazer. A waitress walked by, stopped in front of Charlie, and he helped himself to a crabmeat puff. His drink was ready. As he was having his first taste, he heard someone say his name. Coming toward him in dazzling white pants and a midnight-blue blouse was Lora.

"Charlie, I'm so glad you're here," she said, as if to embrace him, then politely giving him her hand.

"I hate missing a good party."

"Walk with me for a bit."

They moved away from the bar, going around the outside of the tent toward the river. "Everyone's still talking about your match with Wesley," she said.

"You mean how badly I played the first four holes?"

"That did mystify a few people. I meant the last five."

"How's Wesley? He wasn't very happy."

"True, he wasn't. Wesley prides himself on his ability to close—anybody, anywhere, anytime. You turned the tables on him."

"Thanks for the read on the ninth green."

"Thank Granuaile."

Strolling on the soft grass near the river were a man and woman, somewhat older. Paths merged—and Charlie was meeting Liza and Sir Philip Knight, who, Lora said, as she made the introduction, was chairman of the Bank of London.

They had both been at St. Andrews on the day he'd battled Nick Faldo. After his escape from the Road Hole bunker, Charlie should've won, Sir Philip said. It had to rank as one the great shots in golf.

"I was lucky to get out," Charlie said.

"Something I've always wanted to know, had you practiced it or was it pure innovation?"

"I'd tried it earlier in the week on a practice round," Charlie said. "Each time I left the ball in the sand."

"Where are you from in America?" Mrs. Knight asked. She had white hair tinted the lightest shade of violet.

"Right now I live in Atlanta. I grew up in Michigan."

"We do a lot of work with Wachovia Bank in Atlanta," Sir Philip said.

"A friend of mine in college called it the 'Walkalloviya Bank,'" Charlie said.

Sir Philip had a good laugh. "Will you be playing in the Open this year?"

"I'm taking a little time off."

"Well, good luck to you, Charlie."

The Knights moved on and almost immediately another couple was crossing Charlie and Lora's path: the Cochranes from Galway. Douglas Cochrane had a mop of gray hair and a quick smile and his wife, Nell, in an off-the-shoulder blue dress and a double strand of pearls, was equally outgoing. Under his name, Cochrane had an international export company in woolens and spirits; but the topic quickly turned to golf. Charlie's five-birdie charge, Douglas Cochrane said, was really impressive and very exciting to watch.

"A certain tree branch deserves a little credit," Charlie said.

"Ah, rub of the green," Cochrane said. "Helps you or kills you. But you were well-deserving of the break."

"They're old friends," Lora said, when she and Charlie were again walking. "One of the few Irish couples here, sad to say."

****

As the hostess, Lora had an obligation to mix and mingle. She would love to have a dance with Charlie later, she said. Charlie promised her they would and, at the bar by himself, asked for another vodka. A gentleman and his wife were also freshening their drinks, and the man paid Charlie a compliment for his excellent play. Charlie acknowledged the comment, and the gentleman introduced his wife and himself, Karen and Stuart Bentham from London. He was a senior vice-president, he said, of Brotherton Enterprises, Ltd. Tall, dignified in appearance, gray hair cut close to his scalp. His wife had sharply defined features, especially her nose and chin, and had short, brownish-blond hair. She was smiling at Charlie.

Stuart Bentham loved golf and said he was disappointed in his play this morning; almost every other hit was a sclaff. Just off hand, did Charlie have any idea what might be going on with his swing?

Charlie couldn't remember the last time he'd heard the term "sclaff." "In other words, you're hitting behind the ball," he said.

"Precisely."

"Show me how you see yourself as you're making contact, say on a normal 5-iron shot," Charlie said. "The position you're in, or think you're in, and hold it."

Bentham set his glass on the bar and made a valiant effort; it brought a few chuckles from guests gathering around. "What do you see?" he asked Charlie.

"Not Colin Montgomerie," someone put in.

Everyone laughed. Charlie put his hand on Bentham's right shoulder, which was considerably lower than the left. "As I see it, Stuart, you're scooping—no need for it, clubs do very nicely on their own. OK, raise your right shoulder." Bentham raised it. "Now try keeping your shoulders level on the downswing, through contact." Charlie said. They won't *stay* level, but keep that thought it mind."

Bentham attempted to follow the instruction. "Excellent," Charlie said.

People clapped. A woman in her mid-forties, blond, smartly turned out in peach silk, told Charlie she was an incorrigible skuller. Her name was Winsley Hall and half her shots stayed on the ground. "What's my problem?"

"First, do you know the cause of skulling?"

"I just know I do it. Tell me."

"Apprehension. Anxiety. Doubt," Charlie said.

Virtually all the Brotherton s' guests were gathered around. In good humor, Winsley Hall asked, "Are you saying I should see a therapist?"

"Believe me, it's quite normal," Charlie said. "Hitting a golf ball is like walking into a dark room. In other words, it's scary—until we get the lights turned on. Did my ball go into the woods, did it clear the pond? Did it even go? Who doesn't want to end the anxiety? The impulse is to look—to look too soon—and looking too soon raises your whole body and you hit the golf ball on or above the middle. What happens? It goes scooting along the ground."

"You know me too well," Winsley Hall said.

"I know golf. Don't worry where the ball goes. Just swing and enjoy it."

There was another round of even heavier applause. A man with ruddy cheeks wearing an off-white linen suit stepped forward. "Charlie, I tend to smother my long irons."

"That's not good," Charlie said.

****

How the seating arrangements were made Charlie didn't know, but here he was at dinner with Ernestine and Harold Peacock and the couple he'd met earlier, Nell and Douglas Cochrane, for whom he felt a special liking. Whether that was because they were Irish, Charlie didn't know. But he was glad they were at the table. The Peacocks' business was beef. They traveled around the world looking for prize bulls, with an eye toward improving the quality of their own herds in England and beef generally. At appropriate times they would put these magnificent animals on the market. Of the couple, Ernestine was the more talkative but Charlie had the feeling that Harold, a portly man in gray—more plover than peacock—made the final call.

Douglas Cochrane, the only one who wasn't partaking of Brotherton's vintage wines, was a formidable story teller. He liked talking about himself but not in a boastful way; his tales, mostly of a misspent youth, were self-effacing and always humorous. The main course was Atlantic salmon or prime sirloin tips. Charlie was thoroughly enjoying himself. Fine food, wonderful wine, marvelous band. Harold Peacock, suddenly showing a little spark, asked his wife to dance.

Douglas Cochrane turned to Charlie. "How long will you be in Ireland?"

"For the rest of the month."

"You'll have to come out to the Galway Golf Club and have a round with us."

"That's a kind offer."

Cochrane slid a card from his billfold and handed it to Charlie. "I'm the club president, and I mean this sincerely— if you're ever passing through Galway, if not on this visit then on your next, give me a call."

"I'll do that. Thank you, Douglas," Charlie said, and put the card in his wallet.

****

At 10:30 guests were finishing dessert, strawberry short-cake with clotted cream, demitasse. In due time everyone began moving about, socializing. Charlie looked around for Lora, saw her at a table with the Knights; he walked over and, after a brief chat with Sir Philip and his wife, asked Lora if she would like to dance.

"I would, thank you."

They went to the floor, joining two other couples. "It's a great party," Charlie said.

"Your clinic was marvelous."

"Everyone seemed to have fun."

"Including you," Lora said. They were dancing close, not so close as to block out daylight—more exactly, twilight—between them; but almost. "I hope you haven't forgotten our rematch," she said.

"I think of little else."

"How many strokes are you going to give me?" she asked.

"Lora, I was going to ask *you* for strokes."

"You're very charming, Charlie."

"I'm only remembering what you said the first time we played. You were impressed but not intimidated."

"Maybe after today I'm a little intimidated."

He wanted to bring her closer in. "Well, name a day."

"We're going to our house in Inverness on Monday," Lora said. "How's Friday at three?"

"Not soon enough. Otherwise, perfect."

She smiled, came in on her own. "How are you liking Yeats?"

"I'm liking him a lot."

"I thought you would."

****

The party was still going strong but for Charlie it was time to go. In a sense he'd already said good night to Lora; he liked quiet exits. But as he was about to start up the stone steps to the Manor House level, he noticed Brotherton at one of the tables lifting his hand. Not in a wave goodbye but as a signal to hold up. The next moment Wesley was coming over.

"Charlie, I'm glad I caught you. Can you stay another while?"

"Sure."

"Brandy?"

"Fine."

Brotherton went up to the bar, came back with two snifters; he handed one to Charlie and suggested a bench on the bank of the river. One of the many spotlights on the property shone on the first tee, a good distance away. The gas lamps along the river flickered, making the water dance, and the back of the mansion on the higher level was flooded with light.

Brotherton raised his snifter; they both had sips. "I don't know if you set me up this afternoon, Charlie, but I'll tell you one thing—you proved the old saw: 'Pros beat amateurs.' I had some gall thinking I could take you. I'm not a good loser, in case you didn't notice. I owe you an apology."

"I don't think so," Charlie said. "Besides, you almost did take me."

"Looking back, we gave our guests a good afternoon of golf." Brotherton gave his brandy a swirl. "I understand you're going back to the States on June first."

"Yes."

"What's on your calendar, if I might ask?"

"For the rest of the summer, not a whole lot. Later in the year, it's Q-School."

"*You*, Q-School?"

"I lost my card last year—stopped playing actually, family issues. As might be expected, I fell off the money list."

"So you have to re-qualify, a player of your caliber?"

"That's the way it goes."

Brotherton did another swirl. The lamplight gave his scalp a golden glow. "Here's an idea, Charlie. I'm having two more outings this summer: professional people, business associates, government officials." He made a motion with his arm, taking in the party. "Like we're having now. Plenty of golf, great socializing, good times."

Charlie waited for Brotherton to go on.

He went on. "This might interest you, Charlie. I've been looking for someone to take over golf at The Whitridge. This morning—well, it wasn't chaos but it wasn't up to par. My expectations for Dennis were too high. I was watching when you gave your mini-clinic earlier and I had this idea. We have two more golf weekends scheduled, as I said, and I'd like you to take the reins. As summer pro, you'd set up tournament play. The stone cottage on the access road? About a year ago I started working on it, thinking it would make a great pro shop. All it needs is a thorough cleaning and your own personal touches. I'll pay for inventory—shirts, clubs, sweaters, balls, umbrellas; we'll set prices to cover layout plus ten percent. The ten percent is yours. I'm not in this for the money. People will want to see you for lessons. What a bonus for my guests! I'll pay you twelve thousand Irish pounds a month, starting June first—payday twice a month. I'll add £5000 to your first check if you start next Monday. Two days off a week. Do you have a car?"

"No."

"Lora and I have five between us," Brotherton came back quickly. "One, a Saab convertible, doesn't have two-thousand miles on it—call it yours through July. You'll be home in early August. When is Q-School?"

"Late November."

"Perfect. Leave a message with Mrs. Walsh here at the Manor House, whatever your decision. We'll be in Inverness for the week. Think it over."

He already had, and he liked it. Charlie thought the meeting, or talk, might be over. But then Brotherton was saying, "That was a fine lad carrying your bag. It got me thinking. From now on, instead of gas-driven buggies chewing up the course, spewing exhaust and making a lot of noise, we should have caddies at The Whitridge. Golf and walking go together."

"They do."

"We'd need anywhere from fifteen to twenty for one of our weekends. I don't like it when a caddie has a bag on each shoulder, scampering back and forth between golfers; it's not the personal service I want for my guests. Oh, before I forget." Brotherton drew a folded check from his shirt pocket and handed it to Charlie. "Well done."

It was for £1000. "Thank you, Wesley."

"You earned every penny of it."

They shook hands, bid each other good night, and Charlie walked away. He climbed the stone steps. A lot of nice things were happening. On the Manor House level, Charlie passed the great building, the front of it dark by comparison, and walked on the circular drive toward the main entrance-way. A tall, solitary figure was moving in the deep shadows on the lawn. At first thought, Charlie took it as a guest taking a stroll. The figure, clearly a man, looked at Charlie; didn't wave, didn't speak. Just looked.

No guest taking a stroll. Charlie kept walking.

CHAPTER 10

Monday afternoon Charlie returned to Whitridge Manor, walking on the down-sloping cobblestones past the garage. The whole place had a quietness about it: host and hostess, all guests, were gone. Gardeners were trimming the plants fringing the circular drive, upstairs windows in the Manor House were thrown wide, an assistant to the superintendent was cutting in new holes on the practice green. Charlie took the access road past the stone house and after a hundred steps veered toward the great barn. Dennis was at his desk, browsing through a voluminous groundcare equipment catalog, when Charlie knocked and went in.

The superintendent's face broke into a smile. "Charlie Kingston. I heard ye were 4-down after four holes, then rattled off a string of birdies to beat Mr. Brotherton 1-up."

Charlie pulled out a chair. "Something like that."

"I can see the smoke coming out of his ears!"

"He wasn't the happiest guy around," Charlie said. "Anyway, the course played beautifully. Great conditioning, every aspect of it—greens, fairways, hazards."

"It's why I'm here. Not to run god-damn tournaments for the British elite! I told him, I said to Mr. Brotherton, get someone else."

"He has, he's asked me to be his summer pro," Charlie said.

"Now isn't that something?" O'Hea sat back, folded his arms. "You kick his arse on the golf course, then he turns around and offers ye a job. Have ye signed on?"

"No. I thought we might talk about it."

The course superintendent flexed his fingers on his left hand, as if working out stiffness. "Are ye interested, let's answer that one first."

"I am. There's a lot about the job I like."

"I'm a little surprised to hear you say that, Charlie. You're a professional golfer. This makes ye a club pro selling sweaters!"

"A professional golfer who doesn't have his card. And it's hardly a serious position, Dennis —two months, June and July."

O'Hea brushed a few specks of dust from the open page of his catalog. "Your mind is pretty well made up, I'd say."

"I'm here to talk. Tell me something about Mr. Brotherton I don't know. Like the relationship between him and Reggie MacNair—his so-called caddie."

The superintendent chortled. "He's Mr. Brotherton's caddie, sure—like I'm his vice-president at Brotherton Enterprises. Charlie, MacNair spent thirteen years with MI5 in counterespionage—he was one of the most respected and feared operatives of his day."

Charlie felt a sudden spike in his heartbeat. "What is he doing at Whitridge Manor?"

"He's head of security. Anyway, that's his title. What MacNair does is channel Mr. Brotherton's money into Northern Ireland. Up to a £1,000,000 a year to his favorite charities, namely, the anti-Catholic cleric Ian Paisley and his Democratic Unionist Party, and the Orange Order."

"Dennis, you're losing me."

"Let me simplify it, Charlie," Dennis said. "Everything Mr. Brotherton stands for, I'm against."

"Then why do you work for him?"

"Someday I'll tell ye, Charlie."

Charlie was quiet for a good while, looking hard at the greenskeeper. "I think you're telling me to forget the job and go back home."

"I wouldn't want to see ye gettin' hurt."

"How am I going to get hurt selling sweaters and giving lessons?"

"A word to the wise, if I might," Dennis said. "There's more to Whitridge Manor than meets the eye."

****

As he walked toward the door to his house later that same day, Charlie heard young-sounding voices in the back yard. Instead of going in, he went around and down the side. There, standing in the middle of the close-cut grass, were Kevin and Brigid. She had a pitching wedge in her hand and Kevin was telling her that she had to bend forward slightly when she took her stance. Golf wasn't a stand-up-straight game; it wasn't step dancing.

But it was a difficult concept for Brigid to grasp, and she didn't seem to understand why she had to keep her feet more or less planted. Kevin was losing patience but finally got her to bend, as if reaching for a cup on a table. After several "practice swings," he told her to hit the whiffle ball on the grass. She took a good cut at it and missed, immediately trying again. And again. The third time she hit behind the ball, taking dirt and a big clump of grass. Kevin wasn't laughing but Brigid was. Suddenly, looking up together, they saw Charlie standing there.

"I—I'm giving her a lesson," Kevin said.

"How's she doing?"

"It's hard to tell."

"I keep missing," Brigid said.

"Everyone misses to start with," Charlie said.

"The first time I ever tried hitting a ball I whiffed seven times," Kevin said, replacing the clump of grass and stamping down on it.

"Take another swing at it," Charlie said to Brigid. "But shorten up on the club. It's too long for you."

Brigid repositioned her hands on the shaft.

"OK. Now focus on the ball," Charlie said. "Forget me, forget Kevin. Just the ball."

He had a feeling she'd make contact, and she did. The ball popped along on the ground.

"That's the ticket, Brigid."

She made three more swings, each time missing the ball; on her fourth try, she again made contact and the ball actually became airborne—for fifteen feet. "Terrific," Charlie said, holding up his hand for a high-five. Then to Kevin, "I think you have another golfer in the family."

"God help us."

They walked to the terrace. Charlie said he'd make tea, thinking, as he put on water, he was becoming quite good at it. Serving tea was something he'd never done before, ever, anywhere. He carried out cups and spoons, Kevin the sugar bowl and a half-glass of milk. Charlie spread crackers and slices of cheese on a plate; he also had a tin of cookies, purchased from Mrs. Monahan. He dropped a couple of tea bags into the pot, poured in boiling water. Then they were ready to sit down.

He liked the dearness of it, this little bit of formality with two Irish kids. Tea at Charlie Kingston's place. He got Brigid talking on dance, how she got started. Sometimes she wished she didn't take it so seriously, wished she could be more like her friend, Katie Ahern.

"I had a bad dream last night," she said. "They were waiting for me to go on, they'd called my name, and I got lost in the building. I knew the way, the right door, but it was never the right door! And they kept calling my name but I never found it and I never went on."

"That's not a good feeling," Charlie said, "but it's not something to worry about. I had a dream like that once. I was in a tournament, the Western Open in America, and I was near the lead going into the final round. That's the factual part. In the dream: it's the start of the final round and the starter calls my name. I step onto the first tee. But wherever I tee my ball, something always gets in the way of my swing—like a tree branch, or a cameraman, or a security rope. I can't find a good place; my swing is always blocked. Finally the referee disqualifies me for holding up play. I woke up in a cold sweat, never got back to sleep, and later in the day I tied the course record and won the tournament."

Both kids laughed.

Charlie said, "Guess what? I'm taking a job as golf pro at Whitridge Manor, so I'll be staying on through July."

Brigid clapped her hands.

"That's wonderful!" Kevin said.

"I have a plan," Charlie said, mostly to Kevin. "Mr. Brotherton told me from now on he wants caddies at The Whitridge—no more noisy buggies. I want you to start rounding up Castlebantry kids, boys and girls, ages twelve to seventeen. We'll start a training program. If we're successful at it, I'm pretty sure Mr. Brotherton will give you the job as caddie master. And I'd make you assistant to the pro. Practice privileges, playing privileges. What do you think?"

"What do I think? I think I'm dreaming."

"You're not. It'll happen if we make it happen."

"Now you'll be able to come to my feis," Brigid said, her eyes bright with joy.

"That's the best part of all," Charlie said.

CHAPTER 11

From his house, he placed the call on Thursday afternoon. A woman picked up: "Whitridge Manor."

"Mrs. Walsh?"

"Yes."

"This is Charlie Kingston. Mr. Brotherton told me to call and leave a message—"

"I'll be very happy to take it, Mr. Kingston." She had a kind, maternal-sounding voice. "It just so happens that Mrs. Brotherton arrived at the Manor House not ten minutes ago. If you'd rather tell her—"

"Thank you, that would be fine."

"Hold on, please."

After a short while Lora picked up. "Hi."

"What are you doing back?"

"Wesley's mum isn't feeling well, he's visiting her in Glasgow," she said. "I opted out, horrid daughter-in-law that I am, and I don't like staying at our house alone, all these eerie sounds drifting across the moors. So here I am." She paused, then, with great interest, "Are you taking the job?"

"I am."

"I'm really glad," Lora said. "What are you doing? Are you free?"

"I am."

"Then let's play. I'll pick you up."

****

They zipped along, Lora's hair dancing like wind-swept flames. Her clubs, and his, lay on the back seat of the Mustang. She had on cinnamon-brown shorts and a cool lime golf shirt. "Wesley wants to get going on the pro shop," she said. "It's eighty percent done but it never got finished. He'd like you to see it, come up with suggestions, whatever changes you'd like. So maybe we should do that first."

"Sure. Apart from the eerie sounds, how was Scotland?"

"I did a lot of walking. There was a bagpipe festival in Inverness. It's a young city in many ways, for a city that's actually very old," Lora said. "It's right on the mouth of a river, the Ness River. Loch Ness isn't far. It's a very pretty drive—"

"Did you spot the monster?"

"I always look." She laughed.

"Do you think he's really there?"

"No. But why ruin the fun?"

They were passing St. Matthew's, then creeping along through the village center. Arriving at the traffic circle, Lora veered left and after a short distance turned into Whitridge Manor. As they rolled down the cobblestone entrance, Charlie spotted the sun-yellow Saab in front of the garage; even its tires shone. Opposite the Manor House, Lora turned onto the access road and almost immediately pulled in and parked to one side of the stone cottage.

The door was closed, and Charlie noticed the old strap hinges, hand-forged. The main room had a large, glass-fronted display case toward the rear, built-in shelving against two walls, several stands especially made for displaying irons and woods. Two small easy chairs, covered with sheets, were positioned before a black, cast-iron stove.

"I like it," Charlie said.

Off the main room was a second space, just as deep but narrow, with a heavy mahogany desk at one end, an old but once-handsome leather sofa against the near wall, and a sturdy, unpretentious coffee table before it. Behind the desk a large window opened to a stand of trees; through them, easily discernible, you could see the fairway of the first hole.

"The furniture comes from the Manor House, pieces we had in storage," Lora said.

"It'll be a great pro shop. I'll want to set up an area for club repair," Charlie said. "Dennis has a couple of old workbenches in his office. Maybe I can wrestle one away from him."

"Anything else, any alterations?"

"Nothing. It's perfect."

"Then to the tee," Lora said.

****

On the first hole she had a bogey, on the second a double bogey, on the third another double, and playing the fourth hole, the par five over a ravine, she once again hit a drive that tailed off to the right—by any name, a slice. Upset, Lora let the club fall from her hands.

"Charlie, what am I *doing*?"

"Don't worry about it. When we finish, we'll go to the range."

"Let's work on it now."

"Well, I'll tell you what I see," Charlie said.

From his own bag he pulled a 7-iron. "Here's what you do well—shifting your weight to the right on the backswing. But reshifting your weight on the downswing—you have a problem."

"What is it?"

Charlie said, "You have a tendency to stop, where you should keep moving forward." He demonstrated without a ball, clipping blades of grass with his iron. "I didn't stop until my weight was fully on my left side. Note my right foot, on its toe. You try it."

She made a good take away and on the downswing kept moving forward. "Much better," Charlie said. "But rotate your hips on the downswing, Lora. No lateral sway. Swivel your hips. OK, once more."

Lora made another practice swing.

"That's it. Now hit one."

Lora set up to a ball, feet firmly planted. Instead of hanging back, she rotated her hips on the downswing and kept moving forward. The ball flew away—straight, deep, and high—and landed on the far side of the ravine, bouncing down the fairway.

"Charlie, did you see that? Did you *see* it?"

"I saw it."

"You're wonderful!" she said, and kissed him full on the lips.

****

They were on the highest spot on the course, and Lora's long putt fell into the hole for a par. Delighted, she walked quickly across the green and gave Charlie a hug. He hugged her back, happy for her, only then realizing that he could see the Manor House, or a portion of it, on the lower property. Except, as he continued to hold her, he saw it wasn't the

Manor House at all. What he was seeing was the upper floor of the Whitridge Manor garage.

Charlie inserted the flagstick and they walked off the green, stopping to sit on the bench overlooking the Celtic Sea. For a minute they were quiet, taking in the view. Then Lora said, "Here we are again."

"Imagine that."

"I think of you all the time, there in your cabin of clay and wattles made."

He laughed; it was a line from one of his favorite Yeats poems. "I still haven't planted any beans," he came back.

It was her turn to laugh. They sat for a while longer, gazing out. He so wanted to take her in his arms, to turn from the beauty of the Celtic Sea and look into the sea-green eyes of Lora Brotherton. But he knew himself; he'd got into trouble risking dangerous shots too often in his career. She was another man's wife, and that man was his boss.

Don't gamble, Charlie. Play it safe.

"Let's finish, then we'll have tea," Lora said.

****

In the Manor House Charlie washed his hands, combed his hair, then met Lora on the rear terrace overlooking the grounds and the river; they sat at a glistening glass table. A woman of sixty in Whitridge Manor blue brought out an assortment of finger sandwiches on a crystal platter—shrimp salad, egg salad, salmon salad—and, on a smaller plate, a variety of cakes and cookies. Lora introduced Charlie as the American golfer who was taking a summer job as The Whitridge professional. The woman, who had a wonderfully open face, was Mrs. Walsh.

"Well, now, isn't that fine," she said. "It's lovely meeting you, Mr. Kingston."

"It's a pleasure meeting you, Mrs. Walsh."

Lora poured tea. She had changed her clothes and was now in olive pants, a silk shirt with green buttons, and white sandals. The afternoon sun, shining on the back of the Manor House, gave the great blocks of stone a reddish tint.

"This is most enjoyable," Charlie said.

"And such a wonderful day. We've been very lucky, so far."

"You played really well today," Charlie said.

"I have this excellent teacher."

They both had sandwiches, sips of tea. Lora asked him if he had any children.

"A daughter. She died in an accident when she was six."

"Charlie, I'm sorry." Lora pressed his wrist. "What a dreadful thing."

A few seconds ticked by. "How about you and children, Lora?"

"I'd love to have a family, but at this point it doesn't seem likely."

"It could still happen," Charlie said.

"It's not in the cards, I'm afraid."

They each had a sandwich, a scrumptious mouthful. Lora asked him if he'd looked at any of Yeats's poems. He said he had. Poetry had never played a big part in his life, much of any part, really, but he was liking Yeats.

"Name one of his poems you're particularly fond of," Lora said.

"'An Irish Airman Foresees his Death.'"

"I love that one. Can you say a line?"

"I'll try."

After a moment:

> "Nor law, nor duty bade me fight,
> Nor public men, nor cheering crowds,
> A lonely impulse of delight
> Drove to this tumult in the clouds."

Charlie hesitated; he didn't quite have the next line—
Lora came in:

> "I balanced all, brought all to mind,
> The years to come seemed waste of breath—"

He finished:

> "A waste of breath the years behind
> In balance with this life, this death."

"Very nice, Charlie," Lora said, her sea-green eyes
smiling. "Tomorrow I'm driving to Kilcarney for three or
four days."

"I'll want a full account of the match with your father."
He pointed at her. "Put the old man in his place."

"I plan to."

"I should be running, Lora."

"Stay awhile. Let me you show you the house," she said.

****

He could hardly keep track of the rooms, let alone the
furnishings, the paintings, the sculptures, the tapestries, the
carpets, the artifacts. Each room—the library, the dining
room, the living room, the smoking room, the billiards room
(table covered in orange), the drawing room, the morning
room—was its own museum. There was a glass case for

birds of the world, exquisitely mounted, perched; a case for pistols dating to the 16th Century; a collection of golf memorabilia, clubs, balls, scorecards dating back hundreds of years. Not to mention, on walls in all the rooms, classic English and European portraits and landscapes.

Lora and Charlie went up the carpeted stairs to the second floor. All along the corridor were guest rooms. The master bedroom looked out over the river; the room they were now in opened to the great lawn and circular driveway. "I sleep here," she said. "Wesley thrashes about like an elephant."

"It's a beautiful room, Lora."

The ceiling, the faintest shade of rose, was ten feet high; walls were papered in a quiet blue with a thin gold thread; carpet a dandelion yellow. Sunshine poured in through the two front windows. Upholstered easy chairs, lovely lamps, seascapes on the wall. But what most caught Charlie's attention was the bed. It was the first canopy bed he'd ever actually seen, except for pictures. White silk, trimmed with lace—

The bed didn't hold his attention for long. Standing by it, Lora was unbuttoning her shirt.

You'd better think about this, Charlie, a voice—serious, wise, responsible—was saying.

He did, he counted to three, then went over to her, pressing his lips to her neck. Lora tossed her shirt, his fingers worked to unsnap her bra, she gave her shoulders a twist and slipped out of it. Her breasts—he felt momentarily lightheaded, had to catch himself. She undid her pants, her feet dancing free of them in a little step, sweetly executed.

Charlie kicked off his shoes, undressed, followed her into bed. They kissed, long, deep kisses, and she began making sounds, low pleasure-filled purring sounds. Kneeling, he reached forward and pulled on the waistband of her mist-colored panties. She helped by bending one leg and then he let the panties go and they stayed on the other. He had wondered, at times, if she had a superb colorist at a salon in London or Paris. The answer was no. No colorist. He entered her smooth as sun-warmed honey. Her eyes opened, then even wider as he leaned forward and slid fully in. Dangling on her ankle, her panties resembled a sea bird riding the waves.

****

They showered, dressed. Before going downstairs Lora went to the window that opened to the great front lawn and flowering plants. Charlie stood behind her, hands on her arms. "This is my favorite view—I love to stand here in the morning and look out at the gardens," she said.

"I can see why."

They went downstairs. Just inside the main door, Lora said the Saab was waiting for him at the garage. He should ask for Keith Callaghan. "While I'm away, I'll make a few drawings," she said. "Maybe something to use on a Whitridge scorecard."

"That's a great idea."

"See you, Charlie."

They kissed and he went out, walked on the circular drive. As he approached the garage, he noticed the man, whom he'd seen cleaning and maintaining Brotherton's cars, polishing the chrome on the Silver Cloud.

"Keith?"

"Yes, sir, Mr. Kingston. She's ready for you."

They walked into the garage and Callaghan began pointing out the features of the Saab, explaining how to operate the AC and wipers, turn the headlights on and off, lower and raise the roof. Should he leave it down? Please, Charlie said.

Off to the side, a motion caught Charlie's eye. Glancing over, he saw a tall, angular man with a thick mustache whom he recognized immediately. He was standing behind a plate-glass door in what appeared to be a narrow hall, staring at Charlie.

"She's all yours," Callaghan said.

"What's Reggie MacNair doing here?"

"Why, is he looking at us?"

"You could say that."

"He lives upstairs. I don't give him the time of day. Man's a real creep. Any problems with the car, stop by. She needs a wash, I'm here."

"Thanks, Keith."

Releasing the clutch, Charlie backed out of the garage, turned around in the parking area, and drove to the main gate of Whitridge Manor.

CHAPTER 12

Instead of turning toward the Castlebantry roundabout and crawling along in village traffic, Charlie cut across the highway and headed in the direction of Cork, wanting an open road to acclimate himself to "driving left." It always took a bit of concentration until you got used to it. He zipped along—the car handled like a dream, he had a little extra cash in his pocket, and he was in love with a beautiful woman.

Only two miles from Whitridge Manor, he spotted a road sign: *Croghanvale—3 km.* An arrow pointed left. He flipped on his directional signal, down-shifted and made the turn. It was a winding, narrow road through scenic countryside. The Saab danced through the curves. And there, just ahead, was the bridge over the Argideen River; on the other side of it, Pharr's. Charlie liked that he was getting to know his way around. Two miles ahead, if he kept on, he'd come to the crossroads.

He rumbled over the bridge and pulled into a parking space in front of the pub. Four men were standing at one end of the bar, heads together in serious talk. Behind the bar was Emily's granddaughter.

"Charlie, right?" she said, coming over.

"Yes. And you're Mary."

She smiled, pleased he'd remembered. "Murphy's?"

"I'd love one."

As was her custom, Mary rushed the process. "I thought you'd probably left," she said, setting the pint down.

"No. I'm still here. How are you?"

"Too busy for my own good," she said. "I'm finishing my thesis, plus putting in my hours here. Then trouble with my boyfriend. He's always asking me to forgive him, to give him another chance. How many chances can you give someone? Three D.U.I.'s in the past year—he's a child."

"And not a very bright one. Did you break up?"

"We did, and I'm loving it."

Charlie asked her what her thesis was about. She said she was taking a new look at the Flight of the Wild Geese that followed King William's victory at the Battle of the Boyne.

"In 1690 over King James II," Charlie put in, citing the *Cork Examiner.*

"Well, now, I'm impressed."

"Who were these 'wild geese?'"

"They were the Catholic gentry who left Ireland after James II's defeat," Mary said. "James was Catholic. When William of Orange, a Protestant, defeated him at the Boyne, it set the stage for Protestant and British dominance in Ireland. Celtic chieftains, the 'wild geese,' went abroad to regroup, to fight another day. There's controversy over whether they should've stayed in Ireland and engaged King Billy in guerrilla warfare. In my opinion—"

Customers were calling her. "We'll talk again," Mary said. She gave Charlie a smile and moved away.

A minute later someone was saying, "You're Charlie Kingston."

He turned; standing at the bar was a man he vaguely recognized. But couldn't place. "I am," Charlie said.

"I'm John Mulrooney," the man said. He had a deep cleft in his chin and thin, graying hair. "I've seen you walk by my office several times now. The building next to Monahan's."

"Sure, *Surgery.*" They shook hands. "I've wondered what kind of surgery you do."

"In Ireland, 'surgery' means 'doctor's office.' I'm a general practitioner."

"Puzzle solved," Charlie said.

"How are you liking Castlebantry?"

"I've extended my stay, that says something," Charlie said.

"It does. May I ask why?"

"Wesley Brotherton offered me the job of golf pro at Whitridge Manor."

"Well, congratulations—it makes perfect sense," Dr. Mulrooney said. "Kevin Dennehy said you were a golfer. You came very close to beating Nick Faldo in the Open."

Mary placed a pint before the doctor, who had a quick, healthy swallow. "Speaking of Mr. Brotherton," Mulrooney went on, "about a year ago Mrs. Brotherton limped into my office with a cut on her instep—nothing serious but it needed attention. As a physician I shouldn't be commenting, but permit me to say she's a very attractive woman with an exquisite ankle, which, in performing my professional duties, I was obliged to hold."

"My heart breaks for you, Dr. Mulrooney."

The physician laughed. "But there's more to it than that," he said, taking a second swallow. "Mrs. Brotherton reminds me of Mairead McGarrity, who lived in your house. A few years younger Mairead was, with brown hair, but the smile, the eyes, so alike! I remember as a lad riding by her house on my two-wheeler always hoping she'd notice me. Then one day I was pedaling along, in the afternoon it was, and Mairead was struggling with a window box, installing a new one, and I jumped off my bike and gave her a hand. When it was in place, there under the front window, she smiled and asked my name. I told her and she kissed my cheek."

Mulrooney touched the side of his face. "Believe it nor not, I can still feel that kiss."

"What happened to her?" Charlie asked, eager to learn more.

"She went to Northern Ireland, Kieran and she both did."

"Why?"

"It was who they were."

"You mean, they were born there?" Charlie said.

"No, they were born in West Cork. Both grew up in Castlebantry."

If Dr. Mulrooney intended to go on, Charlie didn't know. Just then the group at the end of the bar suddenly became boisterous. Not in argument. One of the men, pint in hand, had started to sing, and soon the others in the party were joining him in song.

"There they go with 'God Save Ireland,'" said Dr. Mulrooney, with a touch of derision.

> *"High upon the gallows tree swung the noble-hearted three*
> *By the vengeful tyrant stricken in their bloom,*
> *But they met him face to face with the courage of the race,*
> *And they went with souls undaunted to their doom."*

Then came a chorus, and ever more lustily the men sang, pints raised:

> *"God save Ireland, said the heroes.*
> *God save Ireland, said they all.*
> *Whether on the scaffold high or the battlefield*
> *we die,*
> *O what matter if for Ireland dear we fall."*

And they went on to a second verse:

> *"Never till the latest day shall the memory pass*
> *away*
> *Of the gallant lives thus given for our land;*
> *But on the cause must go 'mid joy or weal or woe*
> *Till we make our Isle a nation free and grand."*

Emily Pharr, coming out just then, heard the second rendering of the chorus, the men lifting their pints to her as they sang. She talked with them for a couple of minutes, then spotted Charlie and Dr. Mulrooney. "The people have cast their ballot on Good Friday," she announced, walking over.

"But is it to your liking?" Dr. Mulrooney said.

"It's peace in name only," Emily said.

"Ninety-four percent voted yes. I wouldn't call that 'name only.'"

"We'll never have a lasting peace until we take 'northern' out of Northern Ireland, John."

"If a majority in the six counties votes England out, they're out," Dr. Mulrooney said. "That's part of the agreement. What more can you ask for than that?"

"We're deluding ourselves," she said. "The die is cast. It's a sad day in Ireland." Shifting her attention: "Charlie, I was beginning to think you'd gone back to America without saying goodbye."

"I wouldn't do that, Emily."

"I hope not. I said to myself the day we met, now there's a republican. It was in your eyes."

Dr. Mulrooney broke into laughter. "Emily, that's an oxymoron for the ages."

"And what might you mean by that?"

"Professional golfers are conservative to the core."

"I don't see it in Charlie." She looked at him directly. "Correct me if I'm wrong."

He could easily say, "I'm sorry, Emily, to disappoint you." He belonged to a brotherhood that asked no favor, extended no hand. You couldn't so much as borrow a tee from a fellow competitor, or loan him one—the Rules of Golf prohibited it. But Charlie couldn't say that Emily Pharr was wrong. It may have been the moment, may have been Pharr's with its storied past. It may have been Emily, who, from the very start, had seemed to accept him, to take him in—for no reason he could see.

"You don't need to be corrected, Emily," he said.

"Thank you, Charlie."

"On that fine clarification, we'll have another round," said Dr. Mulrooney.

****

When he finished his new pint, Charlie shook hands with the physician and left a couple of pounds on the bar for Mary, who said to him as he was leaving that he shouldn't keep himself a stranger. He said he wouldn't and went out. As he was opening the door to the Saab, a white car with the word GARDA on it rolled slowly by. The man driving it had red hair and a long, pointed nose, reminding Charlie of an Irish setter. He gave Charlie a once-over, the Pharr's parking lot a look, and continued on by.

At the crossroads, he stopped at McCurtain's. Fiona began to draw him a Murphy's but he said he'd already had a couple at Pharr's; all he'd like was one of her specials. She told him what they were. He could see she was stressed, unhappy, and after giving his order to the kitchen she came back and told Charlie that Donal was unrelenting in his insistence that she come to Germany with the kids. It was that or auf Wiedersehen, and she felt herself wavering, giving in to his demand.

"So you can grit your teeth for the rest of your life? Fiona, striking out on your own could be a great new beginning," Charlie said.

"It's not me."

"I don't believe that for one moment."

He thought she might say something but just then Kevin came out of the kitchen with Charlie's dinner, serving him at his banquette and staying for a couple of minutes to tell him that he already had seven caddies lined up, including his girlfriend, Molly.

"Lucky the golfer who gets her. Listen, start coming to The Whitridge after school," Charlie said. "I want you to become familiar with the course—the different tees, the hazards, the general layout."

"I'll be there tomorrow."

"Bring your clubs. We'll play from the blues. How's Brigid doing?"

"Practicing for her feis. Funny thing, yesterday she was in our backyard swinging my 5-iron."

"More likely it was swinging her," Charlie said.

CHAPTER 13

While he and Kevin worked with a dozen neophyte caddies in the vicinity of the practice green at The Whitridge, showing them how to carry a golf bag, where to stand while a player addressed the ball, how to hold the flagstick, Charlie suddenly realized, or remembered, that today was a special day. He glanced at his watch, told Kevin that today was his sister's feis and he was already late. "Take the kids out on the course," he said, "let them see the bunkers, walk the greens," then checked himself. "But you want to see her dance, Kevin. Dismiss the class, have them come back tomorrow."

"Charlie, it's OK, really. You go."

He ran up the path of white stones, then on the access road to the pro shop and jumped into the Saab. In a tournament if you missed your tee time, you were disqualified. Charlie left Whitridge Manor and headed for the traffic circle. If he were to miss Brigid's feis—well, he'd rather miss a tee time.

He had a general idea where the Castlebantry School was but didn't make the correct turn off Adams Street and instead of ending up on Griffith Street he found himself on

Bostwick Road. He did a zig and a zag and finally arrived at the school—a long, modern building of white stucco with a pretty courtyard in the middle. As he might have expected, all immediate parking spots were taken, and he had to drive a good way on Griffith before he found one, rather in a ditch next to pasture land.

From the schedule of events that Fiona had given him, he knew that Brigid, and the other novices in her group, would be performing in the cafeteria. After asking for directions, he found it and walked in, but the girl performing at the moment looked younger than Brigid, as did the boys and girls waiting to perform seated against the far wall. When the girl's number ended, Charlie asked a woman next to him if this was where the novice feis was being held.

"These are beginners doing the jig."

"Oh. Where are they having the hornpipe?"

"I really couldn't tell you."

Charlie went out. A woman in the hall, who was wearing an official badge, told Charlie the novice hornpipe had been shifted to the gymnasium.

"Where's the gymnasium?"

"At the extreme end of the building,"

"Which extreme end?"

She pointed. "But I think it's over by now."

"How do I get there?"

"The quickest way is to go outside."

Charlie went back out, ran across the courtyard, and entered the gym through an outside door. Close to fifty people were inside. Three judges sat at a table in the front of the room. The boy currently dancing had on dark pants, a white shirt and a necktie, and his shoes, with taps, click-clacked on the hard wood floor. A sprightly tune came from a pair of speakers.

When the lad finished he received applause and took his place on a chair beneath a row of high windows. The judges made notes, registered their scores. A woman with silvery-gray hair in a pale yellow pants suit, an official badge on her lapel, stepped forward. "Our final contestant in the novice hornpipe competition," she announced to the gathering, "is Brigid Dennehy from Castlebantry."

Charlie breathed a deep sigh, lifted his eyes to the ceiling. Brigid walked out to the center of the floor in a flared green skirt, a snug-fitting white shirt with embroidery on the sleeves, her hair in ringlets. She had on a touch of lipstick and rouge, her head held high, arms straight at her sides, and when the tune came on her arms stayed at her sides. Only her feet moved, almost in a blur—clickity clack, clackity click—her little legs kicking marvelously, behind her with the knee bent, to the side and in front, knee lifted high. She didn't smile; it occurred to Charlie she was concentrating too hard to smile. He had never seen a golfer making a lob shot over a yawning bunker smile. Charlie was more than impressed. He was thrilled by her performance. When the hornpipe ended, everyone clapped, no one more energetically than Charlie. Brigid took her place beneath the windows.

There was a short wait while the judges compiled their scores. Then the woman with the silver-gray hair took their reports and again stepped to the middle of the floor. "Everyone who danced here today is a winner," she said. "We're all very happy for our contestants. It was a marvelous feis, and we're proud of our children."

Cheering, clapping.

"We have three medals to hand out today in the novice hornpipe—third, second and first place."

Helen O'Sullivan was awarded a third-place medal. Applause. Tim Barstow was given a second place medal. Clapping. Then the woman said, "The winner of first place, who now advances to the national 'prizewinner level' in Irish step dancing, is Brigid Dennehy."

Extended applause, cheering. Everyone, dancers and those who had come to watch, converged in the front of the room. Charlie didn't push but slowly made his way forward. Brigid was standing with her mother in the middle of the excited crowd, and quite suddenly she looked up and saw him. Her eyes, already glowing, brightened with excitement.

"Charlie!"

He wanted to kiss her face, pick her up and hold her like a happy father; he contained himself. "Congratulations, Brigid."

"I didn't think you were here!"

"I was here all right." Then to Fiona, "You have to be a very proud mother."

"I am."

Several people were wondering who he was. He patted Brigid on top of her curls. "You were just great. It was a marvelous performance."

"I still want to learn golf!"

Everyone in the immediate vicinity laughed.

"We'll work on it," he said to Brigid, gave Fiona a last look, and left the school.

****

The next afternoon Charlie reviewed the finalized program for the upcoming June weekend: tee times, pairings, tournament format, local rules, prizes. As part of the program, he would be holding a clinic on the practice range at 2:00: short game, iron play, full swing. (In case of rain, a video of the final round of the 1990 British Open, won by Nick Faldo, with live commentary by the runner-up.) Individual golf lessons by appointment, casual play Sunday a.m., social hour in pro shop—farewell lunch (at Manor House).

Charlie turned to The Whitridge scorecard. When he had started the project of making one, he'd discovered that Sean Harrigan had measured the "out" nine but had neglected the "in" nine. With different tees the second time around, there would have to be different yardages. For example, the first hole measured 355 yards from the whites. Clearly, from the blues, it was longer. Right-angle distance between teeboxes came out to 31 yards. That made the tenth hole 386 yards. And so on around the course. Charlie and Kevin had spent a full afternoon on the project. Some holes played from the blues were longer, some shorter. Total yardage of the front nine was 3421; of the back nine, 3486. Total length, 6907 yards.

While in the process of taking measurements, Charlie had also analyzed each hole's "degree of difficulty" to establish handicaps. On what holes, and in what order, did better players give strokes to less accomplished players? The correct way to judge was by analyzing actual scorecards; let the numbers do the talking. But how many Whitridge scorecards had ever been turned in? So Charlie had taken it upon himself to make the call.

Someone was saying his name. He stood and went out to the front room. Lora was just coming in. "Hi," she said, eyes smiling.

It was painful for him to simply stand there and not take her in his arms. "Welcome back, Lora."

"I have the drawings."

"I'd like to see them."

They went into his office, sat on the sofa; she handed him a 5 x 7 manila envelope. He didn't open it right away. "How's your family?"

"Everyone's fine. It was the first time I've ever beaten my father in golf. Driving home with him, I told him I'd met an American pro who gave me a lesson and he said my 'win' didn't count."

Charlie laughed.

"Actually he was delighted," Lora said. "He hopes you'll drive over with me one day."

"One day I'd like to." When that might be, Charlie couldn't imagine.

He opened the envelope and pulled out three cards of high-quality paper, each with a pen-and-ink sketch on it in color —all bearing the caption: The Whitridge at Whitridge Manor. Two of the drawings were of the golf course; one of the Manor House.

"Do you recognize the holes?" Lora asked.

"The third green and the ninth fairway. They're wonderful. And the Manor House! My God, you're good!"

"Wesley doesn't like them."

Charlie frowned. "When did he see them?"

"Thirty minutes ago when I drove in. He was already here. With weekend guests."

"Oh." He'd thought she was at the Manor House alone. "Why doesn't he like them?"

"He says they're too Celtic."

"Too *Celtic*?"

"I told him, I said, 'Wesley, this is Ireland. You may not like my drawings but don't say they're too Celtic!'"

"I wouldn't know if they are or aren't, I just know they're beautiful." He set the drawings on the coffee table.

"I missed you, Charlie," Lora said.

He reached out, touching her elbow, and she slid closer; then they were holding each other, kissing. Reasons why they should stop stormed his mind; he should pull away, say something responsible; but the words didn't materialize. He reached beneath her shirt, leaned down and kissed her breasts. Lora squirming out of her shorts, her panties. To a clatter of falling items, Charlie threw off his trousers. The old sofa was broad and deep, cool on his knees, and then he was there, a pure and perfect stroke. Her eyes were green agates with blazing black centers.

"Charlie, I couldn't wait."

"Me neither."

"You're wonderful, did I ever tell you?"

"Maybe. I don't remember."

"Will you promise me something?"

"Of course I will."

She was losing her train of thought and he didn't think she'd speak, but then she said, "Never stop making love to me."

"I promise."

"I love you, Charlie." Agates starting to roll.

****

She dressed quickly, stopped for a minute in the restroom, and left the pro shop. In his office, Charlie belted his trousers, picked up several coins, a ball marker and a couple of golf tees off the floor, and went to his desk with her drawings; but he didn't look at them, just sat there letting himself settle down. Finally he took a deep breath and pulled out the cards, studying them, trying to determine what made them "too Celtic." Or Celtic at all. He didn't have the vaguest notion. His phone rang.

Picking up, "The Whitridge at Whitridge Manor, Charlie speaking."

"Wesley here."

Charlie squeezed the receiver, as if clutching a grab handle in a swerving car. "Yes, Wesley."

"Lora told me she forgot to mention tomorrow."

"Tomorrow," he repeated. "I don't recall. She may have—"

"Golf in the morning. We'll need four caddies. Sir Thomas and Buzz Goddard tend to spray their shots, so a couple of forecaddies would help. I'd like you to join us at ten o'clock. We'll make a little match of it. Come up with a format."

Charlie's grip on the phone loosened. "Who's the better player of the two?"

"Sir Thomas, far and away. What do you think of Lora's sketches?"

"I think they're great."

"We might be in Ireland but Jesus Christ she lays it on!"

"The pond, the swans, the rolling third green— that's The Whitridge, Wesley. It's perfect for our scorecard."

Silence. "Well, all right. I know we're short on time," Brotherton said. "Do you have the yardages from the blue tees? Son-of-a-bitch Harrigan never finished his job!"

"I do. The back nine is sixty-five yards longer than the front."

Brotherton inquired about "index." He asked Charlie what he was calling the number-one handicap hole.

"The ninth," Charlie said. "Difficult drive, you have to stay left, you need a high, accurate fade on your second shot. And it's a hard green to hold, maybe the hardest."

"I disagree," Brotherton said. "I'm thinking the fourth hole. Carrying the ravine is a must, and if you don't make it you're shooting three from the drop area. It's a narrow fairway and you have to negotiate four bloody bunkers to make the green."

Charlie was only too glad to give ground. "You're right," he said. "We'll make four the number-one handicap hole and nine the number two; on the back nine, thirteen and eighteen."

"Good, see you in the morning," Brotherton said.

Charlie replaced the receiver, then sat there for a good while, thumb and middle finger pressing against his eyebrows.

****

At 4:30 he got in his car and left for the day. As he rolled by the garage, he saw Keith Callaghan detailing the Jaguar. Charlie braked and pulled in, parking near Callaghan, who set a folded white cloth on the Jag's hood ornament and came over. He had a bouncy step, more jig than walk.

"Charlie, how's she runnin'?"

He opened his door and stepped out. "Like a top. I think my front tires might be low, they tend to squeal."

"Driving straight or cornering?"

"Cornering."

'That could be normal. Let me have a look."

Callaghan had a chrome tire gauge in his shirt pocket; he popped around, applying it to the front valves first, then the rear. While he tested, Charlie glanced at the garage. On the extreme left was a standard house door with a glass panel across the top: entrance to the building. The row of uncurtained windows on the top floor had a strange opaque appearance—

"They're right on the money," Keith said. "Ye might be taking your turns a bit sharp." His left eye twitched, then again. "Would ye like me to check under the bonnet?"

"I'm sure everything's OK. Out of curiosity," Charlie said, making a head motion toward the garage, "what's upstairs?"

"MacNair's apartment. Not that I've ever been in it. Only to the landing, once when his car wasn't here," the garageman said. "Padlock on his door like that." He made a fist. "But that doesn't mean I couldn't get in."

"Really?"

"When we were lads, the Manor House was something of a ruin," Callaghan said. "No one living in it. We knew of a breach in the wall. We'd fish the Argideen, and the garage here was our clubhouse." He gave Charlie a conspiratorial look. "There are ways."

"Is that his car?" It was an old brown Volvo parked at the house door.

"That's it."

"Where's yours, inside next to the Silver Cloud?"

Callaghan laughed. "I'm afraid not, Charlie. My wife works in Cork City, she drops me off in the morning."

CHAPTER 14

On Tuesday, late morning, Charlie delivered the draft Whitridge scorecard, along with Lora's pen-and-ink drawing, to Cork Printing. He talked with the art director, a fine-boned woman, early 40s, with gray hair and several rings on her fingers, named Tara Rowley. After discussing at some length the card's layout, how exactly Charlie wanted it to look, she asked him if he'd like his name on the cover as The Whitridge golf professional.

"No. Just the drawing," he said. "No name."

"Very well then."

"I have a question," Charlie said. "In the drawing here, do you see anything that, well, resembles Celtic art?"

Her eyes fell to Lora's depiction of the third hole. "You couldn't call it Celtic art," she said, "but the influence is there, distinctly."

"Where? Can you point it out to me?"

"The swans," Tara Rowley said, "the over-under inter-lacing of the feathers. The early Celts were a mysterious, complex people—note the water in the pond, the ripples, the avoidance of straight lines. And strongly in the lettering, The

Whitridge at Whitridge Manor. The fonts are suggestive of the Celtic Renaissance."

"It's just what I wanted to know," Charlie said.

Tara said she would send him a proof in three days and he could call in any changes before the final printing.

Charlie thanked her and went out, sat at an outdoor cafe on a busy street, thinking Cork seemed like a lively city, a fun place to live. When he finished lunch, he found 11 Benson Street, address of a component company that had recently sent him three dozen grips at The Whitridge. The owner of The Club Maker, Mickey Fallon, had once played on the European Tour, Charlie had discovered when they had talked on the phone. Now, walking into the shop, he introduced himself to Fallon, who said he remembered Charlie from his win at Mount Juliet. He had tied for seventeenth that day but hadn't picked up a stick in the past five years trying to get his company off the ground.

"How's it going?" Charlie asked.

Fallon had a healthy paunch and wore a Titleist cap on his head. "We're starting to show a little profit."

The store reminded Charlie of an auto parts shop—high counter, shelves upon shelves of boxes, display cases filled with club-fitting tools. Charlie said he wanted junior components. Three iron clubheads: a 6, an 8, and a pitching wedge; a 3-wood clubhead and a putter head; shafts for all the heads, ferrules, junior grips for the shafts, and a small, light-weight golf bag.

Fallon said he carried two sizes in junior components: ages 5-8 and 9-12.

Charlie chose the 9-12 models. The retired Irish golfer opened a glossy catalog. "Are these clubs for a lad or a lass?"

"A lass."

"I have some great new bags, and grips too. In bright colors."

"And a headcover for the 3-wood, something silly, maybe an animal," Charlie said. "Plus everything to set up a shop. A roll of double-sided tape, epoxy glue, solvent, sandpaper, a shaft cutter, a small propane torch, a backup canister—"

****

Back at The Whitridge, he went to work at the sturdy table Dennis had provided. The superintendent had thrown in, and attached, a heavy-duty vise, a key piece of equipment in assembling clubs. Charlie had learned the craft as a kid from the pro at Willow Falls, initially to save money, and it had stayed with him through the years. A few players he knew still fiddled around with clubs, had their own shops, but there wasn't much point to it today with all the manufacturers wanting your business and following you about on the Tour. Charlie slid the hard-rubber guard over one of Brigid's light-weigh steel shafts, tightened the vise around the guard, and started in. An hour and a half later he had finished the entire process, inserting the clubs, one by one, into the dazzling red bag, and sliding over the head of the 3-wood a green-and-yellow cover in the likeness of a friendly lion.

****

When the Dennehy kids arrived at Charlie's the next afternoon, Charlie took Kevin aside on the terrace, telling him to go into the house; he'd see a red golf bag in the corner. Bring it out and give it to Brigid. "Don't say anything. Just, 'Here.'"

Kevin went inside. When he came back out, he went over to Brigid who was standing with Charlie in the back yard.

She stared at the red bag with the clubs in it, then looked at Charlie, eyes wide. "What are these?"

"It's a mystery, suddenly they were in the house," Charlie said.

"Who for?"

"I guess for you. They're too small for Kevin."

"They're beautiful! And the lion!"

"Take one out, Brigid," Charlie said.

She pulled the 8-iron from the bag and gave it a couple of swings. "It's so much lighter."

He didn't want to give her any instruction, not yet. Maybe a little basic coaching. The idea was to make it fun. "OK," Charlie said, "this is the first annual 'Castlebantry Shootout.' Players take turns calling their shots. Closest to the pin wins. Today's contestants are Brigid Dennehy, Kevin Dennehy, and Charlie Kingston. First to play, Brigid. Call your shot."

"What do you mean?"

"Just say 'wildcard.' That means anything goes."

"Wildcard."

The ball Charlie tossed down wasn't perforated plastic; it was a real golf ball. "OK, Brigid, you're up. Swing away."

They were about thirty yards from the flagstick. She took a mean swipe at the ball, topped it and sent it bouncing along; it ended up eight feet from the pin. Brigid raised her hand joyously.

"Next up, Kevin Dennehy," Charlie said.

Kevin hit a good shot, using his own pitching wedge, but it was too long, going well past the flagstick.

"Next up, Charlie Kingston."

He dropped a ball, made a sincere effort to hit it well. The ball took a bad bounce and hit the side of the shed. "Skin for Brigid," Charlie said.

"What's a skin?"

"That means you win the money."

"We're playing for money?"

"Big money," Charlie said. Then, to Kevin, "Your call."

"Bump and run."

"What's a bump and run?" Brigid wanted to know.

"That's what you just hit," Kevin said.

"I did?"

"OK, back ten steps," Kevin said.

They went back pretty much to the limit of the yard. "Big money hole," Charlie said.

Kevin was up. He addressed a ball and came into it with a crisp half-swing. It barely got off the ground, took a hop and stopped fifteen feet from the flagstick.

"Beautiful," Charlie said.

It was Brigid's turn. Charlie suggested she change clubs and go with the 6. He positioned a ball on a tuft of grass and told her to give it a whack. She swung, as if to give it one, but missed the ball completely.

"Too bad," Kevin said.

"We'll give her a Mulligan," Charlie said.

"What's a Mulligan?"

"It's giving someone a second chance."

Brigid was concentrating fiercely. She swung again, missed again. "One more Mulligan," Charlie said. This time the ball went up in the air, just not far enough. He praised her effort, putting out his hand for a high five. Brigid gave it a solid slap. To Kevin he said, "What do you think? The girl's got talent."

But the boy's eyes were directed at the house, toward one side of it, a flat, grave expression on his face. Charlie turned around. Standing there glaring at him and the Dennehy kids was their father, who started toward them in aggressive, unsteady strides.

Oh, boy, thought Charlie. "Hello, Donal."

"What're you doin'?" Words slurred, gravelly.

"We're playing a game. Take a shot. Closest to the pin."

"Don't tempt me to take a shot." Booze on his breath. To his children, "Now go home, this is no place to be hangin' out."

"We're just having a little fun, da," Kevin said.

"Well I'll decide what's fun." To his daughter, "I never want you visiting here again. Now get, both of yeh!"

"Donal," Charlie said, "there's no need to be angry. Come on, be a sport about it."

"You keep your mouth out of this!" The girl hadn't moved and Dennehy said, "Didja hear me, Brigid?"

"I'm not going."

"Oh, you're not. I'll see about that."

"Da, leave her alone," Kevin said.

The veins in his nose swelling, his hand raised in a threatening fashion, Donal Dennehy went toward his daughter. "I'll tell you one last time, Brigid—"

On impulse, Charlie stepped between the two, not so much to fend off Dennehy as to shield the girl. Next he knew he was reeling from a brutally thrown punch to the side of his head. He seemed to hear loud cries, the screams of children...and that was all.

****

When he came to—minutes later, or hours—the yard was empty. Charlie sat up, his brain foggy. Scattered about on the ground were youth-size golf clubs, shafts snapped in two, golf bag kicked and torn. Charlie got to his feet, leaned over to pick up the lion headcover, and almost blacked out.

Inside, feeling dizzy, his face throbbing, he thought to make a compress, but his refrigerator lacked a freezer. A visit to Dr. Mulrooney was called for. He walked slowly, now and then stopping to gain his balance, to the doctor's office.

The waiting room was empty when Charlie walked in. It was a small, clean place—two chairs against one wall, two against another, and a low table in the middle. An antiseptic smell hung in the air. Dr. Mulrooney came out of his office dressed in slacks and an open shirt, took a moment to recognize his caller, then said, "Charlie Kingston, what happened here?"

"Someone's fist didn't like me."

"Come in, come in."

Dr. Mulrooney's office wasn't much bigger than his waiting room. He had Charlie sit on his examination table, checked his eye, his cheek, took his pulse, blood pressure. Nothing abnormal, nothing broken, he said, just a bad bruise. Mulrooney had him swallow a couple of pills with a cup of water, then prepared a compress, ice wrapped in a small towel.

"Lie down," he said, "hold this to your face."

Charlie lay down, and Dr. Mulrooney asked, "Who owned the fist that didn't like you?"

"Donal Dennehy."

"What happened?"

"His kids were at my house, we were making a little game out of hitting golf shots. He showed up, ordered the kids home. They didn't jump and he lifted a hand at Brigid, and when I stepped between them, he slugged me."

Dr. Mulrooney dabbed at the water running down Charlie's cheek. "I'd say you could bring assault charges against him but it wouldn't go anywhere."

"I'm not interested," Charlie said.

"Does Brigid play golf?"

"She doesn't play but she seems to like it."

"Kevin is working with you at The Whitridge," Dr. Mulrooney said.

"He's my assistant, also the caddie master."

The physician dabbed again with a tissue. "Any headache, Charlie? Nausea?"

"No. I'm feeling better."

"Sit up slowly." Charlie sat up. "I want you to take these pills," the doctor went on, "two every four hours. Keep the compress on and see me tomorrow."

"Thanks, Dr. Mulrooney. What do I owe you?"

"It's taken care of; but a word, if I might."

"Sure."

Dr. Mulrooney paused for a moment. "Brigid Dennehy is a lovely girl," he said, "very pretty, very charming. I just want you to understand something, Charlie. No people—" he paused, started again, "—no people are more prurient than the Irish, and at the same time so narrow-minded and judgmental. It's why I go to Pharr's. Not because I'm a republican—I'm anything *but* a republican—but because it's nobody's god-damn business if a physician has a few pints! At any other pub, people would count; they'd watch me, they'd talk. Folks in Castlebantry seem friendly but they're sanctimonious, they're envious, doctors drive around to see how other doctors are doing, counting the cars out front. No one wants you to succeed in Castlebantry; they want you to go on the dole."

"That's depressing to hear," Charlie said.

"Here's what I'm trying to say. Even with her brother along, people will get ideas," Dr. Mulrooney went on. "It isn't becoming that someone, in this instance a visiting American golfer, plays little chipping and pitching games in his backyard with a pre-teen girl. I hope you understand what I'm saying."

"I do, very well."

Back at his house Charlie held the compress to his cheek until the ice was melted, then lay down on his bed, hands covering his face.

CHAPTER 15

He had a fire going the following morning and was sitting before it with a mug of coffee. The medication had eased the pain and throbbing but he'd slept sporadically and had awakened feeling worried, troubled. The good doctor's words had jolted him, shaken him badly. You didn't get yourself knocked out by looking for your great-grandmother's grave!

There was a knock on the door, and Kevin came in dressed in gray trousers and a dark-green shirt under a sweater. He eyed Charlie's face, frowned. "How are you?"

"I wouldn't say I was in tiptop shape, Kevin. I'm doing all right."

"It was a cheap shot!"

"I didn't see it coming, that's for sure. How's Brigid?"

"Watching our da snap her clubs over his knee, and seeing you on the ground, out cold—she was screaming, Charlie. She's very upset."

He pushed gently beneath his cheekbone. "When is he going back?"

"Sometime this morning. But get this, our mum stood up to him. Germany's out, we're not going."

"Good," he said. "I'm proud of her."

Kevin slipped off his backpack, unzipped it, taking out two sandwiches wrapped in foil and a container of potato salad. "Early this morning she put this together for you."

"Thank you, Kevin. Thank Fiona." He paused, then said, "I won't be coming in today. After school, go to my office. Check for messages. If the phone rings, say, 'The Whitridge at Whitridge Manor, Kevin speaking.' Practice it. 'The Whitridge at Whitridge Manor, Kevin speaking.' Take notes on conversations with suppliers. Goods will be rolling in, sign for them. Remember, you're the assistant to the pro. How's Molly doing?"

"Sir Thomas gave her £50! She's my top recruiter. So far we have eleven kids and they all want to play golf."

It hurt like hell to smile, but Charlie smiled.

"Weeds are coming back on the front path, I just noticed," Kevin said. "I'll get to it this weekend."

"It's not a priority. Kevin. You've got your work cut out for you at The Whitridge."

"I'll do it, it's no big deal."

****

Charlie picked up the evidence of Donal Dennehy's rage, putting the broken shafts against the rear wall of the house; he stuffed the brown-and-yellow head cover into Brigid's battered golf bag, added peat to the fire, sat down with one of the sandwiches—sliced chicken with lettuce and tomato, a little mayonnaise. He loved Fiona for caring, mostly for putting her foot down with Donal. Charlie got sleepy and took a nap. Woke up and cleaned the kitchen area, the bathroom, swept the living room. Popped a couple of pills and lay down again.

At two he ate the second sandwich, a ham and cheese, spicy mustard, and half of the potato salad, then visited Dr. Mulrooney who told Charlie what he already knew: Dennehy had given him a real wallop. But he was doing well. "Just take it easy for another day or two, don't tax yourself." Back home again, Charlie thought to do a little non-taxing work on the window boxes. He opened the shed door, waited for his eyes to adjust to the gloom, then went in and rummaged around in the wooden box for a hand-held spade and fork. Suddenly seeing, through a break in the floorboards, what appeared to be another box, really just the top of one. He pulled the box out and sat in the shed doorway. Made of metal, it was dry but caked with grime and dirt. After some effort, he managed to pry loose the top. Inside lay a thick, business-size envelope wrapped in yellowing plastic.

Charlie peeled away the wrap, opened the envelope with great care. Inside were a dozen or so letters, each in its own smaller envelope, all held together with a string. Tucked under the string was a single piece of folded gray paper. Charlie slid it out; unfolding it, he saw a note written in neat script:

> These letters are from Kieran before I joined him in N. Ireland. I didn't want them with me while I was there and I couldn't bring myself to destroy them before I left. They are in your hands now, whoever you are. Do with them as you will. Mairead McGarrity.

He read the note again, sat for a long time looking at the individual envelopes, curious to know what Kieran had written to his wife, thinking he might finally learn who the McGarritys were; but Charlie couldn't bring himself to open a letter. *Whoever you are.* A visiting American golfer is who I am, he thought; out of quiet respect, he returned the box to the hole in the floorboards.

****

He weeded and cultivated the window boxes, then walked toward the crossroads, going into Monahan's. Mrs. Monahan greeted him with a certain cordiality—a customer was a customer; but beneath the surface was disdain. She glanced at his face, and Charlie could almost hear the words she was thinking. *It's a wonder he didn't kill you!* While she went into the back to get his laundry, Charlie picked a few items off the shelves, including a copy of *The Examiner.* Soon she was coming in with a well-wrapped package.

"A quart of milk, please, and a dozen eggs."

She put the items together. He handed her money, went out; at home he made himself a cup of tea and read the paper. The day wasn't getting any warmer and it had started to rain; he kept his fire glimmering. The British Open was next month, at Royal Birkdale in Southport, England, and his friend Gordon Brand Jr., from Ireland, would be playing in it. As would Des Smyth. Charlie looked at the other contestants. Tiger Woods, the favorite. A young Spanish amateur, Sergio Garcia, would be playing; people were calling him the next Seve Ballesteros. Everyone wanted to win a major. Mark O'Meara, who had won the Masters in April, would contend at Royal Birkdale. Nick Faldo was off his game but he was always a threat, a world-class player.

Charlie leafed through the paper. More news on the marching season in Northern Ireland. The Orange Order was adamant on its intentions to march along Garvaghy Road, after church services in Drumcree, as it returned to its lodge in Portadown. British forces were ready to mount major operations to ensure passage of the march, but Catholics on Garvaghy Road were vociferously opposed to it. In a poll, no Catholics were in favor of the march going ahead; virtually all Protestants were for it. Of particular concern to the Parades Commission, as it reported in a statement, was the fear that the I.R.A. would step in to protect the Catholic families. If such were to develop, then the UVF, a loyalist paramilitary group, would likely join the battle, creating in essence civil war.

Charlie closed the paper—so much for Good Friday—and lay down for still another nap.

****

Later in the day Kevin stopped in with a list of calls and messages, all jotted down. "At first," he said, "I made a mess of 'The Whitridge at Whitridge Manor, Kevin speaking,' but then I got good at it. Mrs. Brotherton called from London. She was impressed, she said I sounded like a real pro. She asked for you but I said you were home, you weren't feeling well. I don't know if that was the right thing to say."

"It was fine," Charlie said.

"We got two deliveries," Kevin said. "Three dozen golf gloves, different sizes, men's and women's. A whole carton of Titleist golf balls with The Whitridge logo. And the putters and wedges you ordered."

"Thanks, Kevin. You took care of business," Charlie said.

****

As he was getting ready to turn in—early, nine-thirty—his phone rang. He sat on the side of his bed and picked up. "Hello."

"Hi, Charlie. This is Lora."

He settled back against the pillow. "How nice of you to call."

"Would you like a visitor?"

"Any old visitor?"

"Say it was me."

"I'd love it, but you're in London."

"I was. I'm at the Manor House."

"Then come on out. You might not recognize me. I have a major black eye."

"What happened?"

"I'll tell you when you get here."

He tossed several chunks of peat on the dying fire, shaved, took a quick shower (or what passed for one), tore open his laundry and put on fresh clothes. As he was tying his shoes, he heard a knock on his door; he opened it and Lora was standing there, bracing herself as to what she might see.

"I know, I look like hell," he said.

"It's a shiner, I'll say that. How are you feeling?"

Embracing her, "Suddenly a whole lot better."

"I think I believe you."

He led her into the bedroom. "Here we are, Lora, the beauty and the beast."

"You're the beautiful one, Charlie."

****

Later they sat before the hearth with glasses of wine, the only light from a lamp in the bedroom and the gentle glow of the fire. "While I was lying on the grass, out cold," Charlie said, concluding the Dennehy narrative, "he took the clubs and broke them over his knee."

"I'm sorry—for Brigid, for you."

"I overstepped myself."

"Don't fault yourself, Charlie." Their chairs were close together and she held his hand. "Wesley wants me to go with him to New Zealand."

"What's in New Zealand?"

"Land he wants to look at."

"Where is he tonight?"

"Portadown, exhorting Orangemen to stay the course."

Charlie poured a little more wine. "I've been reading about Portadown," he said. "The Orange Order march, Garvaghy Road. It's amazing, busy as he is, how he finds the time—"

"There's nothing more important to Wesley than his membership in the Orange Order," Lora said. "He hasn't missed a march for thirty years."

Lora glanced at her watch. Curfew at Whitridge Manor, she didn't want Mrs. Walsh to worry, she said. Charlie walked her to the door, they kissed good night, and she was gone. Back in bed, in the dark, he pressed her pillow softly to his face.

CHAPTER 16

In khakis and a golf jacket over his shirt, Charlie left the house the next morning, a chill still in the air. When he passed the Whitridge Manor garage, he noticed that all overhead doors were lowered and MacNair's Volvo wasn't in its usual spot. Charlie pulled in and parked near the garage's side door, walked up to it and peered through the glass panel. In a small, empty hall, maroon-carpeted stairs rose to the second-floor landing; also in the hall, a plate-glass door led to the garage proper, and he caught a glimpse of Brotherton's Rolls; but the garage was dark. He had wanted to have another chat with Keith Callaghan, perhaps press the garageman on how, exactly, one would gain access to MacNair's apartment.

Casually, Charlie gave the knob a twist; that it opened didn't really surprise him. There was nothing on the other side except a staircase. He went in, glanced at the lineup of shiny automobiles—minus the Mustang. Last night, Charlie reasoned, Lora had probably parked directly in front of the Manor House. He began climbing the stairs, curious to see MacNair's door. Fifteen steps in all. Then he was standing before it: heavy oak, reinforced with iron straps.

Hanging in a steel hasp was the padlock, if not quite the size of a man's fist, plenty big. What astonished Charlie was that the lock's U-shaped bar wasn't fully closed, wasn't snapped shut. He could see a hair-line space between the tip of the U-bar and the body of the lock. Should he go in? A voice inside his head was saying, "In golf, there's a stiff penalty for going out of bounds. You're dangerously close here, Charlie."

Thanks for the warning, he thought, and lifted the lock free of the hasp. He turned the knob and gave the door a shove. Noiselessly it swung open.

The room was roughly half the area of the top floor of the garage; at the far end another door probably opened to living quarters. No beds or easy chairs here. The windows in front faced the parking area and the upper reaches of the golf course; a side window took in the first tee, pro shop and superintendent's barn. The opaque appearance Charlie had noticed before? From this viewpoint, it was nonexistent. MacNair could see out but no one could see in. Before both windows a high-powered telescope perched on a tripod. Resting on a ping-pong sized work station in the center of the room were a computer, printer, calculator, fax machine, and other electronic gadgetry—and a pair of telephones, one black, the other orange.

Despite fears that MacNair might suddenly show up, Charlie crossed to the work station. Computer printouts scattered about, scrawled messages on lined paper. He glanced at one of the printouts, recognized the word: "Garvaghy." Looked at a page of calculations, the pound sign here and there, but couldn't make anything out of the scrawl in the moments he had. Just then one of the telephones rang— seemingly the orange one—and Charlie jumped. After three rings, a message came on. "Baskerville here. Where the hell are you, Mongoose?"

Good question, thought Charlie, and headed for the door. But he stopped before getting to it. The telescope at the side window snagged his attention. It was oddly directed, pointing at the large tree adjacent to the garage. A chair with chrome wheels was positioned for viewing and Charlie took an extra moment and sat in the chair, peered through the eyepiece. What he saw sent an electrifying jolt through his body. The telescope, precisely directed, looked through the tree—through a natural opening in the branches—at the Manor House, at an upstairs window in the Manor House, at a canopy bed in a room in the Manor House, where a woman, even as he watched, was stirring, as if soon to get up, perhaps to stretch or dress or whatever else, all too wondrous to imagine, Wesley Brotherton's red-haired wife might do to start her day. Next to the chair Charlie sat in, a box of facial tissues lay on a small table, and in a nearby wastebasket Charlie spied several crumpled pieces.

The table had a single drawer and Charlie gave a tug on the brass pull. Inside were color photographs. He picked them up, stunned by what he saw. They were pictures showing Lora in revealing, sensual poses at her window, all the more erotic because natural, candid. Two pictures had her lying in bed, legs parted, sheet falling between her thighs. Charlie could only wonder if he and Lora might be among MacNair's cache. But such shots, if they existed, weren't among the ones he was holding. Just then, his peripheral vision detected motion outside the front window and he looked over. A brown automobile was rolling down the cobblestone driveway.

In near panic, as he made to return the pictures to the drawer, one slipped from his fingers, sliding beneath the table. Charlie fell to his knees to retrieve it, only to realize that the picture hadn't fallen so much as glided, and was now out of easy reach. In an effort to save precious seconds, rather than circling the table he simply crawled beneath it, snatched up the photo, slid it into his jacket pocket and made for the door. Under stress to get down the stairs to neutral ground, he almost pushed the U-bar into the body of the lock.

Charlie started down. As he opened the outside door, MacNair was coming toward it, a white paper bag in his hand.

His eye flicked to Charlie's bruise. "What do you want?"

"I'm looking for Keith."

In the flat tone of an interrogator, "What do you want with him?"

"The Saab has a shimmy, I wanted him to check it out."

"That's bullshit, it's a new car!" The ex-operative came closer. "You're snooping around."

"I told you why I was here."

"You're lying through your fucking teeth!"

"Reggie, I'm an employee at Whitridge Manor. The garage is not off limits. OK?"

"My place is. Don't fuck with me, Kingston!"

MacNair pushed on by, yanked at the door and went in, leaving behind a whiff of coffee and fresh-baked pastry. Charlie drove away, hands trembling; sure felt like a shimmy.

****

He was shaken but controlled his emotions and carried on, taking several calls during the morning. Merchants making excuses—scheduling difficulties, short on help, mechanical breakdowns. Of all the goods Charlie had ordered, only ten percent had arrived, and he was getting edgy, fearful that his shelves would be empty on opening day. Between calls he reviewed his plans and activities for the big weekend, contingent on the weather. The big tent below the Manor House was a necessity, of course; he had come to the same conclusion for the practice range. Players of all caliber and handicap liked hitting balls (especially free ones), and he had ordered a 60-foot awning set up to offer protection for a hardy, determined group, should it rain. The same would be true of the clinic he was planning for Saturday afternoon, which Wesley saw as a special bonus for his guests.

His phone rang at 10:10. It was a Lora ring and he wanted to say, "Hi. Good morning." But he stayed with protocol: "The Whitridge at Whitridge Manor, Charlie speaking."

"Good morning, 'Charlie speaking,'" she said, a smile in her voice.

Pleasurable ripples flowed under his shirt. "Can you stop by for tea?"

"I'd like to but the chopper's waiting and I'm already running late. I just wanted to say goodbye."

"Have a wonderful trip," Charlie said.

"Stay out of trouble!"

"I'll do my best."

"I dreamed about you all morning."

"I couldn't let go of your pillow," he said.

"See you, Charlie."

He put down the receiver, sat for a moment in a state of blissful listlessness. A ringing telephone snapped him out of it. Charlie sighed and picked up. Heather at Cork Design had a question about the sign she was making for the pro-shop door. "Across the top," she said, "we have 'The Whitridge.' Second line, 'Pro Shop.' Third line, 'Charlie

Kingston, PGA.' Now then, do you want the same type face for line three as for lines one and two?'"

"What do you think?"

"Personally, I see your name without serifs"

He didn't know the term. "Why is that?"

"Variety. Also it's a bolder look.

"OK."

"And 'Charlie Kingston, PGA' goes on a separate panel, do I have that right?" she asked.

"Hanging from brass hooks. When can you have it here?"

"Hopefully by the end of the week."

"It has to be here by one p.m. on Friday," Charlie said.

"I'll do my best."

"Heather, that doesn't do it. I need a commitment."

"I'll get it there, Mr. Kingston."

He thanked her and put down the phone as the whirring, beating sound of a helicopter filled the air. He sat at his desk listening to it fade—only then realizing, in his haste to leave MacNair's flat, he may have failed to close the drawer in the little table. He might just as well have left a note: "Hey, Reggie. Got a neat pad here. Swiped one of the pictures."

Charlie took the photo out of his jacket pocket. It was the one he had thought the most enticing and sensual: Lora standing at her window in a filmy gown breathing in the morning air, straps off both shoulders, her breasts bathed in sunlight.

He put the photo into a small manila envelope, slid it into his desk. Wanting to get out for a while, he grabbed his pitching wedge and walked to the practice range where he emptied a cloth bag, letting the balls roll out. One by one, thinking only tempo—Old Tom Morris...*Bobby Jones!*—he hit high, arcing shots, watching each ball climb into the sky, hang momentarily in the apogee of its flight, then, in keeping with natural law, begin to fall. One of these times—it was a thought he'd had from his earliest days as a golfer—he would hit a wedge so purely, so perfectly, it would defy gravity and just keep soaring.

****

Kevin came to the pro shop with eleven potential caddies (nine boys, two girls), and Charlie worked with the kids for almost two hours, emphasizing etiquette and courtesy over skills. Then he left it to Kevin to walk the kids around the course, hole by hole, and Charlie went home for the day. His cheek was feeling better but it still throbbed and he lay down to rest, soon dozing off. The phone rang. In his mind the New Zealand trip had fallen through and Lora was calling to tell him she was at Whitridge Manor.

"Hello," he said, almost saying, "Hello, Lora." Catching himself.

"Charlie, this is Fiona. I want to apologize for what happened. It was unforgivable."

He sat up, relieved. "Thanks for the care package."

"It was the least I could do. How are you?"

"I'm OK."

"Will you be coming to the pub? Your favorite dinner is cooking," Fiona said.

"I'll be there."

****

Kevin brought the tray to Charlie's banquette: medium-rare roast beef with gravy, baked potato and string beans, side dish of creamed onions. Transferring plates to the table, he told Charlie that many of the new caddies wanted to play golf but they couldn't afford clubs.

"Tell them you'll make them clubs," Charlie said.

"I will?"

"I'll teach you, at a huge savings for the kids—plus you'll make something for yourself."

Kevin went away and Charlie settled into his dinner. Fifteen minutes later Dennis walked in and Charlie observed the interaction between him and Fiona. O'Hea was trying to make a little time with her but Charlie saw nothing to indicate that he was getting anywhere; and Charlie was starting to think that the problem wasn't Dennis—he was a strong, fine-looking man—so much as it was Fiona. Charlie left it there, continued with his dinner. As he was finishing, Brigid came out and sat next to him at the banquette.

"Hi," she said.

"Hi, Brigid. How are you?"

"I didn't know you'd *made* my clubs, Charlie. Kevin told me. It's so unfair what happened."

"It is."

By way of indicating his cheek, she touched her own. "Does it hurt?"

"Some. Not like it did."

They were quiet for a while. "My mum told me about April," Brigid said. "I'm awfully sorry. I'm really, really sorry."

"Thank you, Brigid. I'm sure she would have liked you."

"I would've liked her, Charlie. We would've been great friends."

CHAPTER 17

By Friday afternoon of the golf weekend the pro shop was fully stocked with apparel from top outfitters in Dublin, Cork and London. Against the right-hand wall four sets of irons gleamed; also three sets of woods, eight different putters and an equal number of wedges with varying degrees of loft and bounce. Dozens of golf balls, leather golf gloves, golf towels were on display in the large, glass-fronted case. Different-colored tees, each inscribed "The Whitridge," lay jumbled in a wooden barrel, a sign tacked to the side of it reading: "Take a Handful."

In the calm before the first guests started arriving, Kevin was telling Charlie that school had ended for the summer and he'd advanced with his class.

"Congratulations," Charlie said.

"I'm the luckiest kid in Castlebantry."

"You made your luck, Kevin."

A delivery truck pulled up and the driver delivered a carton. Kevin signed for it and broke it open. "You know what this is."

"The only thing we're missing," Charlie said.

Kevin pulled out a lady's visor with an image of the Manor House on the crown and the caption, The Whitridge at Whitridge Manor. In all, there were three dozen visors, in blue, green, and white, and Kevin placed them on a shelf specifically left empty. Charlie was admiring the look, the exquisite rendering of the Manor House, and who should come walking in, that moment, but the artist herself.

"Look at this place, will you? It's unbelievable."

He had to check the impulse to go over and take her in his arms. "Lora, welcome back!"

"Hello, Charlie. How are you, Kevin?" she said, coming all the way in. "This is amazing." Her eyes went from shelf to shelf, rack to rack. "Oh, visors! Wonderful! I need a new one."

"You've come to the right place, Mrs. Brotherton," Kevin said.

Lora looked over the selection, viewed her drawing, then selected a green visor and put it on. She was in a lemon-yellow skirts and a white blouse with light-green stitching at the neck. "What do you think?"

"Smashing," Kevin said.

"Well then, I'll just have to buy it," Lora said. "Problem is, I don't have any money on me."

"We don't usually extend credit in the pro shop," Charlie said, "but maybe we can make an exception. Kevin, what do you think?"

"I agree."

Just then Kevin's girlfriend, Molly, and a couple of other caddies, were starting down the path. Kevin excused himself and hurried out.

"How was your trip?" Charlie asked.

"The only thing not to like about New Zealand is getting there," Lora said. "And the flight back was agony. I couldn't wait to see you. Do we have time?" She gave a look toward his office.

"Lora, people are all over the place, guests will be coming in."

"There's nothing like the moment, Charlie."

"True, but we'd be pushing our luck."

"I thought you were a risk taker."

"Lora, I love you. Trust me here."

Just then the rumble of a helicopter filled the air.

"After the party," she said, "we have a date."

"Yes we do."

A minute later Wesley came down the path. He walked in, shook Charlie's hand and looked around. "This is it, this is just what I want. And the sign on the door is great." Then to Lora, "Count and Countess von Ludwig are arriving. Let's go welcome them to Whitridge Manor."

"Excuse us, Charlie," she said, and went out with her husband.

****

The following morning at 9:00 Charlie spoke to the sixteen golfers and their caddies assembled at the first tee. Lora and Wesley were among them, though in different groups. "For those who came in late yesterday and I didn't get a chance to meet you, my name is Charlie Kingston," he began. "I'm a Tour player in America, and I'm here to help you enjoy your weekend at Whitridge Manor and, if I can, help you with your game. Our caddie master, Kevin Dennehy, has trained and assembled a group of young caddies, all from Castlebantry and all splendidly attired in their Whitridge T-shirts and caps. Anything you might want to give them at the end of the day, they will certainly appreciate. If you'd like to retain your caddie for morning golf tomorrow, just let him or her know. Now, let me tell you about our tournament."

Charlie looked about at the Brothertons' guests, all eager to start. If he could judge by their looks and their clothes, they seemed brothers and sisters of the guests of a month ago. "It's not quite the Open," he went on, "but we do have fine prizes, and you'll be playing one of the most beautiful courses in Ireland. Only nine holes but different tees for the back nine. The ladies play from the same tees on both nines. Why that's true I don't know. Best ask Wesley."

Everyone laughed, including Brotherton. He was standing with a group of three other golfers: two men in plus fours and a horsy woman in a wraparound plaid skirt and a Whitridge straw hat.

"Our format today is 'Captain and His Crew' or, as it's also called, a 'Scramble,'" Charlie continued. "Here's how it works. Each of you is on a team, four players to a team. The captain of each team chooses the best of the four drives; from the spot where that shot ends up, team members play second shots; using the best of the second shots, third shots are played. Same for putting. Only rule: everyone on a team must contribute at least two drives. We're having a shotgun start. One team will start on the first tee; the other teams will start play on the second, third and fourth holes respectively. We don't have a shotgun but I do have a powerful horn."

Charlie held it up. "When you hear this, in about ten minutes, start playing. Your caddies know the quickest way to your respective teeboxes and will lead you out. OK, to your tees! Good luck, play well, and have fun!"

The throng of golfers and caddies began walking down the first fairway. Left in the vicinity of the first tee were three men, Lora, and their caddies. Charlie had met the men earlier, and he went over to where they were all standing.

Two of the men were wearing Whitridge caps, one the cap of his club in England, Royal Ashdown Forest. Carter Fairhurst, the captain of Lora's team, an amiable chap in his fifties with a goatee, asked Charlie what his philosophy was on "team putting." On difficult, must-make puts, who should putt first?

"That's always a question," Charlie said. "Sometimes the player who's putting badly will hit it just right, and the ball will go in. But I think it's smartest to save your best putter for last. He'll be able to go to school on the first three players."

"I putt like a dog," said Thornton Stockard, a rosy-cheeked man wearing black-framed sunglasses. "So I volunteer to go first."

"And if I know Thornton, he'll sink it," said the third man on the team, Todd Birch, the bridge of his large nose sharply bent, a classic dog-leg. "I've played with him for years, and he makes everything."

"All this is very good to know," said Carter Fairhurst. "How about you, Lora? How's your putting?"

"I'm very good at tap-ins."

After a few more minutes, Charlie said it was time to play. He advised hands over the ears, then raised the horn high and pulled the trigger. It was a strong blast, a cross between a siren and a ship's whistle. "OK," he said to the team members, "the tee is yours."

The three men stayed on the teebox and Charlie stepped away, as did Lora; though she preferred hitting with the men, today she'd play from the women's tees. Carter Fairhurst pegged a ball, then loosened up before taking his stance.

"How are you?" Charlie said to Lora, quietly.

"How do you think I am?"

"Maybe a little tired."

"You never tire me, Charlie." For a second she gave him her eyes. "Just the opposite."

The team captain was setting up to his ball. Carter Fairhurst drifted to the right on his take away, but he hit a decent drive, regardless, maybe 190 yards.

Stockard and Birch teed off, mediocre shots at best, one ball sailing right, the other left. Lora was next to drive but her tee was farther down the fairway. Charlie wished her good luck and she left with her group.

****

The pro shop was a "halfway house" for the players. When they passed it walking in from the ninth hole, they stopped in for cold drinks and snacks brought down from the Manor House, talked about the tournament and how they were doing as a team. Nothing but praise for their young Irish caddies. Several guests asked Charlie for tips. Trying to visualize their problem, he offered suggestions—fuller shoulder turn on the backswing, better weight shift coming through the ball, rock-still head when putting. Don't look until you hear the ball drop.

On the second time around, from the blue tees, players didn't come in when they passed the pro shop—they had only one, two or three holes left to complete their round. The tournament was drawing to a close. When the golfers that had started on the second hole walked by, needing to play the first hole to finish the eighteen, Charlie told Kevin to watch the store; he was going out to see Fairhurst's team come in.

He walked past the superintendent's barn and the practice range, and soon came to the ninth (or eighteenth) green. In the valley where the stream cut across the fairway, golfers were gathered in a small area discussing the approach, talking strategy. The ball chosen for play had stopped just short of the water, and it was going to take a very nice shot to reach the green. Rosy Cheeks, a.k.a. Thornton Stockard, had the first go at it. His ball sliced badly and crashed into the trees. Lora's shot was straight but fell forty yards short. The third man, Todd Birch, chunked his ball, the infamous sclaff. That left it up to Carter Fairhurst; using a fairway wood, he hit the ball well but it too was short, stopping twenty yards from the green.

Charlie stood to one side, well away from the putting surface. When the players reached Fairhurst's ball (as the ball to play), they talked over the shot and Birch redeemed himself, chipping to twelve feet. Stockard's try at it was a disaster; he topped the ball and sent it twenty feet past the hole. Lora had a clean chip but it stopped fourteen feet short. Carter Fairhurst's ball hit the pin but it caromed off, caught a downslope and ended up twenty feet away.

Birch's ball was the closest, but Carter, after a careful look, concluded that Lora's putt was easier to make, slightly uphill and more or less straight in, while Todd Birch's putt was a right-to-left break on a downslope.

"We'll use Lora's chip," he said.

Birch's putt was short; Stockard's ball skimmed the hole by a half-inch and team members groaned. As if to end the stress, Carter Fairhurst putted next; but it was a weak effort, a bad stab at the ball, and didn't come close. Charlie didn't know how the team had done on the back nine, but he seemed to think *they* thought they had a chance to win—if Lora could get the ball to drop.

She put her ball on the spot marked by a coin, adjusted her Whitridge visor. After a quick read she took her stance and without undue delay or deliberation hit the ball; it started off with a couple of little hops—not indicative of a good stroke—but settled into a steady roll, found the cup, and fell. Her teammates hugged and kissed her. Charlie wanted to join in, but of course that would've been unprofessional, at the very least.

"Nice putt, Lora," he said as she and three happy men walked off the green.

"Thanks, Charlie."

To Carter Fairhurst, Charlie asked, "How did you do?"

"Four under, thanks to Lora just now. Saved a par for us. We have a chance."

****

All the Brothertons' guests, players and nonplayers, were in the pro shop. A half-keg of Guinness and several bottles of chilled white wine had arrived, and two young Irish women in blue were passing about delicious tidbits. Everyone was talking and mingling, buying items from Kevin. Already there was a huge dent in the merchandise. Then Charlie, standing in front of the display case, gently tapped the glass with a divot-repair tool. The buzzing stopped.

"It's time to announce the winners of today's tournament," he said. "But first I want to congratulate everyone who played. You're all great competitors. Not all of you who came to Whitridge Manor as the guests of Lora and Wesley knew each other, but it's clear to me you know each other now, and like each other too. Golf brings people together like no other sport or activity in the world... almost."

Everyone laughed. "Now for the results," Charlie said.

In his hands were four scorecards. On the counter rested sixteen handsomely wrapped packages. Charlie put out his hands to quiet the room. "OK. The team that came in last at even par, which isn't a bad score by any means—will the captain, Fletcher York, please come forward with his crew?"

York walked up with two other men and a woman. Charlie shook his hand, congratulated all for fine play. Kevin then gave each player a jumbo box of Slazenger golf balls, eighteen instead of the usual twelve. Everyone clapped. The third place team had a respectable score of two under par. Stuart Smyth walked up and each player received a Waterford crystal candy bowl.

"Now, as for the winner, we have two teams with identical scores of four under par," Charlie said. "The team of Wesley Brotherton and the team of Carter Fairhurst."

Charlie pointed at the two men, started clapping, and everyone joined in. "In golf, as you know, if there's a tie, players face each other in a sudden death shoot-out," he said, "one-irons at thirty paces." Laughter. "That doesn't seems appropriate today, so how do we decide who wins? We match cards. As you also know, there's only one fair way to match cards if play starts on different holes. You start matching at the number-one index hole—that is, the most difficult hole on the course—then go to the second most difficult hole, et cetera. I have Wesley's card and Carter's card before me. Starting at the fourth hole, both cards show birdie 3's. No blood. On the ninth hole, the second most difficult, both cards show par 4's. No blood. But on the eighth hole, one team recorded a 5 and the other team a 4. So the winner is—"

Charlie paused. "But let me put it this way. Second place goes to the team ably led by Carter Fairhurst."

Applause. Kevin handed a silver-blue box to each player. Fairhurst opened his. Inside was a stunning gold-plated table clock, five inches high, from Wallace & Burlingame in London, handsomely engraved: "The Whitridge at Whitridge Manor. Castlebantry, Ireland. 1998." Fairhurst held it up and everyone cheered.

"That leaves the winners," Charlie said, "our host and former member of England's Walker Cup team, Wesley Brotherton, and his crew."

They came forward to loud and sustained shouting and clapping. First-place prize was a mantelpiece clock identical to the clock Fairhurst had just held aloft, only larger. Wesley offered his hand to Charlie, and Charlie asked him if he wanted to say a few words.

"Well, I only want to say this was the most fun I've had in golf in twenty years and I want to thank Charlie for putting on such a splendid tournament," Brotherton said. "Asking him to join the staff as The Whitridge pro was a brilliant stroke on my part, if I do say so myself." The group clapped spontaneously. "I heard about Lora's excellent play, and a putt she made on the eighteenth hole was inspired. Kevin, our caddie master—" Wesley gave the lad standing behind the display case more than a mere glance, "—I don't quite see how you gathered and trained so many fine young people so fast and so well." Then, speaking generally, "All in all, it was a truly great morning of golf. Stay as long as you like in the pro shop—a.k.a. Whitridge Manor Pub; but I believe the Manor House is awaiting us for lunch. At four o'clock Charlie will be giving a clinic on the range. From here on, the course is yours to play whenever the mood strikes." He lifted his clock above his head and merged with his guests.

Several people came up to meet Charlie. One of them was a lively woman on Stuart Smyth's team who spoke with a German accent—the Countess von Ludwig—who told Charlie his putting tip had worked miracles. On three holes, hers was the crucial putt, and she made all three! Two men and a woman signed up for lessons on Sunday morning. All guests were looking forward to the clinic.

Kevin was wiping down clubs in the golf bags stanchioned outside, and from the side window Charlie watched the last of the Brothertons' guests wend their way toward the Manor House. He was glad the golf had gone well, that Wesley's team had won. It was a good start for the weekend. But every so often he felt uncomfortable twinges, never more sharply than just now when Wesley had praised him in the pro shop. Charlie didn't like what he was feeling, couldn't shake the hypocrisy of what was going on....

Kevin came back inside. "What a great tournament, Charlie—and look what we sold!"

"I know, it's something. What are the caddies saying?"

"They're all smiles," Kevin said, "walking around with forty to fifty punt in their pockets!"

CHAPTER 18

Guests were seated in folding chairs set up on the rear portion of the practice range, and a good many of the caddies sat on the grass. A man, maybe 45, in a pale-blue shirt, sparkling white trousers and blue topsiders, sat next to Lora. They appeared to be enjoying each other's company, talking and laughing.

Standing before the guests, Charlie spoke on three aspects of the game: the pitch, the medium-iron, the tee-shot. How to hit each one. Standing near him, holding his bag and handing him the club he wanted, was Kevin. When he came to the drive, Charlie faded the ball, explained how he did it; drew the ball, explained how to make it curve to the left. Hitting a straight ball was the hardest, but he launched a couple of lasers that almost reached the 300-yard marker, and the gathering, as one, gasped.

After thirty minutes, Charlie ended the instructional aspect of the clinic. Were there any questions? A few hands went up.

"Yes," Charlie said, pointing to a large, imposing man with skinny brown eyebrows.

"I have strength, I lift weights at the gym—I'm stuck at 200 yards off the tee. You're hitting it 300. What are *you* doing that I'm *not* doing?"

People laughed. "For one," Charlie said, "your profession isn't golf. Maybe it's your love but it's not your career. That doesn't mean you can't knock it farther. Strength is important, there's no question about that; but it's technique—technique and conditioning. How fast can you bring the club head through the ball? Well, how fast can you uncoil your hips? A new player on Tour, Tiger Woods—no one unwinds his hips as fast as Tiger. But don't belittle two-hundred yards; it's a good drive."

Charlie looked around. "Carter," he said to Carter Fairhurst, whose hand went up; he was sporting a boater.

"After the basics—setup, posture, grip," Fairhurst said, "—what, in your estimation, is the most important aspect of the swing?"

"I'd say mental readiness, but I wouldn't say *after* the basics," Charlie said. "The finest setup, posture and grip won't help if you're mentally at odds with the game. For instance, the practice swing—how smooth, how effortless! Two-fifty right down the middle. But once we stand over a ball we try to kill it or steer it, and we blow the shot. Forget 'ball,' Carter. Think 'dandelion' in your back yard. Make that swing your swing."

Charlie looked around. "Anyone else?"

"I'm sure you've had golf lessons in your life," said a woman in red wearing tortoise shell sunglasses. "What was the best lesson you ever had?"

"The best golf lesson I ever had," he said, and paused. "I'll tell you exactly what it was. It was a lesson I had with the pro at the local course in Willow Falls, Michigan, where I grew up. I was sixteen. The pro was Jake Magliora, a really fine golfer, and one of the best teachers of the game who ever lived. I was having trouble keeping the ball straight off the tee, I told Jake. In other words, I tended toward wildness. He knew my swing, my game; I wasn't a stranger to him. I thought he'd say, 'Tee one up. Let's have a look.' He said, 'Charlie, when you throw a club, what's your technique?' As a kid I had a temper, and sometimes after dubbing a shot I'd chuck my driver or 5-iron into the rough, into the pond. Nothing to brag about. And now Jake wanted to know my *technique*? 'I don't have one,' I said, 'I just grip it and sling it.' A bucket of practice balls was at our feet, maybe now he'd have me hit a couple. No. He asked me what I was thinking when I threw a club. I said I didn't think about anything. I just let the damn thing go, usually with a swear. Maybe if I kicked over the bucket he'd get the idea. *My swing, Jake. I'm hooking, I'm slicing!* But he wanted to go on with how I threw a club. Not why? *How.* And finally I showed him. I grabbed an 8-iron from my bag and chucked it. He said I had a terrific technique. And he wasn't being sarcastic. He wasn't scolding me. He told me I really knew how to throw a club and he walked off the range. I wandered out and looked for the 8-iron, finally locating it. I stooped over to pick it up, then stood there looking at the pro shop and the eighteenth green. And it came to me. That's all I can say. I never threw another club. That was the day I became a golfer. It was the best lesson I ever had and not a single ball was hit."

Guests gave him a long, enthusiastic round of applause. Several came up to him afterwards, shook his hand. Lora waved and smiled as she walked away with the tall, good-looking man in topsiders. The crowd was thinning, and

Wesley, almost the last to leave, drifted over. Beautifully presented, he said to Charlie. Then he said he'd be visiting the Killdoon site Monday morning. "I'd like your view on it."

"Sure. Where's Killdoon?"

"In County Clare, on the Atlantic."

"Oh, the Nick Jarvis course," Charlie said.

"Right. I'll meet you in the pro shop at nine sharp," Wesley Brotherton said. "Then we'll jump in my chopper." He moved on, joining a few of his guests.

The range was deserted. "We can head in now, Kevin," Charlie said.

****

At the party that evening Charlie had to tell several guests, who approached him wanting a morning lesson, that his schedule tomorrow was full; he was sorry, but it was impossible for him to see anyone else. One gentleman, Sir Oscar Beasley, told Charlie that his down-to-earth talk and exhibition had impressed him greatly. Could he come to London for a couple of days and work with him at The Grove. All expenses, of course, plus his fee. Charlie said he liked the idea, and Sir Oscar handed him his card.

A seven-piece band played lively music, guests talked and drank and partook of fabulous hors d'oeuvres. Charlie looked about for Lora, saw her dancing with the man in topsiders, though now he had on slender-soled slip-ons with tassels and had changed from white trousers to royal blue. And so nimble on his feet!

In time, maybe thirty minutes later, Charlie spotted her at a table with a portly man in a teal-blue jacket who was sitting with an elegantly coifed woman in flowing coral silk, and he walked over. After an introduction to the Hon. Archibald Newman and his wife Eloise, both of whom said they had found his clinic very helpful and delightfully entertaining, he requested the honor of a dance with his hostess. Lora took his arm. She had on a backless, champagne-colored cocktail dress and a superb diamond necklace.

"You're a star," she said as they began dancing.

"I hit some golf balls," he said, "answered a few questions."

"It's how nicely you do it."

"Wesley wants me to go to Killdoon with him on Monday."

"He's beginning to rely on you."

"I don't know if that's good or bad."

"How can it be anything but good? Monday afternoon we're leaving for London," she said. "I'll be back Thursday by myself. Let's go on a picnic."

"I know a great spot in the Castlebantry Hills. Can I get anything?"

"I'll have Mrs. Walsh prepare a basket."

They danced quietly. Then Charlie said, "Who's the guy you were sitting with at the clinic?"

"Anthony Whiteley, I've known him for years."

"What does he do?"

"He's the skipper of *Incorrigible*, England's hope in the 2000 America's Cup."

"Is he now?"

The band stopped for a break and Charlie escorted Lora off the floor. "Thursday I'll come by your house at one," she said.

****

In time everyone sat down to a superb dinner of beef tenderloins and broiled lobster tails, the finest wines. At Charlie's table, the wife of the chief financial officer of

Brotherton Enterprises, Eleanor Applegate, a sparky brunette with a dimple in her cheek, mentioned Hillary Clinton's comment about a right-wing conspiracy, and everyone jumped in, thoroughly raking America's first lady over the coals. Charlie might've been sitting with a group of PGA players and their wives. He was quiet on the topic. Finally, as if wanting the American golfer to commit himself, Mrs. Applegate directed her lively blue eyes on Charlie, inquiring, diplomatically, what his take on Hillary was.

He had never said anything good about the president's wife but didn't feel like adding to the tirade. "I really don't have one," he said.

The new topic was global warming, and everyone seemed to agree that Tony Blair's stand on it was strictly political; he didn't believe in the phenomenon any more than they did. Labor was just trying to broaden its base. Charlie glanced toward the dance floor. Lora was again dancing but with Anthony Whiteley.

A fabulous dessert was destined to appear, but Charlie made a small announcement beforehand; his first lesson was at eight and he had better excuse himself and get a little sleep. The guests understood and with great cordiality wished him a good night.

He went up the steps to the Manor House level, walked out to the cobblestone driveway and across to the access road, branching off at the pro shop. Dusk was settling in; the area lay in deep shadows. Then, suddenly, he stopped. Was someone moving about at his car?

Someone was. "Who are you?" Charlie shouted, advancing quickly.

The individual disappeared into the trees behind the shop. Charlie thought to follow after him, to have it out with Reggie MacNair—who else could it be?—once and for all. He stood by the Saab. Strains of lively music filled the air. He looked back toward the Manor House. The sky, over it, made him think the sun was rising; it was dawn at Whitridge Manor. But night was falling.

CHAPTER 19

Forty minutes after lifting off from a corner of The Whitridge practice range, Brotherton's chopper approached the golf course in Killdoon, County Clare—or what was becoming a golf course. Along one long stretch of the rugged, heavily duned property ran a magnificent crescent beach. In the cabin, seated behind Charlie, Wesley spoke to him via the headsets they both had on. "That's the Lodge," he said, indicating a huge, bare-boned structure: no siding, no windows in place. "It'll have twelve suites and fifteen individual rooms. We have plans to build twenty houses with an ocean view and sites are going fast. Those red flags you see, that's how they're marked off; foundations for two or three houses are already in. Over there on the bluff," pointing, "we're going to have cottages at a lower price, with full services and amenities. A basic footprint but interiors to the buyer's wish."

Brotherton spoke to the pilot over the intercom. "Max, start at the first tee, then cruise along going from tee to green, the entire layout."

The chopper banked and moved in. Charlie had never seen so rugged, so dramatic an environment for a golf course.

At first glance, it was a desert wasteland. "OK, this is the first hole," Brotherton said.

It was defined—the whole course was routed—but without a blade of grass. Heavy machinery was moving earth, grading the land, here on the first hole and elsewhere. "Those dunes just ahead? They surround the first green on three sides," Wesley said. "It's a great opening hole. But we have a problem with it. That's the seventeenth green, right there." Over his intercom to the pilot, "Slow it down, Max." Then to Charlie, "The only way a player can get to the 18th teebox after finishing the 17th hole is to cross over the first fairway."

"What does Jarvis say about that?"

"Excuses, rationalizations. I've lost all respect for him. It's bad routing, period. It's why I've brought you along so you could see for yourself."

They skimmed along, Brotherton describing each hole as they passed over it. "Right there," he said, "where those pot bunkers are? Just beyond is the fourth green."

"I see it," Charlie said.

"That teebox hard by? It's the fifteenth."

"So players driving on fifteen have to shoot over the heads of golfers putting on four? Am I seeing that right?"

"You are."

They buzzed every hole. Brotherton pointed out a few additional problems with routing but nothing so striking as the first two. By and large it was a remarkable course with views of the ocean on all but three holes. It reminded Charlie of Pebble Beach, just grander, more dramatic. Brotherton inquired, as they were winding up the fly-over, if he'd like to see any holes again. Charlie said he would—the first and seventeenth, taken as a unit; and the fourth and fifteenth, also as a unit.

Brotherton signaled the pilot. "Max, let's have another look at the one/seventeen trouble spot. Hover over it. Likewise four/fifteen."

The chopper banked. Shortly, Charlie heard Wesley's voice: "OK, here we are again."

****

As a village, Killdoon had a single main street; on it were several shops and three or four pubs. Of the pubs, Casey's was the one Wesley knew and liked, and he and Charlie sat at a table each with a shepherd's pie and a pint, talking about Killdoon, the golf course. Charlie said he realized that links courses frequently had one or two holes that crisscrossed, but in his opinion such design showed a failure of imagination. "It's a crime for a spectacular parcel of land like Killdoon to have competing holes," he said.

Brotherton fed himself a forkful of mashed potatoes and chopped beef, had a swallow of Newcastle. It was the closest beer he could find in Ireland comparable to Chiswick Bitter. "Here's the crux of it," he said, speaking in confidential tones. "Golf is becoming a bigger and bigger piece of Brotherton Enterprises. I have resorts around the world–in Barbados and Tortola, in Tuscany, in Cap d'Antibes, the Scottish highlands, Vero Beach; soon in the Hawke's Bay region of New Zealand–we hope to break ground there in September; on the Riviera, in the Lake Country in England, here in Ireland. As it stands now, there's no oversight; each golf course, with all its varied components, operates independently, much like a fiefdom. Take Killdoon. Those problems never should have happened. What's missing is an overall policy or culture. We offer everything to ensure our visitors' comfort and pleasure but golf is key, and I'm losing confidence that we're doing our best in what's most important to us. We're getting careless, we're not keeping our eye on the ball—I'm getting reports all the time. Charlie, I'll come to the point. I'd like you to take on the directorship of all golf operations in my Resorts Division while keeping The Whitridge as your home course. I want your name and PGA affiliation to remain over the pro-shop door. In your new position you'd oversee all aspects of the game, including the construction of new courses and clubhouses, the hiring and firing of golf personnel, the quality of golf-related service and amenities, such as pro shops and teaching procedures and techniques. It would mean traveling but you'd stay in the best places, play the finest courses—everything first class. Are you still planning on Q-School?"

"I have it chalked in."

"I think you're ready for new ventures," Brotherton said. "The personal attention you give to people, the professionalism you demonstrate at every turn, your easy-going attitude—it's remarkable. Here's how I see it. Through July you'd wear two hats. One you're already wearing as The Whitridge pro; the second would be as vice-president of a new division in Resorts International I'm calling 'Golf.' I'd pay you both salaries through July. Starting August 1, Golf Division only. I'd like you to keep The Whitridge as your home course, as mentioned. The Dennehy lad would take over the day-by-day pro-shop activities. After July, we'll still have golf at The Whitridge but on a smaller scale, fewer caddies, limited merchandise. I'd give Kevin the title 'Pro in Training,' and I'm sure we could find work for him in the off season. As for the new position—I got the idea for it three years ago but no one ever had the requirements, the background I wanted: communications skill, administrative skills, golfing skills. Until I met Charlie Kingston. I'd start you at £160,000 a year, plus bonus and expense account. To a touring pro, that might seem like pocket change, but I can guarantee you in a couple of years as my Golf Czar you'll be making more than most golfers on the circuit— without the sweat, blood and tears! Which reminds me, I never coughed up the £20 I owe you."

"Forget it, Wesley."

"A bet's a bet." Brotherton stripped a note from his wallet. "You and Buzz Goddard kicked our tails."

'Then I'll buy lunch."

"Some other time, Charlie. Today, I just want to get the concept on the table. Bottom line, I'm looking for direction and leadership in Resorts International, specifically pertaining to golf. Personnel will be a major part of the job, keeping good people, thinning out the lazy, the incompetent. I want you to think about it, the rest of the summer if you want—absolutely no rush."

"Thank you," Charlie said.

Brotherton went on in a voice barely above a whisper. "Speaking of personnel," he said, "my head of security has just confirmed what we've suspected for some time." He passed his napkin over his mouth, as if wiping his lips; through it he said: "O'Hea's affiliated with the Southern Command."

"Really."

"He's a great source of intelligence for us and we've nothing to gain by axing him now." Brotherton continued speaking in a low, modulated voice, frequently using his napkin. "What Reggie is picking up, specifically, is the Provos' intentions on July 12. If they step in to protect Garvaghy Road residents, we'll be ready to counter force with force. Charlie, the Orange Order has made the march to Drumcree since 1807, peacefully and proudly—myself for many, many years now—and a band of I.R.A. scoundrels and Catholic nationalists won't dictate our route."

Their waitress, a big-boned woman with strong arms and sturdy hands, came up, asked if there was anything else they might like. Brotherton inquired if she had any cherry cobbler. Last time he was here he'd had a serving and he'd loved it.

"Indeed we do."

"Charlie, you have to try this."

"Sounds good."

"Two cherry cobblers," Brotherton said to the woman, "coffees and two Courvoisier."

The cobbler was indeed excellent. In an expansive mood, Brotherton talked about his days as a Walker Cup player, his win over a fine American golfer named Ted Neighbors in 1975. "I beat him 1-up but I didn't have the drive to turn professional. I had the drive to make money and how much could I make as a journeyman pro? I bought a small company, a manufacturer of quality shotguns and hunting rifles in Birmingham, and a nondescript 18-hole golf course near Kirkcaldy, Scotland, and I nursed them along—that was the best part, watching them grow, bringing them along like kids. Anyway, to wind up our talk, Charlie. Think it over."

Brotherton picked up his snifter. No suppressing his voice now. "There's a saying of Samuel Johnson's I like: 'Claret is for boys, port for men, but who aspires to greatness drinks brandy.'" He held out his glass. "Here's to you, Charlie."

CHAPTER 20

The day after the Killdoon trip Charlie drove to the Bank of Ireland with the pro-shop receipts. He parked his car and walked two blocks to the bank, not nearly so imposing a structure as the cathedral on the opposite corner but, compared to the other buildings in downtown Castlebantry, a fortress.

Inside, a farmer in overalls preceded Charlie in line, soles of his grimy calf-length boots making squeaky sounds on the polished marble floor. An elderly woman currently before the teller's window was negotiating to have the bank rescind a penalty charge against her account. No movement in the line. Charlie glanced at the second queue: a better choice. About to switch, he recognized the man bringing up the end of it—and immediately changed his mind.

Charlie's line began moving and, as it developed, he reached his window just as MacNair was finishing his transaction. He passed behind Charlie, but instead of continuing on he stopped. Charlie could almost feel the man's breath on his neck. Uncomfortable, threatened, he turned fully around.

"You're crowding me, Reggie."

"Am I now?"

"Yes, you are," Charlie said.

"You've got it backwards, Kingston." A sneer on his lips. "And I'm suggesting you move on, while you're able."

The head of Whitridge Manor security walked away and left the bank.

Charlie turned back to the teller, having to steady his hand as he filled out a couple of deposit slips, putting £3681 into Wesley Brotherton's account and £409 into his own. Outside on the sidewalk he looked around, glancing up and down the busy sidewalk. Trying to get his bearings, to remember where he'd parked his car, he found himself staring at the cathedral. Shaken by his encounter, unsure of himself, he thought ten minutes in the church might settle his nerves at least.

He crossed the street, climbed the stone steps, pulled open the huge studded door and entered St. Matthew's, gazing about in the dim clerestory light and spotting a single person, a woman with prayer beads, seated in a pew with a shawl over her head. Charlie scanned the stained-glass windows, then walked down the main aisle nearly to the sanctuary, genuflected, and slid into a pew. A scent from the recent swinging of a censer hung lightly in the air. He waited for his head to clear, his heart to calm; neither happened, and he leaned forward in a lazy man's kneel, thinking to say a prayer, but which prayer? How many did he know? His forehead touched the back of the next pew; he rolled his head against it—

"My son, are ye all right?"

A priest was standing there, and Charlie abandoned his half-kneel. "I'm fine, Father."

"I heard what seemed a groan." The priest had a closer look at Charlie's face. "Well, now, I do believe we've met before. I gave ye a spin to the crossroads some months ago. Playing golf ye were at Whitridge Manor."

"I remember."

"May I join ye for a moment? I'm Father Byrne."

"Charlie Kingston."

The priest entered the pew. "Of course. I remember thinking, some ten days ago, ye were probably back in America."

"No, I'm still here."

"Enjoying your stay, I hope."

"For the most part."

"But something is weighing on ye, Charlie. A groan is the voice of a burdened soul."

Charlie had no answer, other than to think Father Byrne was right on.

"Would ye like me to hear your confession?"

"Thank you, Father. I—I don't think so."

"As ye wish, my son." The priest smiled in a kindly manner. "Perhaps you'd prefer simply talking. What have ye been doing with yourself, Charlie?"

"Mr. Brotherton took me on as his golf pro."

"Well, now, I didn't know ye were a professional player. And how is it going?"

"It's an easy job, a summer job. Only now he wants to keep me on permanently—in a different position, big increase in salary. Do I stay or go home? I'm a golfer, Father. If I stay, it's over."

"Your career is over."

"Yes. But maybe it is anyway."

"How will ye ever know? It might not be."

"It gets complicated," Charlie said. "I've reasons for staying, nothing to do with the job or the money."

"You've fallen in love with Ireland," Preston Byrne said with a smile. "It happens."

"I have." Charlie took in a deep breath. Just say it, he thought. "I've also fallen in love with Mr. Brotherton's wife."

"From a distance, I trust."

"Not from a distance, Father," Charlie said.

"Am I to believe you're having an affair?"

"We are."

The priest's lips moved in silent prayer. After a moment he said, "That clouds the picture, doesn't it?"

"It does."

"Ye know, in your heart, adultery is a mortal sin, Charlie. No good can come from it. Only pain and misgiving."

"I won't try to refute that, Father."

"Furthermore, how can a man work for another man if he's sleeping with his wife?"

Not easily, Charlie thought.

From an alcove, a recess somewhere in the cathedral, came the ceremonial sound of an organ.

"The day we met, Charlie," Father Byrne went on, "ye struck me as a man of honor and decency. And something tells me ye still are. Ye may have taken a wrong turn at the crossroads."

"I may have," Charlie said.

"Don't go too far down it, my son." Father Byrne raised his right hand, made a sign of the cross—thumb and finger touching lightly, as if a petal or a feather were between them he didn't want to hurt. He spoke a few words in Latin, touched Charlie's forehead, and disappeared into the shadows of the church.

****

Charlie spent the afternoon in the pro shop giving thought to the next (and last) golf weekend at Whitridge Manor. He leafed through golf catalogs, scribbled notes—ordered rain outfits for men and women, the newest in sweat-wicking shirts, and a dozen cardigan sweaters of the finest light-weight wool...even as he mulled over his meeting with Father Byrne in St. Matt's. He hadn't walked out of the cathedral with a firmer grasp of where he was, any change of heart necessarily; he just didn't feel quite so—to use the word again—burdened. He answered calls, made a few, spent an hour on the range with Kevin. At 4:30, he called it a day.

Taking the back road, Charlie rumbled over the bridge spanning the Argideen, passed Pharr's and headed for the crossroads, intent on getting home, relaxing on his ter-race and watching his herd of cattle. He turned at the crossroads, and who was outside the Dennehy family door practicing an Irish dance step? Made happy by the sight of Brigid, delighted to see her, he thought to tap his horn, wave, shout a greeting; that same moment the rear door of a dark-gray sedan, parked on the side of Pearse Road, opened. A big, heavy-shouldered man began walking toward the girl. Recognizing the man as Donal Dennehy, Charlie thought OK, it's her father. But something was going on; instinc-tively, he spun the wheel and parked in front of the pub.

Looking over, he saw Dennehy reaching out to Brigid, speaking to her. Charlie couldn't hear his words but Dennehy's expression was kind, unthreatening—fatherly. Good old da coming for a visit. But why was someone in the driver's seat of the sedan, its engine idling? Brigid was moving timidly toward her father, and giving it no further thought Charlie jumped out of his car and shouted, "Brigid, go in the house!" But before she could react, Dennehy grabbed her by the wrist. Brigid began screaming, struggling to break free.

"Donal, let go of her!"

Dennehy looked over, picked Brigid up and began running with her, but Charlie caught him easily, reached for his arm and spun him around. In the melee, Brigid broke away and ran to the house—and Dennehy unleashed a killer punch. Not this time, Charlie thought. He ducked, then drove his fist at Dennehy's nose. At once, it started to bleed. Crazed with rage, the Irishman lunged again, missing, almost falling.

Breathing heavily, he backed away. "I'm not—finished with you—Kingston."

"Then until we meet again," Charlie said.

Pressing a handkerchief against his nose, Dennehy stumbled to the waiting automobile and fell into the back seat. The driver, a man with bristly reddish-brown hair and bulging eyes, made a screeching U-turn on Pearse Road, hooked a right and sped off in the direction of Croghanvale. The door to the household opened and Fiona shouted, "Charlie, come inside!"

He walked toward the door and went in, holding the knuckles on his right hand. Brigid was sitting on the sofa wrapped in a blanket. Charlie sat beside her; she was sniffling, breathing in tiny gasps.

"I was—so scared, Charlie."

"I know."

"I—I'm glad you were there."

Fiona came in with an enamel basin and a small towel. "The water has salts in it. Soak your hand," she said to Charlie.

"It's not necessary, Fiona—"

"No, do it. I'll make tea."

He dipped his hand into the basin. Almost at once he felt the soothing effect. "But I want you to know something, Brigid," Charlie said, looking at the girl. "I know your father wouldn't hurt you, he was just afraid of losing you. I didn't like fighting with him. Fathers love their little girls. I know, I remember. That's the sadness of all this. I'm sorry about today, Brigid. But I'm happy you're here with your mother...." he wanted to add, "...and me." But he caught himself.

"Can I put my hand in?"

"Sure."

She slipped her hand into the basin, just touching Charlie's, her head resting against his arm. "Hi, Prize Winner," he said.

CHAPTER 21

Six or seven men in heavy shoes and work clothes were talking among themselves at the far end of the bar as Charlie walked into Pharr's the following day. Mary McAleer greeted him with a smile that could whisk away any man's sorrows, and he went up to the bar and stood next to a man in blue with a checkered cap on his head.

"I don't mean to be overly personal, but might ye be Dennis O'Hea?"

The superintendent turned at the bar, his face brightening. "Well, now, Charlie! We meet under a different roof."

"I thought I might catch you in McCurtain's later on."

"I've had it with McCurtain's, never again."

Mary came over with a pint of Murphy's. He thanked her, then said to Dennis, "Why do you say that?"

"I'm finished with Fiona. Why else would I go there? Pharr's is my local."

"What happened?"

"Charlie, a man needs a little encouragement, and I'm not referring to the kind that comes in a glass. Though that helps." He gave his head a sad little shake. "I have no one to blame but myself."

"What did you do wrong? You sat at her bar, you were kind, you paid attention to her—"

"What *I* did isn't the issue."

"What is?"

The golf course superintendent had himself a slug of encouragement. "When they were girls, Fiona told my wife-to-be that she'd never sleep with anyone except her husband, even if her husband died. Her father had made her swear to it when she was fifteen, her hand over the family Bible, under penalty of eternal damnation! I thought I might break Fiona down," O'Hea went on. "If I could have her one time, *one time*, she'd see the errors of her ways. Charlie, a man will do a lot for a woman, aye, give up his local! It's all history now."

"You never know, she could change. Give her time."

"I'm turning fifty-three next spring. How much time do I have?"

"Dennis, you've just started the back nine."

The superintendent came out with a robust laugh. Then, never one to let conversation lag, he said, "A few days ago I saw ye walking with Mr. Brotherton, coming in from his chopper. Heads together; thick as thieves ye were."

"He offered me a new job," Charlie said.

"I'm not surprised. And what might ye be doing?"

"I'd be his director of golf, his 'Golf Czar.' I'd travel from one resort to another—visit with the pros and managers, generally oversee all golf operations."

"Charlie, I questioned you about taking the job as summer pro, remember? What you've just described is the kind of job a wealthy man throws his son-in-law! Where's your pride?"

"Dennis, he offered me the job. I haven't taken it."

"Something is going on, I don't know what it is and I don't like it," O'Hea said. "Myself, I'm giving serious thought to leaving The Whitridge. The more I dwell on Reggie MacNair walking the grounds, spying on us from his loft, bugging our lines, the hotter my blood boils!"

"I was in his loft," Charlie said.

Dennis leaned toward him a little. "Did I hear ye right?"

"A while back. The door was open and I went in."

"Where was he?"

"Out getting pastry and coffee, but I didn't know it at the time. Electronic equipment all over a huge desk. I was gazing about and one of the phones—I think the orange one—rang. When MacNair didn't pick up, a voice came on. 'Baskerville here. Where in hell are you, Mongoose?' Then the line went dead."

"'*Baskerville*?'"

Charlie nodded.

"'*Mongoose*?'"

"Baskerville and Mongoose. MacNair drove in just as I was leaving."

"It's a wonder ye escaped with your life!"

"I told him I was looking for Keith."

Mary set them up with a new round and after a while Emily came out. It was always nice seeing Charlie, she said. It was always good seeing her, he said, the sentiment coming from a deep place. Emily didn't waste any time getting down to the issues of the day, asking Dennis if the Orange Order march would likely follow its traditional route. So far he had to say yes, but a detour could still be imposed.

"I dearly hope. It's arrogance of the highest kind, strutting down Garvaghy Road decked in orange!"

"We're working on it, Emily," Dennis said, and Charlie, in a tangential way, felt included in the comment.

Emily wished her patrons a good evening. Dennis and Charlie continued talking, and suddenly Dennis was reminding him of his first day at Whitridge Manor, early in May. "Ye wanted to know who the McGarritys were. I told ye I had a berm to build, do ye recall that, Charlie?"

"Very well."

"I was afraid ye might go running back to America," O'Hea said, a tease in his voice. "But that wasn't really it. At the time I didn't feel right about opening up, sharing what's close to my heart. I knew ye as a golfer. I feel a lot different now, I consider ye my friend."

He had a swig of his Guinness. Looking at Charlie directly, he began to speak, his voice lower, solemn. "Both of them, Kieran and Mairead, were determined to get England to surrender, to say, 'Ireland, take your bloody six for all the grief they've caused us, the huge financial cost, the loss of life and limb.' Kieran had a close boyhood friend in the north named Bobby Sands. The world knows of Bobby Sands. He and Kieran met up in Belfast and Mairead joined them later, and bombs exploded, innocent people died, life in Belfast and London was disrupted, and like so many in the I.R.A.—like today's leader of Sinn Féin, Gerry Adams—they were arrested. Mairead was sent to jail in Armagh, Sands and Kieran to Long Kesh. They were treated as common criminals instead of political activists and were given prison garb to wear, and Bobby Sands and Kieran and eight others in the Kesh went on hunger strike in protest, claiming they had the right to wear their own clothes. How trivial that sounds, but how deep to the heart of the Troubles it went! Margaret Thatcher could've ended the strike by giving them their clothes, but to her they were terrorists and Mrs. Thatcher did not negotiate with terrorists. Sands and Kieran and Mairead wanted their country back—the part of it England in her arrogance had decided to keep; and for wanting to make Ireland one land again—like your own Lincoln fighting to unite north and south—they were terrorists. Sands lasted sixty-six days, followed by the others, in succession. Kieran was fifth— sixty-three days before he gave up his ghost."

Frowning deeply, Charlie gave his head slow back-and-forth shakes.

"As for Mairead," Dennis went on, "it's said she burned with fiercer republican spirit than Kieran. Like the men in the H-Block, she refused to wear prison issue and became leader of the 'dirty protest' in Armagh. Women smeared their cell walls with feces and menstrual blood and wrapped themselves in blankets, wet and stinking blankets at that, and in the morning they might wake to find maggots between their legs. She died of fever. That's all we ever heard. Mairead McGarrity, who stole our hearts in Castlebantry, as beautiful an Irish lass as God ever created, died of fever on a cold and filthy prison floor in Northern Ireland."

Charlie frowned, horrified, angry.

"The status of their house on Pearse Road was kicked around for years and years," O'Hea continued. "Some in town wanted to make it a national landmark, others said tear it down. The furor died away after a spell and the house just sat there, deserted. Oh, it was a sad and lonely sight! Then early this spring Kieran's brother spruced it up a bit and put it on the market like any other property. And an American golfer came along and began living in it."

"Of all people," Charlie said.

****

Charlie unlocked the door to the house treading lightly as he went in. He peered into the bedroom, then continued out to the terrace, sat there looking at the rising field. Today the cows were on the other side. All he saw was waving grass in twilight. He got to his feet and walked to the shed, heaved open the door, and found the metal box where he'd left it, beneath the broken boards. He carried it to the front of the shed and sat down in the doorway, opened the lid and took out the large envelope.

He reread Mairead's comment, then chose the top letter, not knowing if it was the first or the last she'd received from Kieran. In a scribbly but strong hand:

> "Mairead, my beloved, I have joined with Bobby. We are staying in a dim little apt. and already the UVF is watching us and English soldiers are harassing us. It's very dangerous here, death and imprisonment wait on every corner, and Bobby keeps saying tell Mairead to stay home! I would understand if you did. But knowing you, I know you won't. This is an especially nice time of year in Cas'bantry and we would be sitting on the banks of the Argideen tossing pebbles. I love you, Mairead. I love the pilgrim soul in you. Kieran."

Charlie slid the letter into the envelope, slipped it beneath the string. One was all he could read, all he had to read. He returned the box and, at the house, picked up the Yeats volume. Outside, he sat in one of the chairs, opening to "Easter 1916." It wasn't the first time he'd read the poem but he'd never read it with such deep, emotional involvement as now.

His heart was aching as he came to the last few lines:

> I write it out in verse—
> MacDonagh and MacBride
> And Connolly and Pearse
> Now and in time to be,
> Wherever green is worn,
> Are changed, changed utterly:
> A terrible beauty is born.

Feeling a presence behind him, Charlie looked over his shoulder into the shadows of the living room. He didn't know what it was, what pull, what impulse. Whether all was changed, he couldn't say, but something was happening, something had changed. Charlie seemed to see dim forms welcoming him to their house. He stood and went in.

CHAPTER 22

Charlie picked up a loose shaft and club head from the workbench in his office and made to insert the tip of the shaft into the hosel of the iron. Kevin had ordered the components, paid for them, and was now having his first instruction on how to assemble golf clubs—in this instance, for his girlfriend, Molly.

But the tip wouldn't go in. "Did they send the wrong shafts?" he asked Charlie.

"No. It's the right shaft."

"Then why isn't it fitting?"

"The tip wasn't prepped."

Charlie slipped a hard-rubber sleeve over the shaft and tightened the vise around it. "The chrome finish has to be removed," he explained, "for two reasons. "One, to reduce the diameter of the tip, and two, so the epoxy will adhere. So take your sandpaper and rough up the tip."

"How much of it?"

"The depth of the hosel. An inch and three-quarters."

Kevin tried to fold a sheet of sandpaper—

"Take the scissors and cut off a narrow strip," Charlie said.

Kevin cut the strip. "It's a flossing action, back and forth—top, bottom, sides," Charlie said. He took a couple of swipes to demonstrate, then handed the strip to Kevin, who soon had the tip down to bare steel. Chrome gone, it slid perfectly into the hosel.

"Now we epoxy, right?" Kevin said.

Once when he was a kid, he told Kevin, the head of a driver, one of the first clubs he'd ever assembled, had flown off as he'd swung. His friends pointed at it lying in the grass thirty yards away, laughing; funniest thing they'd ever seen. He had laughed also, but he never wanted it to happen again. He asked his pro, Jake Magliora, for advice, and Jake recommended scoring the tip after roughing it. Scoring guaranteed the hold.

"So, what do you think?" Charlie said.

"I think we should score. What is it?"

Charlie drew the edge of a file diagonally across the tip, then repeated the stroke, making a faint but distinct scar in the steel. He handed Kevin the file. "Rotate the shaft about a hundred and twenty degrees and score it again; then a third time."

Kevin made the scores. "Good. *Now* we epoxy," Charlie said.

****

After they had put together the first two clubs, Charlie said he was taking the rest of the day off. If Kevin felt confident, he should continue assembling—don't rush, Charlie told him, think through each step. Leaving the pro shop in Kevin's hands, he walked out to his car and drove home. It wasn't a perfect day for a picnic—overcast, chance of rain—but what did he care? A line from a Yeats poem came to him. *That is no country for old men. The young in one another's arms, birds in the trees—*

At his house Charlie brushed his teeth, combed his hair, put on a new shirt— no sooner done than he heard the honking of a horn on Pearse Road. He pulled on his jacket and went out. Dreary a day as it was, the roof was down on the Mustang. Lora was behind the wheel, arms raised, smiling. Charlie slid into the passenger's seat, leaned across the console to kiss her, then buckled himself in. At the crossroads he told Lora to turn toward Croghanvale.

"Not a great day but I brought an extra blanket and Mrs. Walsh outdid herself," she said as they popped along. "Plus we have a bottle of Côte de Rhone to die for. Who needs the sun?"

"I was just thinking the same thing. How was London?"

"We went to an opening, a new playwright people are talking about, Blair Greenstock. It got great reviews but Wesley didn't like it. He's terribly judgmental and easily bored. A couple of social occasions, friends who were here for the golf weekend. Sir Oscar asked for you. He wants you to come out and work with him at The Grove."

"He's a fine gentleman."

They were rounding a curve. Coming into view was a great expanse of countryside, rolling fields, grazing cattle. Lora's hair was flying. "Isn't this wonderful, Charlie?"

"It's more than wonderful." Pointing through the windshield, he said, "Slow down. Coming up on the right you'll see a narrow road. Take it."

She down-shifted, braked, made the turn and stayed in a lower gear. The road was unpaved, in places rutted; after three minutes it narrowed even more and Charlie said they should stop here; any further, turning around would be difficult, at best. Lora set the brake; he reached into the back seat for the wicker basket covered with a white cloth, and they began hiking. Under Lora's arm were the blankets.

Twice they stopped to take in the scenery, kissing both times. A bit father on they came to the rural cemetery. Charlie opened the little gate and they went in. Passing through, Lora examined a couple of markers but didn't linger. They climbed over a low wall and, quite literally, fell into deep grass on the other side. Charlie set down the basket and Lora opened the blankets.

"What a lovely spot," she said. "How did you come upon it?"

"Walking, looking for my great-grandmother's grave— suddenly there it was."

Lora stretched out her arm. "All counties in Ireland have their special look," she said. "*This* is West Cork."

As they sat there, the day noticeably darkened; a chill breeze came up from the valley, and any minute it might start raining. Best to get under the blanket.

****

The rain held off, but it might have poured; they weren't paying attention to matters meteorological. Lora opened the basket and Charlie uncorked the bottle. The thinly sliced chicken-breast sandwiches, the exquisite wine, Lora barefoot at his side. He clinked her glass a second time, kissed her wine-cool lips—

"This is so wonderful, Charlie," Lora said. "I'm very happy."

"I am too."

She pressed her hand into the cool grass, the blades brushing her palm. "Wesley told me about the new job he offered you. What do you think?"

He wished she hadn't raised the topic. "It's OK. I have a few reservations."

"Like what?"

"I've a commitment to Q-School later in the year," Charlie said. "That means going back to the states. I haven't really decided yet."

Lora seemed disappointed, it wasn't what she wanted to hear. "I see the job as perfect for us," she said. "I could meet you in any of our resorts around the world."

"It would be exciting," Charlie said. "But there's no future in it."

"We've made love, we're having a picnic. Who needs a future? This is the future."

"Something is missing," he said.

"What's missing? Name one thing."

"You."

"*Me*?" Tears sprang to Lora's eyes. "How can you say that?"

"I'm saying it. It's the truth."

"Charlie, explain. *Please*."

"I have you on loan, Lora. That's not having you."

She turned her head, looking toward the distant, rolling fields, but he didn't believe she was seeing them; she was blinking rapidly. "Why are you saying this now? "

"Because in the beginning I didn't care," Charlie said. "Here I was, a visitor to Castlebantry, playing golf, and who do I meet but a very beautiful woman sitting on a bench overlooking the Celtic Sea. We play in and she wants a re-match. Like I was going to say no? Then she comes by my house with a book of poetry. Who brings Charlie Kingston a book of poetry? I'm falling in love with Lora Brotherton. Do I care that she's married, do I even think about it? We have our rematch—I help her with her swing and she kisses me—and later she shows me about the Manor House and we make love in her room."

Rain was starting to fall. "It must've been painful for Des McClure, unbelievably painful for him to have you go away with your father," Charlie went on. "But he wanted you to live and in Killybegs you might die, possibly would die. I want you to live too, Lora. Don't you understand? I want you to come to America with me. We won't have five houses, just one we'll call home. Do you know how I see you, Lora?" He paused, then, catching his breath, "I see you as a wild Irish flower plucked from the shores of Clew Bay and stuck in a London window box."

The rain was coming down hard. They scrambled to repack the basket, put on their shoes. In her car, Lora raised the top. All the way down the bumpy road and on the drive to his house, she was quiet, and Charlie heard himself reaching out to her, apologizing—he'd hurt her, maybe insulted her. But he said nothing. How could you apologize for speaking from your heart? She parked on the side of Pearse Road, shifting to neutral.

Her hands were on the steering wheel and rain flooded the windshield and pounded the vinyl roof. Charlie felt she wanted to say something and was struggling to say it. Of the two women he knew in Castlebantry, he'd always thought of Fiona as the one with problems. Not beautiful red-haired Lora whose husband had bought her a castle in Ireland with its own golf course and a steam running by. Not Lora of the sea-green eyes and freckles touching her cheeks and a red Mustang convertible to pop around in. But now he thought differently. The windshield might have been a wall and Lora was facing it.

"Charlie," she said at last, "I can't see you anymore."

He was stunned, rocked back. "Lora, what I said—I wasn't saying we should break up. I was only saying—"

"I know what you're saying, Charlie." She faced him, tears wetting her cheeks.

"Come in. We'll talk it over," he said, "we'll work it out."

She leaned across the console and kissed him, her lips sweetly on his. "Goodbye, Charlie."

"Lora—"

"Just go, please."

He got out, stood on the side of Pearse Road in the rain as Lora drove away.

CHAPTER 23

During the next week, new merchandise arrived daily at The Whitridge, and Charlie, with Kevin's help, logged the items, then placed them on shelves or hung them on hangers. The pro shop was taking on a look even to surpass the sparkle of the first golf weekend—in women's sportswear particularly, with a selection of high-end shirts and shorts. Also a greater selection of clubs, including a new line of hybrids, a cross between a wood and an iron designed, the industry said, to give players more consistency in shot making and greater accuracy. Charlie could see using one as a rescue club, but nothing would take the place of a solidly hit iron. Nonetheless, the hybrids were here and, priced to sell, would likely go fast.

Not wanting to dwell on his picnic with Lora, specifically the depressing outcome of it, Charlie kept busy. Precise records, careful inventory, focus. He helped Kevin on his club-making and they played golf several time a week; but often Charlie walked to the first tee alone. It was one of the great things about the game, it didn't require a second player. The course always seemed to be saying, Come on, play me, have fun. The swans on the third-hole with their interlacing wings, the magical path to the fifth tee, the steady uphill trek to the green, strap pulling on his shoulder as if he were hauling cargo. He would arrive at the green and stand, for a moment, as if he'd somehow made it to the top. Just ahead was the park bench, and he could never approach it without thinking she might be sitting there and, looking up, would say, *"Charlie Kingston, I presume."*

On the way home late afternoons he often dropped by to visit with Emily Pharr and talk Irish history with Mary McAleer, and almost every night of the week he partook of home-cooked fare in McCurtain's and chit-chatted with Brigid at his banquette and talked with Fiona. News in the Donal department. He was seeing a woman in Hanover, an affair that had started last year, and was agreeing to a divorce.

Toward the end of the second week—Charlie was measuring time by how many days had passed since the picnic— he was in his office, doing paperwork, when he heard young voices through the open window, and he swiveled about in his chair. Through the stand of trees he caught glimpses of Kevin and Molly and two other caddies walking on the first fairway, all with clubs that Kevin had made. It was Molly's turn and she swung mightily. The ball, bouncing and dancing along, never got off the ground.

"What am I doing, Kevin?"

"You're topping the ball."

"I can see that."

"Stay down. You're not staying down."

"What do you mean, *stay down*?"

"Molly, let's just play. Keep swinging. You're doing great."

Charlie left the pro shop. As he drove by the garage he saw MacNair's faded brown Volvo parked by the conventional door. The second-floor window panes had a dull sheen, like the unblinking eyes of a corpse.

****

"You have dinner here every night. This one's on me," she said, pushing away his money.

"Fiona, you run a business," Charlie said, sliding it back.

"No argument now. It's my pleasure."

He returned the notes to his pocket.

"I haven't seen Dennis recently," Fiona said. "Not that I miss him—well, I do miss him, I'm very fond of Dennis; but from the beginning I made it clear—"

"Men don't always listen," Charlie said.

In a quieter voice, "I just couldn't—"

"Enough said, Fiona."

He wished her a good night. Inside his house Charlie crossed to one of the lamps and turned it on, then threw the bolt on the door. He was tired but wasn't ready to turn in. Sitting before the hearth, he picked up the well-leafed copy of Yeats's poetry. Unhurriedly, he went from one poem to another. "Innisfree," "An Irish Airman," "Easter 1916," "Sailing to Byzantium." Every time he read a poem, something was new about it, something came out he hadn't seen before. He was getting sleepy. He'd read one more, and turning the page came to the poem that, of all, seemed to Charlie the dearest: "When You Are Old."

> When you are old and gray and full of sleep,
> And nodding by the fire, take down this book,
> And slowly read, and dream of the soft look
> Your eyes once had, and of their shadows deep.
>
> How many loved your moments of glad grace

And loved your beauty with love false or true.
But one man loved the pilgrim soul in you,
And loved the sorrow of your changing face.

And bending down beside the glowing bars,
Murmur, a little sadly, how Love fled
And paced upon the mountains overhead
And hid his face amid a crowd of stars.

Charlie closed the book, sat for a while, thinking, pondering. With an effort he washed up, then crawled under the covers and soon was in another world. It seemed to him the dream came to him quickly. *He was in his house in the Atlanta suburb hearing footfalls outside his daughter's window; then silence, an ominous silence; someone was outside wanting to take her away. He had to protect her but was deep in sleep, too far under, struggling desperately to waken. Suddenly a loud crashing sound coming from her room, a shattering of glass*—and Charlie woke with a start, sat upright. He smelled gasoline, smoke, caught flickering flames in the living room.

What the hell?

He pulled on trousers, reached blindly for his wallet and passport in the nightstand drawer, shoved them into his pockets and ran through rising smoke to the back door, drew the bolt and went out. Standing on the terrace five steps away, arm outstretched, holding a gun and pointing it at Charlie's head, was Reggie MacNair. Which happened first—whether he ducked or MacNair fired—he didn't know. He heard the report, felt the bullet searing his scalp. Stunned, Charlie fell to his knees.

"I intended to make it short and sweet," MacNair said. "Sorry."

"You won't get away with this—"

Chuckling demonically, "Tell me something before I end your miserable life."

"What is it?" Blood blinding Charlie's left eye. With his good eye he perceived a silvery blur against the side of the house.

Shoes scraping terrace stones, coming closer, "Is it the real thing?"

Silvery blur coming into focus: broken golf shafts, pushed together. "Is what the real thing?"

Moon throwing a shadow of MacNair's outstretched hand, the gun. "You know what I'm talking about! I have a picture of you fucking Mrs. Brotherton, her legs wrapped around your scrawny American arse! Make it your last breath, Kingston. *Is it the real thing*?"

"It's the real thing." He had to keep talking. "A rich, glorious red. But that's not all."

"What? Tell me."

If he reached for a shaft and fumbled it, he was dead. "While I was in bed with Mrs. Brotherton—"

"Yeah?

"—she said she has fantasies about you."

"Like what?"

He was seeing clearly now, clearly enough. He slid his hand forward, fingers closing around the head of an iron. "Your mustache."

"What about it?"

"High between her thighs, she's lovin' it, screaming your name. Then she said—"

"Tell me!"

In balance with this life...

Charlie swiveled low and hard, his right arm shooting upward, the shaft's jagged tip skimming MacNair's chin and entering his mouth. Reeling back, he fired wildly, shot after shot, bullets ricocheting off the terrace and stone siding; toppling one of the metal chairs as he fell, his cry more of rage than pain, shaft sticking out of his head like an antenna. He lay on his back just off the terrace, struggling to pull the shaft loose, hands finally slipping away. His body convulsed, blood gushed from his mouth, and he lay still. In his screaming eyes full moons shone.

...this death.

Panting, sweating, freezing, Charlie staggered around the house. A car was coming along and he stumbled onto Pearse Road, waving both arms. It was all he remembered.

CHAPTER 24

O n Charlie's second day in the Castlebantry Medical Center, a converted mansion with five private rooms in Driscoll Park, Dr. Mulrooney came in at 9:00 a.m., checked the nurse's clipboard, eyed the bandage on the side of Charlie's head and asked him how he was feeling.

"Like hell."

"You're lucky to be alive."

"Thanks."

It was a small, clean room with a high ceiling, walls painted a light green. Through a window you could see the park—lawns, trees, pathways, a fountain. Three kids were chasing about, playing tag; an elderly man and a woman sat on a bench, facing the sun.

"Another day or two, we'll have you out of here," Dr. Mulrooney said. "Chief Dunn wants to see you."

"I'm not surprised."

"What will you be using for clothes?"

"I haven't thought about it."

"You're close to my build, my height," the physician said. "What's your shoe size?"

"Nine."

"Let me see what I can do," Dr. Mulrooney said. "Here, read all about it." He set a newspaper on the bed. "I'll be in later."

Charlie dozed for a while, then unfolded the paper—and was startled by the front-page picture, in color, of Reggie MacNair lying on his back, eyes mirroring the moon, blood spilling from his mouth, a steel shaft between his teeth emerging, gore-darkened, from the back of his head. Banner headline: AMERICAN GOLFER SLAYS EX-MI5 AGENT. In a two-line subhead: *Tour Player Wounded by Agent's Bullet.*

Charlie pressed his hand lightly over the bandage to calm the sudden throbbing. He read the article on page 3, which said that MacNair and Kingston both worked at Whitridge Manor in Castlebantry, owned by British industrialist Wesley Brotherton—MacNair as chief of security, Kingston as the professional at the private golf course on the estate. According to local authorities, Kingston's rented house on Pearse Road in Castlebantry was fire-bombed. As the pro golfer ran out the back door, MacNair stood on a small terrace and fired a handgun, grazing Kingston's head. "At the time of this writing," the article concluded, "no motive has been established for the attempted murder. How Kingston managed to pick up a section of a broken golf-club shaft and drive it through MacNair's head remains a mystery. A thorough investigation is under way. Kingston is recovering from his gun-shot wound in the Community Medical Center in Castlebantry."

The door opened and Charlie's nurse, a 60-year-old woman with auburn-colored hair came in to take his temperature and blood pressure and to give him his medication.

Everything was holding, she said. If he wanted anything, just ring.

Charlie thanked the good woman. He leafed through the *Examiner*, coming to an article on page 5 that caught his eye. "In a statement, the Northern Ireland Parades Commission has said that it has prohibited the Orange Order from using its traditional marching route to commemorate King William's victory at the Boyne in an effort to prevent the possibility of riot and injury if the parade were to proceed along Catholic-dominated Garvaghy Road.

"The Rev. Ian Paisley, leader of the Democratic Unionist Party, was said to be deeply disappointed in the ruling, which, he contended, showed the growing power and influence of the I.R.A. in Northern Ireland affairs. Paisley contended that the I.R.A. had brought undue pressure on the Commission by threatening to intervene if the Orange Order march proceeded on its customary path.

"Paisley concluded by saying that The Good Friday Peace Accord was a useless document. 'Only when I.R.A. decommissioning is a verifiable fact will there be lasting peace in Northern Ireland,' Rev. Paisley concluded."

Charlie folded the newspaper, having the good feeling that his side in the political battle had prevailed, and that he'd played a small part in the victory—clearly the drugs he was on had to be messing with his brain. Just then there was a quiet tap on his door; it opened, and coming in holding a small vase with wild flowers in it was a young girl in a yellow dress.

"Hi, Charlie."

"Brigid, how nice of you to come see me."

She handed him the vase. "I hope you're feeling better."

"I am. Suddenly I'm feeling a lot better." He poked his nose into the flowers. "Ah, wonderful. So much nicer than the medicine Dr. Mulrooney gives me."

Brigid laughed.

"Do you know what would make me feel better still?"

"What?"

Charlie touched his cheek, closed his eyes, hoping she'd get the idea. She did. It was a longer, dearer kiss than he had any right to expect. When he opened his eyes, Brigid's mother was just entering the room.

****

The next day at three in the afternoon, attired in John Mulrooney's clothes—the physician's brogues were probably tens—he walked into the single-story office building on Doolin Square, turned right in the lobby and entered the office of Garda Chief Edward Dunn.

"Mr. Kingston, good morning," the chief said from behind his desk.

"Good morning."

"This is Detective Healey."

Charlie recognized the red hair, the Irish-setter look of the man who had driven slowly by Pharr's some time ago, scanning the automobiles and the individual in the parking area. The two exchanged glances.

"Please, sit down," Chief Dunn said.

Charlie took the chair in front of the chief's desk; to one side of it sat Healey.

"How are you doing?" Dunn asked.

"I'm doing all right."

"Dr. Mulrooney said if the bullet had hit you a quarter-inch closer in, we'd be sending you home in a box."

"So I understand."

Edward Dunn, in a blue suit, had dark, neatly combed hair. Charlie recognized a similarity with Fiona, mostly in the round chin and deep brown eyes. "Mr. Kingston," he said, "we've called you in to ask you what happened as you saw and experienced it at your house three days ago. Let me say, to start, that postal worker Brian Lynch stopped to pick you up on Pearse Road. He reported the fire on his mobile and drove you to the medical center."

"If I don't get to see him and thank him personally, tell him I'm indebted," Charlie said.

"I'll be glad to." Dunn picked up a copy of the newspaper on his desk and held it up for Charlie to see; on the front page was the photo of MacNair with a golf shaft through his head. "Is this scene familiar to you, Mr. Kingston?"

"Yes."

"Can you identify the man?"

"Reggie MacNair."

"Did you kill him?"

"I did."

"Why and how did you kill MacNair?"

He was awakened by a loud crash, he said, as of a rock breaking through his window. Smoke and fire began building in the living room. He pulled on a pair of pants and ran out the back door. MacNair was waiting for him on the terrace with a handgun and fired.

"How far away was he?"

"Twelve to fifteen feet."

"At that range, how did you escape with a wound?"

"I ducked."

"You ducked a bullet?"

"I ducked before he fired."

"Then what happened?"

"I was on my knees facing away from him but saw his shadow as he came closer."

"Because of the fire," Detective Healey put in, "his shadow would've fallen away from the fire."

"The fire hadn't fully caught," Charlie said. "The shadow was from the moon."

Dunn continued his questioning. "Did MacNair say anything as he came toward you?"

"No."

"Did you say anything to him?"

"No."

"What happened next?"

"Broken golf shafts were lying on the terrace. I picked one up, made a quick turn, and jammed it at his face."

"It went into his mouth. Were you aiming for his mouth?"

"No."

"It would take an extraordinarily powerful jab to have a golf shaft pierce a man's skull," Dunn said.

"When a shaft snaps, the tips are razor sharp. With the club head in my hand I had a solid grip." Charlie made a fist and gave it an upward thrust.

Dunn asked his assistant to step in. Looking at Charlie, Healey said, "When the golf shaft caught MacNair in the mouth, what did he do?"

"He fell back, firing, bullets bouncing off the terrace, the siding of the house. The gun fell from his hand and he tried to pull the shaft out. Blood was pouring from his mouth, he thrashed about, then...then he died."

"What were the broken shafts doing there?"

"I work with a lad at Whitridge Manor named Kevin Dennehy. I'm the pro, he's my assistant. His sister became interested in the sport." Charlie shifted his eyes to Dunn by way of acknowledging that he was talking about the chief's nephew and niece. "She's an athletic girl, a competitor, so I made her a set of clubs," Charlie went on. "One afternoon the three of us were practicing golf shots in my yard and the kids' father showed up, furious; to me he seemed drunk. He knocked me down with a heavy, deliberate punch, then broke Brigid's clubs over his knee, snapping them like twigs. Later on I collected the pieces and laid them on the terrace."

"And you picked up one of those pieces and stabbed MacNair with it?" Healey asked.

"Yes."

"If you're up to it, could you demonstrate the move?"

Charlie slid off his chair onto his knees, simulated picking up a shaft, then twisted his torso and gave it an upward shove.

"How many seconds do you suppose that sequence took?" Healey asked.

"Two to three," Charlie said, seated again.

"And he didn't fire?" Healey said.

"He fired, just too late."

"His finger's on the trigger, he's on edge, he could've expended three or four rounds!"

"He could have. He didn't," Charlie said.

"He didn't wait to fire when you stepped out of your house."

"That's true."

"He was there to kill you, why didn't he finish the job?"

"I was on the ground, wounded," Charlie said. "Where was the rush? Maybe he was savoring my misery."

Healey looked at Dunn, who came in. "To backtrack a minute, Mr. Kingston," the chief said. "Before running out of your house, did you take anything with you, any personal effects?"

"My wallet and passport."

"Where were they?"

"In a nightstand by my bed."

"Was there anything else in the nightstand?"

"I don't remember."

From his desk's center drawer Dunn pulled out an envelope, singed around the edges. "How about this?"

"It's an envelope."

"Do you know what's inside it?"

Sweat was building on Charlie's chest, under his arms. "I'm not sure."

"How about a photograph?"

"Could be."

"Would you say who it's of?"

Charlie didn't want to say anything he didn't have to say. "I'd be guessing."

"Let me help you then," Dunn said. "It's a revealing shot of a woman with red hair standing before a window in a transparent gown. Does that help?"

"It's of Mrs. Brotherton," Charlie said.

"We were looking for valuables in your house, what remained of your house," Dunn said, "anything we could take for safekeeping." He gave the envelope a shake. "So, tell us. How did this picture end up in your nightstand?"

"I was in Reggie MacNair's office above the Whitridge Manor garage maybe three weeks ago," Charlie said. "He wasn't there, he'd gone out for coffee and hadn't closed the padlock. So I went in."

"Trespassed," Detective Healey said, cutting in.

"Well, I wasn't invited."

"Under what authority did you enter Mr. MacNair's office?"

"My own," Charlie said. "One time I saw him snooping around my car at night, and several times I saw him glaring at me. He had a pair of telescopes set up with telephoto lenses. I found a cache of photographs, all of Mrs. Brotherton. One of the pictures dropped to the floor just when he was coming back to his office. In my rush to get out, I slipped it into my jacket."

"So the missing photograph was his motive in wanting to kill you, is that what you're saying?" Healey asked.

"Possibly. It was a kind of leverage I had on him," Charlie said. "How would it look to Mr. Brotherton if his head of security was taking sexy photographs of his wife? More than anything, though, I think MacNair was threatened by me, angry. Who was this American stepping on his turf, getting a good job, driving one of Mr. Brotherton's new cars, and maybe more than anything else spending time with Mrs. Brotherton, playing golf with her, giving her lessons, while all he had was a telescope? MacNair didn't like me, to be generous about it."

Healey and Dunn nodded. The chief said, "We appreciate your comments, Mr. Kingston. No charges will be brought against you. Clearly you acted in self-defense. I am concerned, however, about your safety here in Castlebantry. MacNair isn't the only man who would like to see you dead. Detective Healey—" Dunn gave his assistant a glance, "theorized that MacNair was planning to pin the murder on Donal Dennehy, who spends most of his time in Germany. Why else would MacNair use a Walther, a German handgun, when he shot you? And the bottle thrown through your window once contained Riesling wine, also a product of Germany. The point I'm making is this. I've known my brother-in-law for many years, and no one holds a grudge, nurses a wrong, like Donal. I'm referring to the punch you threw at him when he came to take his daughter. For your own safety I'm suggesting you leave town. Fiona told me you came to Ireland to invite your soul. What you've invited, it seems to me, is trouble; and I'm not sure we've seen the last of it. Having said that, I appreciate the time and attention you've shown my sister and her kids. I believe you've been good to them. As for the picture—" he picked up the envelope, "—I don't want any part of it. It's yours."

Dunn slid the envelope across his desk. "Oh, stay away from Pharr's. You might find yourself answering questions of an entirely different nature. Go back to America, Mr. Kingston."

****

An hour later he was sitting at his desk examining a couple of invoices when his phone rang. By the sound of the ring, the time of day, he seemed to know who it was. With anticipation, he picked up. "The Whitridge at Whitridge Manor, Charlie speaking."

"Everywhere I go it's Charlie Kingston, the American golfer."

Right family, wrong spouse.

"I don't know whether to fire you or make you the new CEO of Brotherton Arms!" Brotherton said. "What do you know about guns and ammunition?"

"I had a .22 when I was a kid."

"How are you, Charlie?"

"To quote the doctor who treated me, I'm lucky to be alive."

"The picture of MacNair made the front page of every tabloid in London," Wesley said.

"It made a few here also. Anyway, the pro shop looks great. We're ready for the weekend."

"Charlie, I've canceled it," Brotherton said.

"Wesley, I'm OK. Seriously," Charlie said.

"My golf pro wounded, my security agent dead, an investigation under way. I'm not sure our guests would be comfortable," Brotherton said. "I'm moving it ahead to August."

"I'm disappointed, Wesley."

"I understand, but it's best if we keep a low profile. Lora and I will be coming out Saturday, late—not so late that we can't get in a little golf, if you're up to it."

Charlie's disappointment vanished. "Not a problem. It'll be good seeing you."

"Let's meet in the pro shop at five o'clock. After golf, stay and have dinner with us."

"Thank you, Wesley."

"Oh, I've been rethinking Golf Czar," Brotherton said. "It's beneath you, Charlie, so forget the concept. I've got something you're going to love, we'll talk about it."

The line went dead: Brotherton's signature way of signing off. He sat for a few moments deep in thought, then went into the shop and told Kevin the weekend was canceled. "We're pushing it ahead to August."

"A lot of the kids will be on holiday in August."

"We'll manage. I'm leaving for the day, Kevin. Line up three caddies for Saturday, late afternoon. For Mr. and Mrs. Brotherton and me."

Charlie took the back road across the Argideen, passed Pharr's, turned at the crossroads and parked alongside his house, or what remained of it. Its crooked teeth had with-stood the fire but more than a few had fallen out. The roof, except for a portion over the bedroom, had collapsed. In the air hung the pungent smell of a charred, water-logged wood.

He walked down one side of the ruin and stepped onto the terrace, moving carefully over debris; scattered about were the broken shafts of Brigid's clubs, except for one. He picked them up and put them together in a pile. The heads were like new and Kevin would be able to use them. In the living room, blackened timbers lay criss-crossed on the floor, in a few places smoldering. Fireplace still a fireplace. Charlie peered into the bedroom, its furnishings barely holding on—injured, bedraggled veterans of war. From his pocket he pulled the singed envelope and set it on one of the smoldering rafters. It began smoking. Flash point reached, it burst into flames.

CHAPTER 25

His room, a small single on the third (top) floor of the Castlebantry Hotel, had a look about it that reminded Charlie of a poet's or scholar's garret, as he envisioned one. The knee-hole desk, the slanted ceiling with a window in it. You could sit in the small, upholstered easy chair or lie in bed and see the sky.

It was his second morning in the hotel. Charlie got out of bed, in the bathroom turned on the shower. For a change, plenty of hot water. He stayed under it for a good while, used one of the big towels, and began dressing. Yesterday he'd gone to Seaton's and purchased pants, shirts, shorts and a pair of shoes, then had stopped by John Mulrooney's office to thank the good doctor and return his items, neatly placed in a box.

Ready for his day—Wesley and Lora would be coming in later on—Charlie went downstairs and walked into the hotel dining room, sat in a booth and gave his order to a young waitress with thick dark hair and an accent that wasn't Irish, maybe Italian. She brought him coffee. He sat there, working to keep his mind focused; it was like trying to control an unruly child who insisted on having his way.

Breakfast of scrambled eggs and toast, refill on coffee. A man walked in and sat down at a table across the room. Charlie thought nothing of it but as the man gave his order, Charlie glanced over, seeming to think he'd seen him before, somewhere. Not wanting to stare, he went back to his breakfast. Somewhere…but where? The short, bristly hair, the protruding eyes. Then, at once, it came to him. He remembered, vividly. Charlie's head, all but healed, began pulsing. It was the man who'd driven the gray sedan, who'd made a violent U-turn on Pearse Road the day Donal Dennehy had tried to kidnap Brigid.

Charlie didn't look again. He signaled his waitress, told her to bill his room, and left the restaurant.

****

Dennis was sitting in a motorized cart with one of his assistants when Charlie visited him later that morning. The worker, a man Charlie knew as Dennis's top greens cutter, said something to his boss and walked into the barn.

"Is it an apparition I'm seeing," the superintendent asked as Charlie came closer, "or the living, breathing Charlie Kingston himself?"

"Himself, I think. I could be wrong."

Dennis put his hand on Charlie's chest as he sat down. "It is, glory be to God!" Glancing at the bandage, "Ye went and almost got yourself killed!"

"Almost."

"How are ye?"

"Dr. Mulrooney kicked me out of the medical center so I guess I'm OK. You heard the weekend was called off."

"Aye, and I'm disappointed," Dennis said. "The celebration at Whitridge Manor should go on for a week! Everyone is saying it, talking about the difference coming to work in the morning, the freshness of the air again. Thanks to Charlie Kingston."

"It was self-defense, Dennis."

"You say. Loyalists have their Battle of the Boyne, republicans now have their Battle on Pearse Road."

O'Hea reached into the slot to the left of the steering column and pulled out a folded newspaper. Opening it, "This isn't a photograph, it's a statement," he said. "It sends a message to the likes of Ian Paisley and the Orange Order and the UVF and to Mr. Brotherton himself. Fuck with the Irish, you'll end up with a spear through your skull! I've heard via the network that Paisley has put a price on Charlie Kingston's head. Because what this American golfer did, ye see, was kill the man who funnels Wesley Brotherton's financial contributions to Paisley, said at this time of year to be in the vicinity of £300,000; and now where the hell is it? The Reverend Dr. No is not amused."

Irishmen loved to spin a tale, and O'Hea was spinning a honey. "Help me out, Dennis. How do I go about my business if someone is after my head?" Charlie wasn't thinking of Ian Paisley.

"Let me relate a little history," O'Hea said. "During Ireland's War of Independence, the entire British force in Dublin was on the alert, day and night, to capture Michael Collins." O'Hea leaned in a little and spoke, for some reason, in a quieter, more respectful voice. "Do ye know what Collins did?"

"No."

"He rode the streets on his bicycle, going wherever duty called, never apprehended, never even seen. They would have shot him on sight! But those who sought him were lesser men, lacking both vision and will. Do ye see what

I'm saying, Charlie? Go fearlessly about your business like the man who made Ireland!"

"Dennis, the comparison honors me but I think it's something of a stretch," Charlie said.

"What would ye say if I was to recommend ye for honorary membership into the I.R.A.?"

"I'd say you were a crazy fucking Irishman."

"Here's how I'll present it to the Army Council," Dennis said. "'In keeping with the great tradition of Wolfe Tone, Padraig Pearse, and Michael Collins, Charlie Kingston struck for Ireland's national unity with one inspired thrust of a golf shaft! As evidence, I present this picture of Reggie MacNair, loyalist of the first water, enemy of the Republic. Let it be said that Charlie Kingston's courage, fortitude, and dedication to the goal of *one Ireland* qualify him as an honorary members of the Irish Republican Army."

Charlie hadn't laughed so hard in years. "Dennis, you're too kind, too thoughtful," he said. "However, I don't see how—"

"Sorry, there's no backing out," O'Hea said. "You're in. Speaking for all members, both the living and dead, welcome to the I.R.A.!"

****

Later that day Charlie was suddenly aware of a pounding, a rumbling sound in the air. Kevin was outside with the day's caddies and he poked his head into the pro shop. "They're here, Charlie."

"OK. We'll meet you on the first tee."

Charlie stood at the counter, shop door open, waiting. Shortly the Land Rover, with Keith Callaghan driving, came in from the helipad. Charlie thought it might stop but it continued on and followed the circular drive to the Manor House.

Charlie fiddled with merchandise, straightened sweaters on a shelf, adjusted the lineup of putters on display. In fifteen minutes the Land Rover started back, turned in at the pro shop, and Brotherton got out. Charlie waited for the other door to open but it didn't, and Callaghan turned the all-drive vehicle around and drove away.

"Charlie, you're looking fine, none the worse for your ordeal," Brotherton said, coming in. They shook hands. "Do we have caddies?"

"They're on the first tee."

"Give me a stroke on the fourth and ninth hole and we'll play for twenty pounds."

"You're on." They left the pro shop. "Isn't Lora coming out?"

"I'm by myself. I'm glad we canceled the weekend," Brotherton said. "It would've been too much, way too hectic. Maybe even scary. I see where the local garda absolved you of any wrongdoing, and rightly so! I want to hear everything and I have a lot to say—an exciting proposal to make, as I mentioned."

They were on the path of white stones that sloped gently down to golf-course level. Three caddies, each toting a golf bag, were waiting on the first tee; to one side stood Kevin. Wesley gave a second look at Charlie's head. "You sure you're up to this? Doctor says it's OK?"

"No problem."

"If I beat you, I want to beat you fair and square."

Molly, Kevin's girlfriend, had Brotherton's clubs; a rangy kid Charlie remembered from the first weekend was on his bag. Not wanting to send Lora's caddie home, Kevin relieved young Barry Smith of her clubs and assigned him the job of forecaddie.

"Take the honor, Wesley," Charlie said.

Brotherton turned to Molly. "Three wood. And keep your eye peeled. I'm not sure where this is going."

The ball, savagely struck, hugged the right side of the fairway, running through the dogleg into the first cut of rough. Charlie put a decent swing on his ball; at the bend it curved left toward the green. "You and your fucking draw," Brotherton said.

Brotherton was a fast walker; didn't like dawdling. Charlie wanted to press him on his better half as they moved down the fairway, but before he could form a query that didn't seem too inquisitive, Wesley was filling him in.

"I'm sorry Lora isn't playing with us. She couldn't make it."

Charlie pictured her in her room, resting, possibly ill. "Is she OK?"

"She's fine, Brotherton said, "sailing with friends in the Adriatic. You may have met the chap at our last party, Anthony Whiteley. Only a so-so golfer but a world-class helmsman, looking to challenge New Zealand in the 2000 America's Cup. They're in his own 45-foot sloop. Yesterday a string of foul weather drove them south and they made port in Corfu."

The news threw Charlie off stride; his thoughts got tangled and he almost stumbled.

"She left London on Monday, saying she'd be back Saturday and we'd pop over to Whitridge Manor," Wesley went on. "Last night I got the call."

They were approaching Brotherton's ball in the first cut of rough. Using an 8-iron, he muscled it to the green.

"Are you—well, you know—concerned?" Charlie asked as they walked across the fairway.

"It's a party of six, not in the least," Brotherton said. "Sailing's in Lora's blood, maybe more than golf. As for Whiteley, who do you think put up eighty percent of the capital to build *Incorrigible*? He'd never have an English yacht again. Here's your ball."

Bill Feeley slid the golf bag off his shoulder and Charlie pulled his pitching wedge. He set up for the shot—feet, hips, shoulders well-aligned—and swung. Made contact, looked up to locate his ball in flight. Didn't see it. "Where'd it go?" he asked his caddie.

"It just kind of scooted into the trees."

"How far in?"

"Way in."

"You shanked it, Charlie," Brotherton said.

He didn't shank again but he played badly, hitting into the water on number three and the woods on five, and on the ninth hole he three-putted from fourteen feet for a double bogey. As they walked off the green, Charlie took a £20 note from his wallet.

"Forget it, you were way off your game," Brotherton said.

"A bet's a bet," Charlie said, and handed him the money.

****

They sat on the broad terrace overlooking the river, Wesley with a single malt, no ice, Charlie with an Irish whiskey hoping, with each sip, to dull the hurt; and he was hurting badly. Mrs. Walsh brought in hors d'oeuvres on a handsome crystal platter. Engraved around the edge of it: *Walker Cup, 1975. Wesley Brotherton, Undefeated.*

"Getting back to MacNair," Wesley said. "He had an elaborate, highly sophisticated system of money-laundering worked out. For years I've been sending money to Reverend Paisley and his Unionist party, also the UVF–the paramilitary group in Northern Ireland that serves as a counter-force to the I.R.A. It's who I am, it's what I passionately believe in. And MacNair was robbing me blind. In box after box of documents we carried out, the evidence is there; and he likely would've got away with it save for a midnight duel with a visiting American golfer."

Wesley spread black caviar on a cracker and popped in into his mouth, had a swallow of Scotch. "I owe you a big thank you, Charlie."

"You don't owe me a thing."

"And that's not all," Wesley Brotherton said. "Not only was MacNair a crook, he was a pervert. Up there in his loft pounding his miserable little pecker over lusty photographs of Lora, shots he took himself. Looking out her windows, early sun shining on her breasts, sleeping in her bed. Three hundred shots in all, maybe more."

Charlie was sitting very quietly, one hand over the other at his belt.

"I looked at ten," Wesley said, "that was it, that was enough. I burned each and every one, chucked the photographs on the flames ten at a time, twenty at a time. Son-of-a-bitch was violating her, Charlie. In his sick and twisted mind, raping her!"

Charlie didn't say a word.

Brotherton pressed his fingers against his eyebrows, then, inhaling, went on. "When the news broke, and it broke like a thunderclap over London, I couldn't imagine what Reggie's motive was in wanting to kill you. Then when we found out he was cooking the books, it occurred to me maybe you had something on him, knew something about his scheme. Giving him a reason. Am I even close?"

"I had nothing on MacNair."

"Then what was it, as you put it together?"

He told Brotherton what he'd told Chief Dunn. MacNair was jealous. Who was this American golfer stepping on his turf? Giving Lora lessons, driving one of Mr. Brotherton's cars, going away with him in his chopper. "In his demented way," Charlie said, "he had to take me down. Whitridge Manor wasn't big enough for the two of us."

****

Mrs. Walsh served a wonderful dinner on the terrace. Medium-rare double-thick lamb chops with mint jelly, roast potatoes and peas fresh from the shell, a bottle of fine French burgundy. As they were finishing, a damp wind came up, then the first drops of rain, and Wesley said they should have their coffee inside. Inside they went, sat in handsome leather armchairs in the billiards room. Mrs. Walsh placed a sterling service on a low marble table.

"Thank you. And two brandies," Brotherton said.

They talked awhile longer, or Wesley did. Dennis O'Hea, he said, had written him a letter saying he'd be leaving on September first. No reason given, but Wesley suspected it was because the superintendent knew his days at The Whitridge were numbered. "I kept him close, he kept me close, to our mutual benefit; but I suffered him quite long enough," Brotherton said. "Recently he got hold of some intel that hurt us pretty bad. But enough of O'Hea. The job I offered you as Golf Czar—"

Mrs. Walsh brought in their brandies. Wesley thanked her, then continued, "—as I said, it's not for you. Here's how I'm thinking now. I fired Nick Jarvis. He defended his cross-over holes and I called him incompetent and lazy. You showed more insight in a twenty-minute flyover than he showed me this whole past year! I want you to go to Killdoon and fix Jarvis's fuck-up. I see three months' work, largely on site. I'll give you £75,000, plus all expenses, for the job. Not bad pay, but more important, as I see it, you'll be honing your architectural skills. Now here's the exciting part. Have you ever played Carnoustie?"

"I have."

"It's one of the great courses in Scotland, world class. An American won the Open there last year. Right now I can't recall his name—"

"Justin Leonard."

"Right. My division, Resorts International," Wesley continued, "has just closed on a magnificent parcel of land near Carnoustie, twelve miles up the coast. Charlie, it's an unbelievable site. Jack Nicklaus is dying to get his hands on it but I can't stand the man, pompous arse that he is. And for what he charges, how much time would he spend on site? Fucking blowhard! Charlie, you'd put your heart and soul into it from day one. *Dunellen, A Charlie Kingston Golf Course*. Now that's a credit. Fix Killdoon along the lines we've discussed, it's yours. You could schedule flyovers, start walking the land by the middle of November. Hiring people, lining up a staff. I'll pay you £800,000 over two years. Plus housing and expenses and a yearly trip to the States to see your mum."

Charlie could only wonder what was behind it. If something was too good to be true—

And then, in moment, it flashed on his mind. Taking on Dunellen would make him one with the skipper of the *Incorrigible*. The man who put up the capital to have her built held Anthony Whiteley in his hand. You could borrow Wesley Brotherton's wife, but heaven help you if you defaulted on the debt.

"It's a hell of a package, Wesley," Charlie said.

"Right down your fairway."

"But I won't be able to take it."

"What are you talking about, Charlie?"

"I have an appointment with Q-School."

"Where are they holding it?"

"La Quinta, California."

"First-class travel back and forth," Brotherton said. "All expenses, rent yourself a suite for the week. Get your card, stick it into your wallet, and get yourself back here."

"I just—I won't be able to do it, Wesley."

"One million pounds over two years," Brotherton said.

"Money isn't the problem."

"What is, then?"

"It's just time for me to go."

Brotherton sat back, fingers linked but the back of his hands were flat, a bridge with a log jam in the middle. "OK, then," he said, an air of finality in his voice but not a trace of anger, "do what you have to do, Charlie. Just know I won't make this offer again. If it's time for you to go, it's time for me to let you go. When you leave here, Dunellen is off the table. So are you. Is Kevin ready to take over in the pro shop?"

"Yes, all aspects. He just won't be able to give lessons."

"Are you leaving Castlebantry?"

"In probably a week."

"Leave the Saab off with Keith before you go."

"Thank you, Wesley. And thank you for everything."

Brotherton picked up his snifter. "Good luck."

Charlie lifted his glass, had a taste of the brandy, and went out, down the marble steps. At the great front door of the Manor House he stopped, as if giving himself a chance to reconsider. *Dunellen, A Charlie Kingston Course.* He gave himself the chance, then opened the door and left the Manor House.

Lights on, wipers going full, he drove away in the Saab. Outside the Whitridge wall, he merged onto the roundabout and was soon passing the Castlebantry Hotel. But instead of pulling over, as planned, he drove through the village and after a couple of miles on Pearse Road came to McCurtain's. All spots in front of the pub were taken and he had to park near Monahan's, long closed for the day, and hurry back through the driving rain. The strains of a fiddle, the toot of a pennywhistle, reached his ear as he pulled open the door.

He made his way to the bar, stood among a crowd of tourists, many of them American, who were laughing, talking, taking in the music. Fiona spotted him and walked over.

"When did you come in?"

"A few minutes ago."

"You're soaking wet."

"It's really coming down."

"Can I get you anything?"

"I'm fine. Thanks."

"How was your day?"

"As days go? Nothing special," he said.

"I'll get you a whiskey. You look cold."

"Really, I'm OK. I just wanted to stop in."

"It's nice seeing you, Charlie." Fiona went away to take care of her customers.

Charlie stood at the bar. The tenor was singing:

> *"To all the kind people I'm leaving behind,*
> *To the streams and the meadows,*
> *Where late I have been,*
> *And the high rocky slopes round the cliffs of Doneen."*

CHAPTER 26

Three days later he was sitting with Kevin on the matching chairs in the pro shop. An afternoon sun, shining through the side window, gave the many assorted items, on the shelves, in the cases, a warm, inviting glow. "The only thing you can't do, I told Mr. Brotherton, is give lessons," Charlie said. "My feeling is he'll give you a good raise."

"It won't be the same without you."

"You'll do just fine, Kevin," Charlie said. "Count every penny, show every penny—earn his trust. On golf weekends, your primary job will be watching the shop. So start thinking about someone taking over as caddie master. Talk man-to-man with Mr. Brotherton, you'll have no problems."

They stood up. Kevin picked up the golf bag lying on the floor and carried it out. Charlie took it from him and set it in the trunk of the Saab. He looked at the pro-shop door, or just above it. "I remember when I had the sign made, saying the pro's name should go on a separate panel. So, take it down. Do what you want with it."

"As long as I'm at The Whitridge, it stays right there," Kevin said.

****

Pharr's was empty when he walked in the next afternoon. No one on either side of the bar. Charlie went up to it, not minding the wait. If he were to draw himself a Murphy's, no one would care. His eye caught the pegboard with the nicknacks on it. He should buy an item to bring home. Just then Mary McAleer came out from an inner room in stone-washed bluejeans and a pale yellow T-shirt.

"Charlie, all we've been hearing, all we've been seeing! How are you?"

"I'm OK., I'm doing all right."

She stood across from him, pressing against the bar. "Emily was very upset, and so proud. Spinning around and putting a golf shaft through the head of that former British operative! Can I get you a Murphy's?"

"I'd love one."

Mary worked the tap, came back, stout faintly aswirl. Charlie asked her how her thesis on the flight of the wild ducks had turned out and she broke into laughter. "Flight of the Wild *Geese*, Charlie."

"Sorry."

"It received high honors."

"Congratulations." There was a slight pause. "How's Emily?"

"She isn't doing too well, last couple of days. Dr. Mulrooney came by and wants her staying in bed."

"Would I be able to see her? I'm going home."

"Home, like in America?"

"Like in America," Charlie said.

"We'll miss you. Let me go inside for a minute."

Charlie stayed at the bar, looked around. The banquettes seemed new; stuffing no longer visible. Then he noticed black tape over the splits in the vinyl.

Mary came back out. "Emily would be happy to see you, Charlie. Dip under the bar, there at the end."

He did and, inside the Pharr residence, she led him in and out of a kitchen, then along a corridor, through a doorway and into a secluded room where Emily, in a nightgown and robe, was resting in a chaise beneath a light blanket. A window opened to the bridge over the Argideen River.

"Hello, Charlie," she said in a low voice, indicating to Mary she could leave. "Please, sit down."

A stiff-backed chair was near the chaise. "Thanks for seeing me," he said, seated.

"I always said you'd better not leave without saying goodbye."

"I remember, and I haven't. How are you feeling, Emily?"

"Life is catching up with me, Dr. Mulrooney says."

"You look fine," Charlie said. "A little rest, you'll be like new."

Emily glimpsed his bandaged head. "You wear your badge proudly."

"Someone fired a shot at me."

"Someone indeed—Dennis says MacNair was a link between Brotherton's millions and loyalists in the north."

"I've heard he was."

"You made him see the error of his ways."

"I really didn't have a choice, Emily," Charlie said.

"It's how history is written." A smile touched Emily's thin lips. "Let me tell you a little story."

Charlie was afraid he was tiring an already tired woman. Without a pause, she went on. "It goes back a good way, I was a child," Emily began. "A gang of Black and Tans stormed Croghanvale one afternoon, looking to smash the rebels they knew were here, and from the roof of Pharr's my mother fought them off with the rifle Michael had given her, a Mannlicher it was, one of his own. Four of that scurrilous lot lay dead on the ground, and the others fled. Gretta took a bullet in her shoulder, she lay there on the roof, bleeding, almost died."

Emily reached out and held his hand. "She didn't have a choice but it made history. Some call it a turning point in the war." She squeezed ever so lightly. "I'd better rest a little."

He leaned in and kissed her face. "Goodbye, Emily."

"I hope to see you gain, Charlie."

"I'll come back."

She smiled and closed her eyes. In the pub, Charlie saw that three men had come and Mary was busy filling pints. On the patrons' side of the bar, Charlie waited for her to come over. When she did, he told her that he and Emily had had a very fine talk. "I'm glad," she said. "Another Murphy's?"

"No, thank you." He handed her a £10 note. "This is for my first."

"Charlie, it's on the house."

"Well, for yourself then," he said. "I'm wondering if you can tell me where Gretta's grave might be."

She explained where he'd find it. "It's a bit of a climb. When you get there, her stone sits by itself."

"Thanks." Starting to leave, Charlie had a thought. "Mary, something else," he said. "I feel very close to your grandmother. If I gave you my address, would you drop me a note and tell me how she's doing? I think you know what I'm saying."

"Of course I will, Charlie."

She gave him a sheet of paper and a pencil and he wrote his name and address. Outside, he walked through the parking area and circled the building; toward the back, he spotted a narrow path winding upward through a rocky field. He followed it, and after several minutes of trudging came to a level, grassy area, site of a small cemetery above the river; glancing about, he saw a marker rather isolated from the others. Charlie walked over to it, stood there looking down—name and dates going in and out of focus. He dropped to his knees. Lettering clearer now but were his eyes lying? Resorting to touch, Charlie reached out with his fingers:

Margaret Russell, 1891-1963.
The Spirit of Ireland's Fight for Independence.

He stayed for several minutes, absorbed in the wonder of it, kneeling at her grave.

CHAPTER 27

At the hotel bar, Charlie's last night in Castlebantry. The bartender had slick brown hair and wore black trousers and a starched white shirt. Three other men, Charlie guessed from out of town, were at the bar, and a man and a woman sat at one of the little tables near the street-side windows that looked out onto Wolfe Tone Way. No one was talking, even whispering; no one was looking at anybody. The bar reminded Charlie of a bus station, just cleaner, nicer appointments. Maybe he should ask the man nearest him what his views were on the Flight of the Wild Geese. See if he could get something going. Or he could say, "My great-grandmother knew Michael Collins. With the rifle he'd given her, a Mannlicher, she repelled a band of Black and Tans in Croghanvale." That might work. Or he could casually drop that he was an honorary member of the I.R.A. That would stir up the Castlebantry Hotel bar. It could bring the garda. Chief Dunn himself might come running in.

Charlie was about to leave, wanting to get in six or seven hours' sleep; tomorrow would be a long day starting with breakfast with Fiona and her kids. Just then a new customer pushed open the street door and, standing several spots from

Charlie, asked for a schnapps. He polished it off, ordered another, and spoke in subdued tones to the bartender. Charlie glanced over; to his alarm, if not horror, it was the man he'd seen at breakfast, the driver of the car idling on Pearse Road—

Charlie lowered his head, turned away. Leaving two pounds on the bar, he headed for the lobby door, walked to the elevator. In his third-floor room, he attached the security chain, finished packing, and crawled into bed at 10:15. An hour went by and he wasn't anywhere near falling asleep. An hour and a half. From time to time the sound of footsteps in the corridor. Guests returning to their rooms. The opening and closing of doors. Silence. Then new footsteps—coming closer... slowing...stopping....

Charlie sat upright. A knock. A second knock. Terrified, he reached for the phone, thinking to inform the front desk... and a voice came through the door. A woman's voice.

"Charlie?"

The tease. Open the door and get shot. Then, "Charlie, are you there?"

"Who is it?"

"Fiona."

Fiona? "Hold on, give me a second."

Still dubious—a con was a con—he pulled on a pair of trousers and a T-shirt and opened the door, leaving the chain in place. Standing there was Fiona. Charlie released the chain and she came in, holding a silver bag in her hand with a red drawstring.

"Dropping by like this, Charlie, don't think me awful," she said.

He saw that she was nicely dressed in smooth-fitting tan slacks and a silk, bluish-gray blouse. "Fiona, not at all. I—I'm surprised." He locked and chained the door.

"This is for you." She handed him the silver bag.

Inside were a split of champagne and two glasses. "Now I'm really surprised. Thank you. Sit down."

He thumbed loose the cork and poured, handing Fiona one of the glasses. She was sitting in the upholstered chair and Charlie pulled out the little chair at the desk.

"To you, Charlie," she said.

"And to you, Fiona." They tasted the champagne.

"It seems like yesterday that you walked into McCurtain's," she said, "and now you're going home. Are you excited?"

"Not really. There's nothing for me at home. Picking up the loose ends of my career."

"That's important to you, isn't it?"

"Less important than it used to be."

"Still, it's your main reason for going home," Fiona said.

"It's a reason," Charlie said. "I'm also leaving because your brother strongly recommends it. I've caused enough trouble."

"But he didn't say you can't come back, did he?"

Charlie laughed. "No."

"So come back," Fiona said.

"I'm sure I will." Charlie refilled their glasses, emptying the bottle. "You were really busy the other night," he said.

"A bus load of visiting Americans came in. They wanted to know about Michael Collins. Did he really have his last pint in McCurtain's?"

Charlie laughed. "Dennis mentioned Collins's 'last pint' my first night in McCurtain's."

Fiona was sitting back in the easy chair, one leg loosely crossed. "You've come full circle, Charlie."

"You know, that's true. I found my great-grandmother's grave."

"How wonderful! When? Where?"

"In Croghanvale. Earlier today. There's an inscription on her stone, '*The Spirit of Ireland's Fight for Independence*.'"

"How proud you have to be!"

"I am. It's so unbelievable. Emily Pharr is my great-aunt."

"Now I know you'll come back," Fiona said. "It's so amazing. Whatever you think of my brother, he's convinced your stay here would make a great movie. *The Charlie Kingston Story, An American Golfer in Ireland*."

They both laughed. "Tell him I hope he gets rich on it."

They had the last taste of their champagne. "Do you know why I came to see you, Charlie?"

"To say goodbye."

"I have tomorrow for that."

Charlie stood, took Fiona's glass, set it on the desk and led her to the bed. They undressed, held each other, kissed; he sensed a loosening, a willingness in her to let go. Charlie moved over her and sooner than he might have thought Fiona's long legs were reaching upward, as if to kick in the floor of heaven so the shall-nots could come tumbling out, halos and all. She was looking at Charlie, her eyes warm, but then her hands rose to her temples coming together like slow-moving curtains. She could only go so far. No one should see the face of a married Catholic woman committing adultery, making love to a divorced man she would probably never see again, as she reached for a moment. Through her fingers Charlie saw anyway. He prayed that he might hold on, hold on for Fiona, and then, at once, her face softened, she became truly beautiful, as if the God she feared was now blessing her, saying, *It's all right, Fiona. I'm happy for you! Yes, Fiona!* And from her lips, between her fingers, came a deep, wondrous cry of rapture.

****

"I left my house two times and two times turned around," she was saying to him at the door of his room.

"I'm glad you persevered."

"I am too," she said, her eyes glowing. "See you in the morning."

She went out, and Charlie peered the length of the corridor; once again he locked and chained the door. Back in bed, he looked up at the window in the slanted ceiling, watched clouds drift along, revealing to him as they passed stars in the sky.

CHAPTER 28

In the morning he carried his suitcase and clubs to the main floor and stood at the checkout counter, looking over one shoulder, then the other, while waiting for the middle-aged woman with gray, tightly set hair, to tally his charges. He signed the credit-card slip, and the woman gave him a slow, judgmental look. He was not someone whom she would miss. The Castlebantry Hotel was a place of high, ethical standards, and she did not condone illicit, hour-long visits such as occurred in Room 309 last night. Charlie picked up his suitcase and golf bag, and went out. A taxi was waiting for him. The driver, a young man with a ponytail, stowed the items, and in no time was pulling up to the Dennehy family door.

Brigid came running out. She insisted on pulling Charlie's suitcase and Kevin lugged his clubs. Charlie paid the driver and went in. Fiona greeted him with a warm hug, last night's glow still on her face, in her eyes. Then she said, "To the table," and they all went into the dining alcove.

Fiona served a traditional Irish breakfast: two eggs over easy, bacon, sausage links, black pudding, white pudding, brown bread with sweet butter and strawberry preserves, and a pot of tea. They talked, reminisced, now and again sharing a laugh; but for the most part the table was quiet, as if when one is leaving there isn't much to say. It was the single best breakfast Charlie had ever had, and he told Fiona, and from time to time she would look at him and smile.

When they finished breakfast, Charlie said he had gifts. In the living room, the family sat on the sofa while Charlie unzipped one of the pockets on his golf bag. Whatever he took out first, he held behind his back, only bringing it forward when he was in front of Brigid. It was the head-cover that had gone with her 3-wood, in the image of a friendly lion.

She hugged it to her chest. "I'm so glad you found him!"

"He found me. He woke me up one morning whispering in my ear, 'Take me to Brigid.'"

"Charlie, thank you!"

He went to his golf bag again, unzipped another pocket, and withdrew a stout, business-sized envelope wrapped in protective plastic. "I found this buried in the tool shed behind the McGarrity house," he said, giving Fiona the packet.

She was perplexed. "What is it?"

"Open it and see."

She unwrapped the outer piece of plastic, then slid the isolated note from under the string. As she read, her eyes zeroed in more and more intently; her jaw dropped. To Charlie, "My God, these are Kieran's letters to Mairead!"

"They are. I read one, the first one he sent."

"They could be very valuable, Charlie. Are you sure—?"

"Fiona, they're yours," he said.

From outside came the honk of a horn. Everyone got up and he hugged Brigid first, lifting her off her feet. "Dance well," Charlie said, the taste of salt on his lips. "I love you, Prize Winner."

He went to Fiona; before he could say anything, she said, "Thank you for coming into our lives, Charlie."

"Thank you for inviting me."

He held her for another long moment, kissed her on the lips, thcn went to the door. Kevin followed him out. Jimmy O'Sullivan had the boot open and put in the suitcase, then relieved Kevin of the golf bag. But before he lowered it in, Charlie took the bag from his hands and passed it to Kevin.

"I'm taking my putter and sand wedge," he said, pulling them clear.

"Charlie, what are you doing?"

"Giving you a good set of clubs."

Charlie got into the car and waved at Fiona and Brigid in the doorway and at Kevin still standing there, shaking his head. Jimmy started his cab and drove away. He took the country road that ran along the foot of the Castlebantry Hills, through the hamlet of Croghanvale, past Pharr's and over the Argideen.

"So you're going back, Charlie," O'Sullivan said.

"I am."

"Do ye remember our talk? It was your second or third day in Castlebantry and I was driving ye to Whitridge Manor. I was telling ye about my golf grip."

"You were using your old hurling grip."

"I decided to change."

"Did it do anything?"

"For the first ten days I couldn't hit the ball ten feet."

"So you went back to left hand low," Charlie said.

"I did not," proudly spoken. "I stayed with it, worked at it, and I've taken seven strokes off my game."

"That's fabulous, Jimmy."

They were now on the main road to Cork. Jimmy talked about his daughter, Helen, taking a third place in the recent feis. Oh, she performed beautifully in the hornpipe. Next year she'll be a prizewinner sure. Charlie offered congratulations, kept looking at fields, the grazing cows, the rolling hills and hedgerows....

Soon enough they came to the airport and Jimmy let him off at the main entrance. Charlie put £50 in his hand.

"Many thanks," Jimmy O'Sullivan said. "Ye never came by for your pint."

"I thought about it."

"Well, the offer stands. So come back."

"Good luck with your game," Charlie said.

He walked into the terminal, checked his suitcase through, sat in an area that overlooked the main entrance absently watching as vehicles came in, either parking or letting off passengers. Suddenly he leaned forward, feeling his heart jump. A small red car rolled in and parked. But it wasn't a convertible and the person who got out was a man in a baggy gray suit.

A copy of the *Cork Examiner* lay on an adjacent seat and Charlie picked it up. On the first page was a photograph of three Catholic boys, Richard, Mark and Jason Quinn. The article said they had perished in their home in Ballymoney, Northern Ireland, victims of sectarian violence. Protestant and loyalists were angered by the altered route of the Drumcree march, and in retaliation a member of the Ulster Volunteer Force set fire to the Quinn house—

Charlie closed the paper, troubled by the event, saddened. Hardly the note he would choose to leave on, and he felt it was a bad omen. Aer Lingus announced Flight 319 to Dublin. Putter and wedge in hand, Charlie filed out with other passengers to the jet.

CHAPTER 29

I t was hard getting started on a golf regimen when Charlie got home. He visited his daughter's grave a couple of times, telling April about a girl he'd met in Castlebantry; she does this Irish dance, the arms don't move, just the feet, like lightning. Clickity clack, clackity click. Brigid won a dance competition when I was there; she's now a "prize winner." What sweet outfits they wear, hair in curls. Charlie was starting to tear up, thinking of the little friend he'd left behind, and of the little friend he'd laid to rest.

He called his mother in Willow Falls. "Oh, hello, Charlie." By her greeting, it was as if she'd forgotten he was away. Gretchen did ask him to come out for the Willow Falls Library Fair, of which she was the chairwoman, but Charlie said he'd just got back and was too busy, he'd fly out for Thanksgiving. That was fine by his mother. If emotionally removed, she was almost always agreeable.

Charlie had dinner with his friend, the priest Phil Reardon, who told him, after listening to Charlie's Irish adventure, that he would be in the confessional all this week between 7:00 a.m. and 8:00, and he would like Charlie to come by.

"Sorry, Phil. I'm not up for it."

"Charlie, you slept with two married women, you killed a man—"

"I know what I did."

"And you don't think you should make a confession?"

"Phil, I'll come to terms with my sins my way."

"What way is that, letting them blow away like leaves?"

"In the first place, I don't think they're sins," Charlie said.

****

Going on his third week, thinking it was high time to starting swinging a club, Charlie called his rep at Callaway, Kurt Rosborough. They chatted for a while. Rosborough mentioned an article he'd seen in *Golfweek* about Tour player Charlie Kingston who speared a man to death with a golf shaft while vacationing in Ireland. Clearly in self-defense. "But it had a lot of people talking," the Callaway salesman said.

"I didn't think it got back," Charlie said.

"Oh, it got back. Big time. Because no charges were filed, it blew over pretty quick. What can I do for you, Charlie?"

He wanted to say, "Nothing. I'm just calling to say hello." He told Rosborough that he'd left his clubs and bag with a young Irish golfer. And he wanted to start hitting the ball again.

A small pause. Charlie thought the rep might say he wanted to clear it with Callaway, now that it was known that Kingston, hardly a big draw anymore, had violently thrust a broken shaft through a man's head. "Not a problem, Charlie. Specs the same?"

"Same."

"I'd like you to try our new Big Bertha," Rosborough said.

"Sure."

"I'll drop the clubs off with Larr Peters in a couple of days."

"Thanks, Ros."

The next day Charlie drove to his home course, the Wenatchee Golf Club, seven miles west of Atlanta. He parked, walked along a shaded path to the magnificent Tudor-style clubhouse. Just before getting to it, he veered left and entered the pro shop. Twenty sets of woods and irons lined one wall, rack after rack of sweaters and shirts, shorts and pants, shelves of golf shoes all with the new "soft spikes." Three men and two women were walking about, looking at this, picking up that. No one seemed interested in buying, just looking. An assistant pro in his early thirties, in pastels, was standing behind a large, curving counter.

"Charlie, good seeing you," he said.

"Hi, Brad. Is Larr in?"

"He sure is. Hold on."

In a few minutes a tall man with graying hair and smiling blue eyes walked, with a small limp, into the shop. "Charlie, how in hell are you?"

"Larr!"

He didn't shake hands with Charlie; he looped his big arms around Charlie's shoulders and gave him a bear hug. "Where'd you play in Ireland, all the great courses I imagine. Lahinch, Ballybunion, Old Head—"

"On a small local course in Castlebantry," Charlie said.

"In other words, you took time off. Glad to hear it."

Charlie asked him how things were going at the club.

"A couple of kids on the Georgia team came by and one of them had a 66," Larr said. "People were talking 'course record.' I squelched that in a hurry. Charlie Kingston held the record with a 65 in a pro-am four years ago, I said, and his college fraternity brother wasn't keeping score!"

They both laughed and went outside and sat in chairs overlooking Wenatchee's eighteenth hole. "Atlanta papers carried a story about you last month," Larr said. "None of us knew what to make of it. Our new club president, Harmon Bleier, raised the question of—I'm not pulling any punches here, Charlie—of whether we should keep you on as Wenatchee's touring pro. He thought maybe you were prone to violence. That you'd lost your card was also brought up and didn't help. But a majority of members and Executive Board members supported you, citing hardships, and the motion was defeated by a two-to-one margin."

"That's heartening to hear," Charlie said.

A foursome was coming up the eighteenth fairway. "But to more important matters," Larr Peters said, "in two weeks we're having our first Wenatchee Open. Two days, stroke play, winner takes home three thousand. We've got some good area names. There's a cracker-jack assistant pro at Peachtree, Dave Anders; the pro at East Lake who won the Georgia Open last year, Al Yeager; then a former Tour player who's coming up from Savannah, Layton Furey. Plus a lot of good amateurs. The kid on the Georgia team I told you about, Billy Randolph."

"Furey won at Phoenix three years ago," Charlie said.

"Can I sign you up? It'll cost you two hundred bucks."

"I'll likely fall on my face," Charlie said, "but sure."

On the eighteenth fairway the first player advancing to the green put a horrid swing on his ball and dumped it into deep grass forty yards short. The next golfer topped his approach, a low screamer that ran the green and ended up in a bunker.

"I should probably hit some balls," Charlie said.

"Do you have clubs with you?"

"I've got an old set in the trunk of my car."

"Let me have your keys," the Wenatchee pro said. "A kid will meet you on the range."

****

A bony-shouldered 17-year-old named Pete Wynn was standing with Charlie very near the spot where he and Buddy Hewitt had stood when Debby had called, saying April had had a bad spill. As best he could, Charlie shook off the memory of that morning. Pete handed him the clubs he asked for, starting with a pitching wedge, then a 7-iron, then a 4. He hit half-a-dozen 3-woods and three drives. That was it. He gave Pete ten dollars and told him to leave the clubs and car keys with the pro.

"OK, Mr. Kingston. Thanks."

"Can you meet me here same time tomorrow?"

"Sure."

Several benches lined the hitting area and Charlie sat on one in no rush to leave. He was finally sleeping through the night but Ireland wasn't going away. He missed his pro shop, the Castlebantry Hills, Emily Pharr and Dennis O'Hea; Brigid, Kevin, Mary McAleer; Keith the garage-man, Dr. Mulrooney. Fiona. Ah, Fiona! They all walked through his mind. Wesley Brotherton, Reggie MacNair, Donal Dennehy, Mrs. Monahan, Chief Dunn. It was a procession. Some stopped, lingering momentarily. How clearly he saw Fiona and Dennis, Emily and Brigid. But the person he wanted to see, wanted most to see, wasn't there. He couldn't beckon her to his mind. Yesterday he'd dropped into a bookstore and bought a book of Yeats's poetry, kept it by his bed; certain poems he knew by heart and he would say them with the book closed. She was away, hiding somewhere, invisible. And he began thinking that those you loved most you could never see their face. It was written that way. Why, he didn't know. Theirs would be the face most easily brought to mind, wouldn't you think? Sometimes he thought Lora was close to appearing, might do a walk-by, give him a smile. But no. It was like trying to capture a dream; you might be on the verge of having it only to have it elude you time and time again.

The only man on the range, besides Charlie, shouldered his golf bag and started to walk in. It was someone Charlie recognized, a club member he'd gotten to know fairly well in recent years. They had played the Wenatchee course together three or four times. Ned Brewster. Seven handicap, pretty good amateur. A nice guy.

"Saw your swing just now," Brewster said, drawing close, "told myself that's Charlie Kingston. Who else? You're back!"

Charlie stood and they shook hands. "How are you, Ned?"

"Not too bad, better than the alternative." He laughed loudly—a tall, well-fed man with fair skin, in patchwork pants and a shirt that picked up the predominant color of the patches: lime. He let the golf bag drop from his shoulder. Charlie recalled that Ned was president of a large auto-parts manufacturing company, with a nationwide chain of retail outlets.

"You've been away," Brewster said. "Where was it—?"
"Ireland."

"Right, I remember now."

If Charlie had it right, Brewster was on the club's Board of Directors.

"I know it's late to offer condolences but I'd like to anyway," Brewster went on, "about your daughter, I mean. What happened was very distressing for Muffin and I."

Charlie gave a small nod. "How're you hitting 'em, Ned?"

"I'm playing to a five. Still a bit quick from the top, tempo needs work. Whose doesn't, right? Unless your name is Charlie Kingston."

"Playing to a five handicap is nice golf," Charlie said.

"We're having our first Wenatchee Open next week, I'd like to get low amateur."

"No reason you can't."

They were still standing. Charlie wasn't in the mood for socializing and he hoped Ned would move on. "Muffin's dad finally gave me the reins," Brewster said. "Great old guy but a bastard to work for all these years. Now I'm calling the shots and lovin' it—if I could only get OSHA off my back! Clinton is killing us, Charlie. Where's Reagan now that we need him?"

"Somewhere."

"You should see the new place Muffin's folks have in Dolphin Bay," Brewster said, continuing in an intimate manner. And why not? He and Charlie Kingston were tight. "We were there earlier this year, over Easter. I don't know what he and Jill are going to do with all that space but that's for them to worry about, not us. Biggest house on the back nine at the new Jack Nicklaus course. Lou goes out after dinner with a Sunday bag and plays fourteen, fifteen and sixteen, then cuts over and plays twelve, thirteen and halfway down fourteen he's back home, sitting there on his deck with a Tanqueray and tonic. He could've ran the company another three years but suddenly retirement seemed right. Muffin's happy as a clam at high tide. I'll say this for Lou. He worked hard all those years growing his business, everything he has he deserves. How about yourself, Charlie? I heard you'd quit the Tour."

"No. I just haven't played for a while. I lost my card."

"Well, that's too bad," Brewster said, as if he didn't know. "Hope we can get out one of these days, I've always enjoyed our rounds."

"Good luck in the Wenatchee Open, Ned."

"Thanks."

He hoisted his bag and continued on his way, and Charlie sat back down, thinking Ned Brewster had really changed. Because he couldn't think of one nice thing to say about the man. Who could change that much? Talking about his father-in-law drinking Tanqueray and tonics overlooking the fourteenth hole at Dolphin Bay, bragging on it. Old Lou, everything he has he deserves....

Maybe it's just me, Charlie thought.

Old Tom Morris... *Bobby Jones.*

****

Charlie's group in the Wenatchee Open included the Georgia star, Billy Randolph, whose etiquette was impeccable even as he played a take-no-prisoners style of golf. But too often he found himself in jail and ended up shooting rounds of 75 and a 76. Coincidentally, Ned Brewster made up the threesome. He had an opening round of 77 and blew up the next day with an 84.

Dave Anders, the assistant pro at Peachtree, had an even par 144, for third place; the Savannah pro, Layton Furey, finished second at 138; and Charlie's 137 won the tournament. Drinks in the Wenatchee Lounge. Ned Brewster offered his congratulations, but Charlie sensed that the CEO of World

Auto Parts, Inc., wasn't saying all that was on his mind; and a few days later Larr Peters told Charlie, as they sat in the Wenatchee pro's office, that Muffin had commented that Charlie Kingston owed Ned an apology.

"What?"

"Halfway through the second round he asked you for a tip, is how she put it. Wheels had fallen off his swing, how could he get them back on? You gave him a look and kept on walking."

"Did he really think I was going to say anything?"

"He hoped you were. As it was, you 'threw him under the bus'—quote, unquote."

The Wenatchee pro picked up a copy of *Golfweek* from his none-too-tidy desk. "I have an idea." He flipped through the pages of the golf world's weekly newspaper. "Playing in tournaments like the Wenatchee Open is fine but I think you should give the Nike Tour a shot," Larr said. "Three thousand is chump change by comparison. A couple of wins, a top ten here and there—you'd bypass Q-School and grab yourself a spot on the Tour starting in January."

Larr moved down a list of upcoming tournaments. "OK, the Omaha Classic, August 2; the Fort Smith Classic, August 16, in Fort Smith, Arkansas; the Permian Basin Open, August 23, in Odessa, Texas; the Boise Open, September 13—"

"I'm not interested," Charlie said.

"What's this about you and Q-School anyway? I remember in '71 making the cut by one stroke. I was a happy kid but half-dead from the stress. Three months later they were shooting at me in 'Nam. I made it back with my Purple Heart and spent the next five years in an alcoholic wasteland. Q-School's not 'Nam, but I wouldn't wish it on my worst enemy," Larr said. "Let me place a call for you, Charlie.

I know the pro in Omaha, Wally DeWitt." He reached for his phone.

"Larr, don't bother."

"How about sponsors' exemptions? You could pick up two or three—win a Tour event between now and December, add a top five or a top ten, you'd be playing the Bob Hope in January."

"I'm not sure that's true."

"Charlie Kingston would get an exemption. You have a great record, you were always a fan favorite—"

"I'm going to La Quinta," Charlie said.

****

At Thanksgiving Charlie visited his mother in their old brick house on Keller Street. She was never one to need or ask for help, but her hip was bothering her and he did a few jobs around the place, pruning her forsythia bushes, cleaning gutters, renovating the brick path between street and front door. She cooked a turkey to perfection and served all the trimmings. Two couples who knew Charlie came over for the feast. His mother only bought jug wine, and she had a couple of glasses of Paisano as did everyone else. It was a happy gathering. He slept well in his old bed, and before he left he visited Jake Magliora, the Willow Falls pro, at his house on Chestnut Hill Road. Jake had a basement workshop filled with all kinds of club-making paraphernalia, four shelves of books on golf—the game, its history, the lore. He'd always had a beard; it was gray now but he didn't seem any older. Well he remembered the lesson in which nary a ball was hit; but what a magnificent demonstration Charlie had given on the fine art of club-throwing.

"I'm sure you were impressed, Jake."

"You're starting Q-School in the final stage, I take it."

"I am, thank God."

"Were they going to make you start from scratch? Come on. When I tried for my card," Jake said, "just twenty-five, I'd won a couple of county tournaments. I made it through the qualifying rounds—first the regionals, then one in the Memphis area, then a semi-final tournament in Tulsa—and I was in the finals at Torrey Pines. I needed to go low on the last day, a 68 would put me on the projected cut line—I double-bogeyed the first hole, never got it together, and shot a 79. I thought it was the end of the world, but do you know something? It wasn't. I got a job here in Willow Falls, we raised kids here, what a great place to live! Willow Falls used to be nine holes, remember? Then the Mills family asked me to build a new nine, make it an 18-hole course—you were a kid, you'd come out and help. Oh, you wanted to be a golfer! It was in your blood from day one. I remember your first win...at Doral. How happy we were, the Mills family, we all toasted you in the club bar. I'm proud of you, Charlie. Jesus, I thought you were going to beat Nick Faldo in the British Open!"

Back home, Charlie played golf at Wenatchee and other area course, hit the practice range, ran three miles every morning, worked out in the nearby gym on Lenox Street. Occasionally he had dinner out, by himself or with a friend, but mostly he stayed in and read—history, a couple of novels, on Ireland or by Irish authors.

Fall. Leaves on the course conspiring to hide your ball. A game within a game. Days getting shorter. In preparation for his trip, Charlie bought new shirts, a new travel cover for his golf bag, had his clubs regripped. Taking mail from his box two days before leaving, he found an envelope with Irish stamps on it. Upper corner: Mary McAleer, Croghanvale. It couldn't be good new. In a fine young hand Mary told him that Emily was very ill with pneumonia. Dr. Mulrooney was deeply concerned but said recovery was possible with treatment and rest. Mary had come home from Dublin to stay with her grandmother. The day Charlie had left, Mary said, Emily had spoken of him in the fondest of ways.

He mulled it over—to go or not to go—for half a day, finally deciding that his card took priority. In the back of his mind he could hear his ex-wife screaming at him: *Charlie Kingston and his career. Well you and golf can rot in hell!* But this seemed different to Charlie, he wasn't sure why. It just seemed different.

On the morning, just before he left, Larr Peters gave him an early call, wishing him good luck. He should show those young blades what it meant to be a golfer. Charlie caught a taxi for the Hartsfield-Atlanta Airport and boarded a flight for San Diego.

CHAPTER 30

L a Quinta. The Stadium Course, PGA West, at the foot of the San Jacinto Mountains—palm trees and lush grass surrounded by barren land, site of the final stage of the Tour Qualifying Tournament—a.k.a. Q-School. On the practice green, Charlie stroked ball after ball, frequently tapping back a competitor's putt that had rolled too far. "Where you from?" "Hit 'em well." "Keep it in the short grass." Such cordialities, Charlie knew, were unlikely to be on anyone's lips tomorrow.

After forty minutes of practice—working to keep his head rock-solid still in the stroke—he sat on a bench casually observing the twenty men in his immediate area, though over a hundred and fifty were here, each looking to win a spot on the Tour. Most had advanced through a series of nation-wide elimination tournaments; a small number, like Charlie, were starting at the final stage. But however players had made it to the Stadium Course at PGA West, they were the best of the year's Tour hopefuls and, come next Monday, could find themselves among the thirty or so golfers eligible to tee it up at the Bob Hope Classic or Phoenix Open or at

Pebble Beach with the likes of David Duval, Jim Furyk and Tiger Woods in January.

****

Charlie's caddie, Felix, who had a near-perpetual smile on his face, worked a trio of locales—Palm Springs, Palm Desert and La Quinta—to make his living. He was very familiar with the Stadium Course, and at 7:40 sharp on Wednesday morning, under perfect conditions, Charlie teed a ball on the first hole, a par 4 at 377 yard. His drive drifted left and ended up in the rough.

With Felix and two fellow competitors, both in their twenties, Charlie left the teebox. Ben Stokes, the older of the two, had a wife and kids, and Charlie knew that Q-School wasn't merely a challenge for him—the rest of his life depended on how he did. The younger player, Jeff Simone, had no family; what he had was a dogged set to his jaw and no one, let alone a 44-year-old dude trying for a comeback, was going to beat him out of a spot on the PGA Tour.

Charlie's approach from the rough landed in a greenside bunker; his sand shot left him twelve feet to the hole and his putt to save par slid by. Bogey. Stokes and Simone both had fours. On to the second hole.

And the third and the fourth and the fifth.

Charlie wasn't playing well. His irons weren't zeroing in; on his first fourteen holes he missed five greens. Stokes was steady, Simone had started mumbling to himself, and Charlie needed to par the last three holes to come in with a 73. Carding an opening-round 73 was no way to start. To make the cut, a player had to average 70 stroke per round over the six rounds played; if he averaged 71 strokes, he was out of it—he could try again next year. If the weather became a factor—winds, rain—all that would change; but the forecast for the week was sun and more sun, daytime temperature hovering around 80.

On the sixteenth hole, a par 5 at 566 yards, Charlie had a strong drive and a good fairway wood, leaving him fifty yards to the pin. Felix told him to play to the left and above the hole. If his ball caught the slope, it would funnel toward the cup and he'd have a good chance at birdie. Charlie's ball caught the slope, drifted toward the flagstick, hit it squarely and dropped for an eagle 3. Felix grinned, gave Charlie a lo-five. Ben Stokes muttered "Nice shot" and Jeff Simone said nothing (that you could hear) on his way to making a double-bogey.

Charlie finished the day with a 71, Simone with a 75, and Stokes, whose pretty dark-haired wife was standing just off the green, had a three-footer on the last hole for a 70. He took his time lining it up and the ball lipped out, stopping five feet away. His wife squeezed her hands, closing her eyes in pain; when his next putt skimmed the hole, her head went back in agony. Ben, Charlie thought, just get the fucking ball into the fucking hole. *Please.*

****

After each round as the tournament progressed, Charlie spent thirty minutes on the practice range, then thirty minutes on the putting green; had dinner in La Quinta, watched a little TV in his room at the Embassy Suites Motel, and went to bed by 10:30. In the morning, he pulled on fresh clothes and caught the minibus to the course, chipped and putted while waiting for his call to the tee with two other golfers. He had successive rounds of 72 and 73. It was the halfway mark, and he wasn't doing well.

On the fourth day, one of the golfers in Charlie's group decided he'd had enough; no way could Al Williamson make the cut. He played along, thoroughly enjoying himself and the course. The other golfer, a 30-year-old Florida pro named Bobby Joe Koop, had a good chance of making the number; a few breaks, no bad bounces, he'd qualify. On the twelfth hole, the shortest par 4 at 363 yards, Koop pulled his tee shot into deep rough, and he and his caddie began looking for it. You were allowed five minutes for a search; after approximately three, Charlie told Felix he was going over to help, but just as he started across the fairway he saw Koop lean over, as if to identify a ball he'd just spotted, possibly his. What Charlie also saw was a ball drop from the Florida pro's hand.

"Got it!" Koop cried out.

His caddie walked over and handed him a club. Charlie went back to his own ball, took a couple of deep breaths to quell the hurt, the anger He finished the round with another 71, thought of confronting Koop but let it go. Woke up in the middle of the night faulting himself for not saying anything, but then put the incident behind him. Golf wasn't a game of tattletale; you called rules on one person and one person only: yourself.

The following day Charlie had his best round, a four-under-par 68, and on the sixth and last day—with golfers pulling hats over their faces to hide their anger and muffle their cries of despair—he was having another good round. The projected cut now stood at 424, and to make that number he would have to have a 69. Going into the last hole, a long par 4, he needed a birdie. A par wouldn't do it.

He smoked a drive and had a 6-iron going in. "Nice and smooth now, Charlie," Felix said. "Left of the flag is best."

Charlie struck the ball crisply. It landed shy of the green, rolled on, and stopped some fifteen feet from the pin and to the left of it. "Good shot," Felix said.

Walking up to the green, Charlie wondered how many times in his career a final putt had decided the outcome. Many times. Except in this case, right now, it wasn't a trophy on the line, or money. It was Charlie Kingston; he was on the line. This was it. Sink this one, Charlie, you'll be a big-time Tour player again.

Behind his ball on one knee, he sized up the line. Crouching directly behind him was Felix. Both saw it as a double-break. Thirteen feet, tricky but makeable

Speaking to him privately, Felix said, "Start your ball to the right, it'll follow the break, and near the hole will catch the second break. Do you see it?"

"Yes. Looks good."

"Give it a nice touch."

Charlie took his stance, firmed up his grip, suddenly realizing that he saw a different line, not Felix's read at all. It was more direct, taking out the first break almost entirely and picking up the second break at the hole. He liked it; clearly it was the line to follow. Giving it no more thought, he angled his feet and putter more to the left and made the stroke. The ball started rolling; as it drew near the hole, Charlie waited for the second break to bring it in but the ball changed direction only the smallest amount and missed the hole by two feet and rolled another two feet before stopping. He stood there wondering what he'd done, what he'd just done, then walked up and tapped the ball in.

A non-smiling Felix spoke to him as they walked off the green. "I told you start it *right*, Charlie."

"I know you did."

"What happened?"

"I saw a different line."

"It wasn't even close!"

"What can I say?"

Charlie checked and signed his card in the scorer's tent. Some thirty players were still on the course. Those golfers who had already finished, whose scores were one stroke higher than the projected cut, walked about hoping (and praying) that the scores not yet entered would adjust the number favorably. It didn't budge. Mike Weir, a Canadian, was the winner of the 1998 Tour Qualifying Tournament with a six-round score of 408. More than thirty players advanced, among them Ben Stokes with a 418, which Charlie was glad to see, and the Florida pro Bobby Joe Koop, whose 424 put him directly on the cut. Charlie Kingston, the 17-year veteran of the PGA Tour, had taken one stroke too many at 425.

With all scores formally posted, he handed Felix a check for $600. "I'll never know what happened," the caddie said, "but good luck, Charlie."

They shook hands and Felix drifted away. Elated shouts from newly crowned Tour players drifted out from the club bar. "See you at the Phoenix, Joe!" "You sure will, I'm gonna win it!"

Ten minutes later the golfers riding to the Embassy Suites in the minibus with Charlie might have been prisoners heading to a work detail. In his room, Charlie showered, put on his last shirt and pair of trousers, and had a drink at the Embassy bar. Standing next to him was a young man still in golf clothes who was drinking Budweiser from the bottle.

"Long day," Charlie said.

"Sure was." He had a sun-battered face, skin on his nose flaking.

"How'd you do?" Charlie asked.

"Missed it by a stroke."

"That's tough."

"Tell me," the young man said. "My wife's home cryin' her eyes out. I've already put in two years on the Nike Tour—driving from one backwater town to the next, sometimes sleeping in the car, lucky to bring home a thousand dollars. I don't blame her but I'm not giving up. One stroke, a bad chip on the eleventh hole today. Stubbed it. Fuckin' stubbed it!" He pressed his head with his hands, then said, "How about you?"

"Didn't make it."

The young man looked at him closely for the first time. "You're Charlie Kingston."

"I am."

"I followed you when I was a kid, I tried copying your swing. I'm Steve Hooker. Laugh if you want to."

Charlie chuckled, had a taste of his vodka and tonic.

"Did you really miss the cut?" Hooker said.

"I did."

"That's hard to believe. Tell me something, you've been there. Is it one or the other? Golf or family?"

"It depends on who you are," Charlie said. "Maybe you're better at balancing the two than I was."

"I'm terrible at it. She wants to leave me. I'm putting her through hell." The young man's eyes filled with tears. "I'm sorry, the week took it out of me."

"You'll be OK. Love your wife and kids," Charlie said.

Hooker glanced at his watch. "I have to run, nice meeting you, Charlie."

He had a quiet dinner. On the red-eye to Atlanta, Charlie thought about his putt on the last hole. Felix's read would've given him a good chance at it, seven out of ten. His read took any chance away. Charlie closed his eyes, seeing the ball run by the hole. He seemed to feel a smile on his face, and then he was asleep.

CHAPTER 31

On his day home, Charlie called Aer Lingus, booked a flight for Cork and reserved a car. Flight leaving in two days. He spoke with Larr Peters, who said he couldn't believe the report from PGA West saying Charlie Kingston was among the notables who had missed the cut at Q-School. What the hell happened? Charlie said he didn't have an answer. He'd made some good shots, missed too many others. Larr said he didn't know how the Board of Directors would take to it; he wanted to let Charlie know he'd heard some rumblings. Charlie said he wasn't worried; they should look elsewhere.

Phil Reardon wasn't thrilled that his friend was going back to Ireland. If he might ask, what was prompting Charlie to return to the place where he had so lost his moral bearing? To find it, Phil. Why else? Father Reardon trusted that Charley was not speaking facetiously. How long would he be gone? Hard to say. Maybe a week. Maybe, who knows? He wanted to visit his ill great-aunt and some friends, and he had a strong desire to set foot on Irish soil again. There was a line from a Yeats poem that said it so well. It was something he felt in the deep heart's core.

Charlie gave his condo a cursory dust and pickup on the afternoon he was leaving. He packed a couple of warm sweaters (no short-sleeved golf shirts), trousers, socks, a couple of turtlenecks, set the suitcase by the door. Traveling without golf clubs was a rarity, a pleasure. The pure ease of it. Two hours before leaving he picked up his mail, sat down on the living room sofa, and looked it over. The only letter had Irish stamps on the envelope, and he thought it was another note from Mary; it couldn't be good news. But then he saw the name in the top corner—

His heart took a crazy leap. Wildly excited and at the same time filled with anxiety, he waited a moment, then opened the envelope and began to read:

> Dear Charlie,
> Kevin had your address and last week I called him at the pro shop. "The Whitridge at Whitridge Manor, Kevin speaking." It sounded so like you! Charlie, I've done so much thinking these past months. The things you said to me in the Castlebantry Hills hit me deeply; they were hard truths and hard to take. I probably always knew them but it was you who made me face them. I've left Wesley. I'm no longer a woman on loan, I'm not his window-box flower anymore.
>
> Right now I'm staying with my parents in Kilcarney, probably through Christmas. The other evening at Clew Bay I cried—in sadness at my years as Lora Brotherton, joyfully because I'm Lora Fitzgerald again. Come see me, Charlie. We'll play winter golf, then sit by a fire. My telephone number in Kilcarney is 353 98 27077.
>
> Love,
Lora

Charlie leaned back, letter on his chest, eyes closed. *Winter golf. My clubs.* But first things first, and he reached for the phone.

****

After landing in Cork and stowing his suitcase and golf bag in the trunk of his rented Toyota Corolla, Charlie drove away from the airport and was soon spinning through familiar, if winter-quieted, countryside. Houses and places of business, trimmed with Christmas decorations, sought to brighten a cold, overcast day. A couple of miles outside of Castlebantry, he began looking for the cutoff, the back route to the crossroads. Seeing it, he switched on the directional signal, made a right turn and followed the curving road to the Argideen River, crossed over it, and pulled into the parking space outside Pharr's. No cars were out front; the place seemed deserted; a gloomy atmosphere hung over the building.

Charlie tried the door: locked. He walked behind the building, hopefully to speak to someone. Two men were sitting in a battered pickup truck in the service area. Speaking through a half-opened window, Charlie asked what was going on.

"Pharr's is closed," said the man behind the wheel, in his forties, heavy stubble.

"For the day?" Charlie enquired.

"More like forever."

"Is...Emily all right?"

"She's fine where she is, I'm sure of that."

The second man, younger, nodded in agreement.

"What about Mary McAleer?" Charlie asked

"She went back to Dublin."

Charlie thanked the men and walked away, sat in his car looking at the building of many rooflines, a dull ache in his chest. After a while he twisted the key, soon parking in front of the pub. Christmas lights wreathed its door and windows. He stepped out of the car, eyed Michael Collins in the entryway (still striding purposefully along), and entered McCurtain's. Green and silver ribbons swooped between paper lanterns hanging from the ceiling. Charlie stood at the bar, and soon the inside door opened and Fiona came out.

"How may I be helping you?" she asked, looking right at him; but then she stopped short. Her eyes widened. "Charlie!"

"Hello, Fiona."

She reached across the bar and held his hands. "Well, my goodness. What a surprise! Come inside, I'll close the pub."

Charlie walked through the opening in the bar and followed Fiona into the kitchen. They gave each other a long, generous hug, then continued into the Dennehy living room and sat on the sofa, facing each other.

"You look really well, Charlie."

"So do you, Fiona." Her hair, no longer piled on top of her head, fell well short of her shoulders.

"What brings you back, Charlie?"

"I heard Emily was ill. I stopped by Pharr's just now—"

"She died ten days ago," Fiona said, "but she hadn't been well. Hundred of people showed up for her funeral, from all over Ireland."

"I—I'm sorry I missed it," Charlie said. "The place seemed deserted."

"They're already fighting over it. Some say preserve, some say tear it down."

"Like the McGarrity house," Charlie said.

She smiled. "I call it the Charlie Kingston house."

"Fiona, the 'Charlie Kingston house' burned ignominiously to the ground."

"I disagree, it went down in flames, and I believe Mairead and Kieran would say the same. As for his letters," she said, "they're in the National Museum in Dublin."

"That's wonderful," Charlie said.

"A handsomely scripted card in the display case reads: 'These letters from Kieran McGarrity to his wife Mairead were donated by Fiona Dennehy of Castlebantry and were discovered by Charlie Kingston, an American golfer, on the McGarritys' property on Pearse Road.'"

"You're putting me on, Fiona," Charlie said.

"One day in Dublin, go have a look," she said. "But let me get you something."

He put out his hands, covering hers. "Just sit with me. How are Kevin and Brigid?"

"They're doing very well, neither here at the moment. Brigid's with her friend, Katie—her mum took them to the shopping mall in Cork City. Kevin's at The Whitridge fulfilling golf-club orders, I think he's made a dozen sets since you left."

"Tell him I'm proud of him," Charlie said. "So Mr. Brotherton has kept him on."

"He has," Fiona said, "but everything's in flux. As I hear and read about it, this is the last year of Whitridge Manor as a private residence. Next year it will open as one of Mr. Brotherton's resorts—tennis, horseback riding, hiking, and of course golf."

Charlie tossed the news around in his head. "How's Dennis?"

"Dennis is Dennis. He has a good job in Skibbereen, fine course, he tells me. He stops by occasionally. But, seriously, you must be starving. I'll make you a bite. Would you like a Murphy's?"

"I'm afraid a Murphy's would do me in, Fiona."

"I have a nice guestroom upstairs. After lunch, please, stretch out."

"I won't be staying," Charlie said.

A faint shadow, as when a cloud passes across the sun, covered her face. "You just got here, Charlie."

"I'm going to Kilcarney," he said.

She looked at him as if suddenly seeing the full picture of his return, and recognizing that she was only a small part of it. "I'm glad you're being honest with me, Charlie," she said. "It's the only thing I ever wondered about. You listened to me enough, I would've listened to you—and I knew from the beginning, from the day last spring when you came by with a golf bag on your shoulder looking for lunch. You had just played at Whitridge Manor, you told me. I saw it in your eyes—you'd done more than play golf at Whitridge Manor. And I remember wondering how it would all turn out with you and Lora Brotherton."

She smiled. It was a lovely smile that seemed to come from her soul. "Well now maybe I know and I'm happy for you, Charlie. We'll be friends, I know we'll always be friends. Now let me put up a pot of good strong tea and make you a sandwich. It's no small spin to Clew Bay."

****

With darkness coming and a chill rain starting to fall, Charlie drove north on N20 past Mallow and Charville heading for Limerick. Nothing to see, just the road ahead, headlights coming at him, occasionally the twinkle of Christmas lights in a village. At Limerick he picked up N18, his window down a couple of inches, cold air and rain coming in to keep him going, radio blasting, jet lag catching him despite Fiona's good strong tea. Galway. He got temporarily lost in the city, somehow found N84 and began singing, to keep himself awake but also because he felt like singing. Sleepiness suddenly went away, it had no business with Charlie. One important turn remained. Somewhere ahead R330 would take him west to Clew Bay while N84 continued north into County Sligo...and there it was, R330! The last leg of his trip.

Kilcarney—2 km. Into the darkness, the rain, he drove on. In the town—he sensed it was more town than village—he found the monument Lora had told him about when he'd phoned from his condo, and he followed Devlin Road for a mile looking for the sight he would definitely recognize, as she'd said. She wasn't going to tell him what it was. Then, just as he was beginning to think he'd gone too far, he saw it. He braked, turned into the driveway and parked next to her red Mustang convertible.

Charlie got out and began walking in the rain on the brick path and the house door opened and Lora came out in her yellow slicker, smiling, hair tossing in the wind. He increased his step, the sooner to have her in his arms; and then she was in his arms.

ABOUT THE AUTHOR

A nthony Robinson, the author of six novels, grew up in the Maverick Art Colony in Woodstock, New York. He graduated from Andover and Columbia, served three years in the U.S. Navy as a junior-grade lieutenant, and published his first novel, *A Departure From the Rules*, in 1960—the year he earned his Master's degree at Columbia. He joined the English faculty at the State University of New York at New Paltz in 1964, where he taught American Literature and was the director of Creative Writing. Retired since 2000, he is currently working on a new novel called *The Floodplain*. Anthony Robinson and his wife, Tatiana, make their home in New Paltz and New York City.